ZIG ZAG WOMAN

by Roberta Tracy

Historium Press

All rights reserved. No part of this book may be reproduced or transmitted in any form or by any means, electronic or mechanical, including photocopying, recording, or by any information storage and retrieval system, without written permission from the publisher.

This is a work of fiction. Although many of the characters, organizations, and events portrayed in the novel are based on actual historical counterparts, the dialogue and thoughts of these characters are products of the author's imagination.

First Edition published by Historium Press

Images by Shutterstock, Imagine, & Public Domain
Cover designed by White Rabbit Arts

Visit Roberta Tracy's author page at
www.thehistoricalfictioncompany.com/roberta-tracy

Library of Congress Cataloging-in-Publication Data on file

Hardcover ISBN: 978-1-962465-25-0
Paperback ISBN: 978-1-962465-26-7
E-Book ISBN: 978-1-962465-27-4

Historium Press, an imprint of
The Historical Fiction Company
Macon, GA / New York, NY
2024

To my family for giving me joy and inspiration,
and in loving memory of Mary Gesing Asbury and Richard Tracy who
made it all the way through the first draft and still saw possibilities.

TABLE OF CONTENTS

Preface	7
Chapter One	9
Chapter Two	12
Chapter Three	15
Chapter Four	18
Chapter Five	22
Chapter Six	27
Chapter Seven	33
Chapter Eight	36
Chapter Nine	44
Chapter Ten	52
Chapter Eleven	58
Chapter Twelve	61
Chapter Thirteen	63
Chapter Fourteen	66
Chapter Fifteen	72
Chapter Sixteen	77
Chapter Seventeen	82
Chapter Eighteen	86
Chapter Nineteen	91
Chapter Twenty	93
Chapter Twenty-one	98
Chapter Twenty-two	102
Chapter Twenty-three	106
Chapter Twenty-four	112
Chapter Twenty-five	115
Chapter Twenty-six	120
Chapter Twenty-seven	126
Chapter Twenty-eight	133
Chapter Twenty-nine	137
Chapter Thirty	143
Chapter Thirty-one	146
Chapter Thirty-two	151
Chapter Thirty-three	161
Chapter Thirty-four	167
Chapter Thirty-five	173
Chapter Thirty-six	179

Chapter Thirty-seven	186
Chapter Thirty-eight	191
Chapter Thirty-nine	193
Chapter Forty	201
Chapter Forty-one	206
Chapter Forty-two	210
Chapter Forty-three	215
Chapter Forty-four	219
Chapter Forty-five	224
Chapter Forty-six	228
Chapter Forty-seven	232
Chapter Forty-eight	234
Chapter Forty-nine	238
Chapter Fifty	241
About the Author	245

PREFACE

From an official casebook of the Los Angeles Police Department, September 1910...

On Tuesday afternoon last, Detective Charles Tyson and I came upon an elderly gentleman sprawled face down on South Broadway, just outside Swanson's Restaurant. Once we hoisted him back to his feet, he described how two young lads knocked him down before snatching his wallet and pocket watch. When a kindly waiter stepped in with a pint, mug of soup, and shoulder to lean on, we took off in the direction the old man had been pointing.

The culprits must have stopped to count their loot, or we would never have spotted the two boys, barely out of knickers, running full speed ahead not more than a block away. The pair turned down an alley behind Pantages Theatre and might have eluded us altogether had a long, thick roll of carpet not blocked their way.

A stench of rotting flesh and swarm of flies set the pair reeling and gave me time to overtake and hold them fast. Tyson came up close behind and gave the carpet one strong, swift kick.

Human remains rolled out, not those of some modern-day Cleopatra on her way to Caesar, but a body so brutalized it was impossible to identify, though bone structure will surely lead the coroner to identify it as female. The girl could have met her doom in a fancy house or the back alley where we found her. In my disbelief and shock, I relaxed my grip and the thieves scampered off. Along the way, they dropped their ill-gotten goods, which we returned to the grateful owner.

Respectfully Submitted, Seamus McManus

CHAPTER ONE

And so, with the stroke of a pen, a man who would soon be her partner forever changed the course of Margaret Morehouse's life. She would never lay eyes on the body in question, but discovering its identity became her mission, and for some time, obsession.

One foot planted in tradition and the other extended towards the unknown, she was a woman at a crossroads without a clear destination. If she'd followed family tradition, Margaret would have already reached the pinnacle of womanly success on the arm of a wealthy man.

Goodness knows, Mother tried. She could never fully tame her young daughter's wild copper curls or confine those long lean legs within a tent of crinoline petticoats. She showed her how to run a household without raising a hand and engage in polite conversation without sounding overly intellectual.

Neither lesson applied to Margaret's marriage to Edmund Morehouse, a man steadfast as they come but far from affluent. Any abundance in their lives came about through hard work and love. Privately, they shared similar passions and views. Publicly, the role of pastor's wife never quite fit, but Margaret wore it with grace and a few alterations.

They had their work cut out for them. By 1910, the United States was the richest nation in the world. The prosperity enjoyed by a chosen few only deepened societal divides and threatened public safety.

For the first time since its founding in 1869, LAPD was under intense public scrutiny. When an officer mistook a child for a hardened criminal and shot him in the back, eager reporters scooped the story. The department issued a formal statement declaring the boy to be "large for his age" without one word of apology.

Compounding the outrage, rumors of inappropriate treatment of female suspects behind jailhouse walls became grist for journalistic mills. Never had such titillating tales appeared as front-page news, and the public wanted more. Although a spokesman from the mayor's office labeled the stories and banner headlines "salacious muckraking," complaints amplified into moral outcry throughout every level of local society.

City officials demanded immediate reform. Their efforts could not have been timelier. As the population rose to over 300,000, so did the number of young women on the brink of poverty and exploitation. Captain Clarke convinced his peers the best way to avoid accusations would be to have mature women with unassailable reputations question female suspects, especially the pretty ones.

A parishioner recommended Margaret for this role to Mayor George Alexander, who shared that endorsement with his wife. A week later, the Morehouses found themselves washing down lemon scones with gold-rimmed cups of oolong tea at the home of the city's most prominent couple.

The very next day, an envelope bearing the City of Los Angeles emblem appeared on their doorstep. Inside was a letter from Captain Clarke, offering Margaret the position of policewoman with arrest powers, subject to Edmund's approval. She would be only the second woman so named in his jurisdiction.

A decision to join the force would mean abandoning her own seven-year effort to improve the lives of women and children. In the end, Margaret knew she was not the only human being in the world with a willing heart and capable hands. There should, and could, be others.

Her still loving marriage had become maddeningly chaste. Margaret longed to be held, not merely admired, and blamed Edmund's lack of intimacy on long hours devoted to the welfare of others. It was as if he had closed the covers on the album of their lives, shelving all the tumbling, fumbling, blissful times that might never come again.

Throughout her beloved City of Angels there was much work to be done, enough perhaps to subdue any natural urges.

Margaret had no idea how to work alongside men who might not share her sensibilities. Asking too many questions could make her sound mindless. Making suggestions would make her sound bossy.

Margaret silently vowed no hint of scandal would ever tarnish her reputation. She soon came to wish a guardian angel or goddess of hearth and home had been listening.

CHAPTER TWO

Edmund always claimed Margaret had entered his life in the guise of a red-headed goddess, too intelligent and beautiful for the likes of a poor mortal. Their physical and intellectual harmony should have made for a rock-solid union, but fissures began to form after Edmund's nephew returned to the West Coast.

As a child, Edmund idolized his brother Jack, eleven years his senior. Their parents, though loving, focused most of their attention on the firstborn son. Whenever Edmund's academic or athletic achievements did not measure up to Jack's, their father would throw up his hands and ask, *Why can't you be more like your brother?* a question neither of them could answer.

Edmund's six-inch growth spurt at age seventeen brought him to manhood almost overnight. Emotional maturity lagged far behind. Debutantes and scullery maids caught his eye. He became a notorious rake.

One of the women he frequented died after prolonged labor, along with her baby. No one could be sure the child had been Edmund's, but his parents paid the grieving family dearly for their silence and sent him nearly 350 miles north to preparatory classes at Jesuit-run Santa Clara College.

It took a generous donation for the good fathers to turn a blind eye to Edmund's Episcopalian roots, but they could not overlook the liquor and women he brought with him. He was sent packing after a single semester.

Desperate to salvage family reputation, the senior Morehouses begged Jack, by that time a renowned international import and export attorney, to take Edmund along on an ocean voyage. Saltwater and sea air would turn their reprobate son into a responsible man, they reasoned, and a few months' time might make everyone forget the scandal.

Jack was reluctant at first. Years of global business dealings had forced him to neglect home and family. His wife Elvira was wealthy in her own right, a fact she never let him forget.

Their young son Leland rarely saw his parents. Father was always abroad, and Mother devoted her energies to business and social advancement.

Nevertheless, when a group of trusted advisors approached him with an opportunity to open trade relations with Japan, Jack seized the opportunity. Assured of a relatively swift journey, he agreed to take his brother along.

Edmund flatly refused to go until his father threatened disinheritance. Travel halfway around the world sounded far more appealing than having to work for a living.

Aboard the schooner Calliope, the brothers found time to talk to each other in ways they'd never explored before. Conversation flowed between them, free as the gulls above, deep as the waters below. Jack's world view spanned several philosophies and he never passed judgment. Edmund listened, learned, and felt valued at last.

Business in Japan concluded with prospects of abundant future earnings for all parties. Halfway home, the ship anchored near an island in Micronesia. Jack stayed on board but encouraged his brother to go ashore. Edmund complied willingly, mostly to partake of the native women's delights.

That night, in the darkest imaginable turn of events, pirates boarded the ship, slashing the throats of the crew on watch and all who slumbered, including Jack.

The Calliope's provisions were more precious than gold to brigands whose existence depended on vagaries of wind and weather. They stripped the vessel of ropes and sails and left it to moor in place. Only the men who'd gone ashore survived to cast the victims' bodies into the ocean and steer the ravaged ship back home.

Guilt-ridden, Edmund returned to California. One night of passion had saved him from his brother's fate but cast him to the lowest rungs of a personal hell.

His parents could not bear the loss and died within a week of each other. The small fortune Edmund inherited weighed on his soul until he dedicated it to improving the lives of society's discards.

Vowing never again to tarnish the family name, he entered the seminary and a decade of self-imposed celibacy.

Until he met Margaret. Their souls recognized each other from the very start. Had Leland not come back to Los Angeles wearing his father's face like a living death mask, they might have been sitting round the dinner table with a passel of children instead of debating the merits of her taking on new responsibilities.

On one issue they both agreed: never in Los Angeles's history had an experienced police force been more essential. A ghastly round of killings flared up around the infamous parlor houses located in the poorer parts of town. The victims were all fallen women brutalized in the same methods used by London's Jack the Ripper.

Edmund feared any danger lurking in the streets might soon equal the threat to their marriage if he stood in Margaret's way. He reminded himself how unlikely it would be for the Whitechapel murderer to come to America thirty years after his last bloody rampage. Still, experts declared the recent round of strikingly identical mutilations were the work of one man, recently branded in newspaper headlines as the Parlor House Horror. A man sick enough to reenact monstrous crimes could be lurking anywhere.

Two bombings heightened the atmosphere of widespread terror. The first turned out to be a hoax fashioned from a manure-filled gas pipe left at the Alexandria Hotel; the other genuine, defused before it was detonated at the Hall of Records.

Colonel Harrison Gray Otis, owner of the *Los Angeles Times*, boasted vocally and in print that "labor-union wolves" had been stopped in their tracks. Unions, in turn, accused corporate bosses of planting explosives to undermine efforts to improve workers' lives.

Edmund prayed for a sign, but none appeared. Words of consent spilled out of his mouth like vomit, not the support he knew Margaret so richly deserved.

In the end, all he could do was mutter some inanity about going to bed before ten because they would both need to be up and about early. She patted his cheek and kissed his brow. He trudged off to his bed and buried himself in the blankets.

CHAPTER THREE

Margaret yanked down the tambour of her roll-top desk. Had any of those flat wooden slats gone off track, she would have taken it as a sign, but they aligned perfectly. She turned the key, locking in pen, paper, and at long last, a decision.

Staying up past midnight to list reasons why she should or shouldn't join the force had been unproductive. In a little over twenty-four hours, she would either be making history or a fool of herself.

"If my soul really is off on some distant cloud writing the story of my life, I need an editor!" she proclaimed to the moon and closed the curtains on a cloud-streaked sky.

Margaret depended on Edmund's backing to make her projects possible and herself, a progressive woman caught up in a traditional setting, acceptable. His initial lack of support undermined her confidence. That, and the eternal question, "What would mother think of me now?"

Reading about her daughter's appointment on the front page of the L.A. Times, and knowing her friends would too, would have driven Sarah Ellison to drink or, at the very least, distraction. Pillar of church and family, she expected nothing less from Margaret.

Even their house resembled that matriarch, from alabaster stucco walls pale as her skin to twin dormers arching like eyebrows high above a dark red door. The wrought iron crest atop the center cupola heightened this effect, particularly when she wore a tiara on special occasions. Inside, Margaret's father and brother brought warmth and an occasional touch of disarray, but outside — ah, that was pure Mother.

Margaret and brother David had begun formal education under the tutelage of their mother's nephew, a man too inept and careless of appearance to be hired by institutions of higher learning, but family after all. She did well in all subjects, often outshining David. On her fourteenth birthday, the tutor proclaimed her too smart for a girl.

Worried signs of intellect would scuttle marriage prospects, Margaret's mother decided the young lady should take up music, a more maidenly pursuit. When vocal and pianoforte instructors reported Margaret's lack of interest and ability, she took up dance class with lawn tennis and archery lessons thrown in to subdue her budding athleticism.

On occasion, Sarah Ellison praised Margaret's Grecian profile and auburn hair. More often, she expressed doubts about finding a suitor tall enough to control her headstrong daughter.

Margaret's figure, another cross to bear, remained coltish until shortly after her sixteenth birthday, when puberty began to fill out her form. Mother determined to keep Margaret under lock and key and abandoned all plans for finishing school.

Her father, Peter Ellison, was a titan of industry and peacekeeper at home. His son might fare well at a military academy, but Margaret was another case entirely. Her mind was eager to learn and quick to retain. Doors that flew open for a boy with her talents would remain shut for Margaret.

In the privacy of his library, he engaged his daughter in the kind of literature and philosophical discussion men of learning normally reserved for their sons. Margaret soon came to associate the musky scent of leather-bound books with her father's eyes twinkling above his muttonchops and rich voice guiding her on the path of knowledge.

She thought no man could ever be his match until Reverend Morehouse officiated at her mother's funeral.

A sudden attack of apoplexy took Sarah Ellison down. She left the earthly realm in style, hair coiffed, pearls in place, raising a champagne toast with her husband to the New Century.

Eager to come to the aid of a wealthy widower, Margaret's mother's friends began bringing around eligible bachelors. All were identical as tin soldiers to a girl hoping for a husband with the courage of Abraham Lincoln and wit of Mark Twain. She entertained them politely and wondered if the ladies were wagering to see who would be first to rescue "dear Sarah's" gangly offspring from spinsterhood.

When lackluster youths came to call, Margaret and her father drove them away, she by flaunting intellect and he with scowls and harrumphs loud enough to exorcise demons.

Edmund Morehouse met with a warmer reception. From the moment he turned to her with admiring eyes, Margaret felt an attraction. By the time they were trading lines from Barrett, Browning, and Shakespeare, she was completely smitten.

Their twelve-year age difference did not matter. He projected character no younger man could match. Margaret could only wonder if devotion to calling had kept him from marrying earlier.

A full bristly beard offset a fine brow but did not obscure his handsome profile. His slight tendency to portliness and the one-inch height advantage she had over him made no difference. He was the first suitor to appreciate who she was, rather than some ideal of what a woman should be.

One year after they met, he asked for her hand. Margaret's father was modern enough to let her decide for herself, but she'd already made up her mind. In the early spring of 1901, they were wed before a select group of family and friends. Brother David was amongst them, resplendent in a naval uniform.

Waves of nostalgia crossed Peter Ellison's face when he proudly gave his daughter away. Showered with rice and blown to disarray by a sudden storm, Edmund and Margaret raced down the marble-topped stairs, laughing as raindrops bounced off his hat and her veil.

A shimmering rainbow arced above in heavenly sanction. Before nightfall, they took the train to Long Beach and boarded a ferry headed for their honeymoon destination, the seaside paradise of Avalon on Catalina Island.

A decade later, inspired by the memory of that day's promise and relieved to have Edmund's reluctant blessing, Margaret resolved to forge ahead.

CHAPTER FOUR

The Morehouses' world turned upside down on a warm September day when Captain Hiram Clarke of the Los Angeles Police Department welcomed Margaret to the force with a book of rules and first aid kit. Had he included a crystal ball, she might have been able to predict the way murder and deception would riddle her life for the next twenty years.

On her first official day of work, Margaret tried to take advantage of a long-standing police department privilege, free trolley rides to Central Police Station on First Street. The pot-bellied conductor, who always tipped his hat to policemen and waved them aboard, eyed her up and down with suspicion.

"Anyone *not* wearing a badge must pay!" he declared.

Assuming he had not had a chance to read the morning paper, she handed him the fare.

If she'd left home a few minutes later, Margaret would have ridden to work alongside Alice Stebbins Wells, Los Angeles's first female policewoman with arrest powers, who *never, ever* paid to board a trolley.

Margaret and Edmund had followed the former minister's narrative in the newspapers with great interest. Years of social welfare work had brought her into direct contact with vulnerable populations.

Local newspapers featured Alice's persuasive views, particularly the urgent need for female officers to counter widespread mistreatment of incarcerated women. The most thorough pieces described how these poor unfortunates became enmeshed in their male partners' misdeeds, leading to disgrace, wrongful imprisonment, child abandonment, and suicide.

In May 1910, she petitioned the police commissioner and Los Angeles City Council to create a new strong role for women on the force. Implicit in the text and signatures of 100 local citizens was a strong suggestion she be the one to fill it.

A stack of morning editions featuring Alice's front-page picture landed on the desk of Mayor George Alexander. The astute politician declared to city council members and any reporters within earshot how impressed he was with the quiet resolve he observed in her eyes. Once his remarks went public, the police chief made the unprecedented appointment.

Margaret's first live encounter with the amazing Mrs. Wells came as LAPD's first policewoman with arrest powers came barreling down the street directly towards her, arms extended somewhere between a handshake and an embrace.

"How do you do, Mrs. Morehouse?" she began, offering a gloved hand. "My name is Alice Wells."

Margaret had been mentally preparing herself for the moment but never expected it to happen while she stood quivering like a willow outside the station door.

"Much better now that I've met you. I'm grateful someone with your reputation paved the way for me, and hopefully many more women, to enter public service."

Dark curls tucked under a wide-brimmed cloche and every seam of her camel-colored coat smoothly aligned to her form, Policewoman Wells epitomized perfection. The flowers and veil on Margaret's hat, while secure, were more appropriate for a tea party than police work. A short cape hastily thrown on before leaving the house barely concealed mends in her best lace blouse.

Alice's high-necked top and slender tie conveyed authority while her cinched waist, slight poof to the upper sleeves, and gently flared skirt revealed femininity. She couldn't have chosen a better outfit for work or a worse one to make a nervous newcomer feel comfortable.

With only minutes to go before their workday officially started, Alice began to brush lint from Margaret's shoulder.

"You look fine, my dear. It's so hard for a woman to know what to wear for our groundbreaking work. Armor perhaps, but how would we ever get around? The men have uniforms and one day, I am determined, so shall we! Back home on my sewing table are designs I'm working on for our very own uniform. I envision a floor-length dress and jacket in a khaki color, I think. I was toying with gray but it's far too somber."

"Khaki? I've never heard of that color."

"It a dusty hue, leaning more toward beige. Comes from the Persian. Will look stunning with your hair."

Margaret smiled and shook her head.

"I'm so glad the powers that be found you first!"

"All those newspaper articles made it hard for them to ignore me. That was my intention, of course!"

"You're breaking new ground for all of us and doing it so well. I almost didn't make it here. The conductor would not believe I was an official member of the force, but thankfully I brought my coin purse."

Alice chuckled and folded her collar back to reveal a badge engraved with the words *Policewoman's Badge Number One*.

"I had similar problems on my first day; perhaps we ran into the same pig-headed man. The Chief had already given me a standard police badge, but the conductor insisted I was wearing my husband's. My Frank is a businessman and former farmer, not likely to join the force. I reported the incident directly to Captain Clarke, who had this made up."

"Do you think I could ask him to do the same for me?"

"It's more effective to *insist*, my dear. Since it's your first day on the job, I'll be happy to do the talking."

Alice took Margaret by the hand and marched to the Captain's door, knocking lightly first, then barging right in. He rose immediately and gestured towards two cushioned office chairs.

"I see you two have met already," he said in welcoming tones.

Alice shook her head and remained standing.

"We have no time for chitchat. I would like Mrs. Morehouse to accompany me on my rounds today, and for many days until she is fully acquainted with her job description."

The Captain's bristly moustache spread atop his smile.

"Take her under your wing? Excellent suggestion, and may I say how attractive and efficient you two look together?"

"You can say whatever you wish. For my part, I'll settle for efficient," Alice responded, letting her eyes twinkle just a bit. "And speaking of efficiency, Mrs. Morehouse deserves to have the proper equipment to do a proper job."

"Equipment? Please, Mrs. Wells, don't bring up that subject again."

Alice tossed her head and rolled her eyes.

"I'm not talking about firearms this time, but mark my words, one of these days a policewoman will be caught up in a desperate situation and all it would take ..."

Margaret's horrified expression prompted the Captain to interrupt.

"I promised your families neither of you would ever be assigned to dangerous places and I mean to keep my word."

"Harm finds its own way but, I must admit, so far I have avoided it," Alice muttered. "Firearms for women will be a topic for future discussion. Right now, all Mrs. Morehouse needs is a badge like mine."

The Captain heaved an audible sigh of relief.

"Of course, easily done. I'll have a Policewoman Number Two badge made up today."

"I'd prefer to have it inscribed simply with the words *City of Los Angeles Policewoman*," Margaret interjected in a decisive tone that surprised everyone, even her.

"That way, Mrs. Wells will always retain the distinction she so richly deserves and the same badge can be made for all the women who follow."

With a quick flick of her wrist, Alice removed her badge and pinned it on Margaret's cape.

"Most people know who I am by now. Wear this until yours arrives. Keep your streetcar fare handy, my dear, but flash the badge whenever you can. It's the only way we shall ever gain acceptance."

CHAPTER FIVE

Margaret ran her fingers over the raised metal engravings and wondered if anyone would ever take her seriously.

Once the Captain dispatched his assistant to the local tinsmith and shut the door, Margaret and Alice proceeded to Clune's Broadway. It was a lovely day and but a short walk to the newly opened picture playhouse, the last place on earth Margaret would have expected to begin training. Her head was still reeling from their encounter with the Captain.

"How in the world do you keep up such an easy banter with your superior, who's a man at that?"

Alice regarded her in mock dismay.

"Please don't tell me you never question anything a man tells you!"

"I don't have that many men in my life. Edmund and I always talk things out and, oh dear..."

Margaret hesitated and bit her lip. Edmund and she always engaged in meaningful discourse, but not once in all their time together had she challenged him. If he hadn't given grudging approval, she wouldn't be out that day on her first assignment with such a plainspoken woman.

Alice softened her tone.

"I'm sure your husband is a good and considerate man, so is mine. And so is the Captain but getting to know and work with each other hasn't been easy. At first, this position seemed merely a watered-down version of what I'd had in mind."

"You seem happy now. How did you, as I believe you phrased it earlier, learn to stand up for yourself?"

"It's a habit born of necessity when you're from a large family. For the first week or so, Captain Clark and I engaged in heated debates. Eventually we found ways to communicate with each other.

Many of our discussions have led to positive outcomes."

"Was I one of those outcomes?"

"I urged him to recruit more women daily and even used what the Mayor said about my resolve to back my claims about womanly virtues."

"How did he respond?"

Alice dropped her voice at least two registers.

"Impressed with your *resolve*, was he? In my book, *resolve* is a very nice word for it."

They locked eyes and laughed.

"To be fair, only one week later he made sure I was first on the force to learn of your appointment. I thanked him from the bottom of my heart. The addition of another woman implies permanence. Your position is equal to mine and just as important."

Fluttering flags atop Clune's Broadway diverted their attention. The impressive structure had been open for a year, but Margaret had never been inside. Lavish posters near the entrance intrigued her. She was drawn to one for Mr. Edison's "Frankenstein" showing an image of the poor disheveled monster above the words, "If I cannot inspire love, I will cause fear!"

Much as Edmund and Margaret had enjoyed Mary Shelley's classic novel, she wondered what his reaction would be to seeing it in a theater. He refused to go to storefront nickelodeons with their showy facades and loud piano music but might find the 600 seats and respectable atmosphere at the Clune more acceptable.

The ticket seller, already familiar with Alice, waved them through without charging admission. D. W. Griffith's "As It Is in Life" was playing. Margaret found it hard to take her eyes off actress Mary Pickford's incredible curls but reminded herself to focus on the audience.

Alice bustled up and down aisles, breaking up furtive kisses, and escorting an inebriated youngster out of the theater. Her stern attitude was as prominent as the badge on Margaret's cape and no one questioned Alice's authority.

How could I ever judge others so quickly? Margaret wondered. Unless behaviors became too out of hand, she would prefer to leave affectionate couples alone and counsel young people, however tipsy, before escorting them out to the street.

She continued to observe in place until a small ruckus began, loud enough to be heard over the incessant noise of cranking projector and pounding piano. From the corner farthest removed from the screen, a tiny girl bolted into Margaret's beckoning arms.

A man emerged from the same corner. He bounded up the aisle faster than a woman with a sobbing child wrapped around her torso could follow.

They made it to the lobby, where Margaret tried her best to soothe the little girl.

"Is that your Papa? Should we run after him and let him know I found you?"

"Papa is good. That man is bad. He tried to kiss me! Please don't take me back to him."

Margaret didn't know what or whom to believe, but intuition favored the child.

"How about we just see where he's going, and we'll run the other way?"

The girl stopped crying and burrowed her head into the nape of Margaret's neck. When they emerged from the lobby, the man was still in sight, dancing down the street like an impudent scoundrel. He turned around to give them a look of triumphant malice, cocksure she would not put the girl down to give chase. Rage and inadequacy immobilized Margaret until a hand came down on her shoulder.

"What have we here?" asked Alice.

The girl wriggled in Margaret's arms. She must have begun the day turned out neatly in her navy sailor dress. At that hour she looked more like a discarded Dresden doll with undone ribbons in her flaxen hair.

"My name is Eleanor and I want my mama."

"I'm Policewoman Morehouse and this is Policewoman Wells. We're here to help."

"That's what *he* told me. Mama and I went to Hamburger's Department Store this morning to buy new shoes. I don't know how I got lost. The magic man said he could help. First, he took a dollar out of my ear. Then he bought me an ice cream from the street wagon and took me to the picture show."

"Am I a bad girl?" she whimpered as Margaret lowered her to the ground.

Alice grasped the situation immediately.

"You are a good girl. If you're ever lost again, look for a policeman or a policewoman with a badge like the one she's wearing."

Eleanor traced the letters and number on Alice's badge, still pinned to my coat. "Policewoman Number One," she read. "I'll remember. When I grow up, can I be Policewoman Number Three?"

Margaret laughed.

"Oh, my dear, I hope by the time you are old enough to join the force we'll be up to badge number twenty-five!"

"At the very least," added Alice.

The women escorted Eleanor back to the station and into the arms of her worried mother, who'd been searching Hamburger's and the surrounding neighborhood for hours before coming to the police.

With growing admiration, Margaret watched Alice counsel her.

"Those fancy store displays are so distracting! I have admired those bonnets and jewels, even imagined myself wearing them from time to time. Trouble is, while we're daydreaming, evil is out there waiting, ready to steal our most precious belongings."

Shaking her head in gentle reprimand, Alice turned her attention to Eleanor.

"And when they're out in the world, pretty young ladies must never, ever, lose sight of their mothers."

"Until I'm big enough to go to the store on my own?"

"Not even then," Eleanor's mother murmured, hugging her daughter even tighter.

Alice and Margaret watched as they left, hand in hand.

"How can we be sure Eleanor's magic man won't try his tricks on some other trusting child?" Margaret.

Alice looked thoughtful.

"I might be able to post a 'Seeking the Whereabouts' flier, "Did you get a good look at his face?"

"Just a sneering profile as he ran away. He moved, I would almost say slithered, in a most curious way."

Alice caught Margaret up on the rest of her afternoon activities. She'd bought coffee and a sweet for the drunken boy and sent him home with a warning. Two positive outcomes in one afternoon convinced Margaret she had, at last, found her proper calling.

They were about to leave the station when the largest, most Irish-looking policeman Margaret had ever seen barreled through the door, cheeks florid with excitement.

"We've another dead girl on our hands. Found the body in the alley behind the Pantages Theater," he announced, "wrapped up in one of those Persian rugs. Young lady, I think. Her guts are still inside, that means no ties to the Parlor House Horror. Flesh is mostly gone, and the flies and rats tell me she's been there more than a few days."

The man's lyrical Irish cadence failed to soften the image he described. Nausea welled within Margaret visualized his words as nausea welled within her.

Alice flashed a sweet smile on her way out the door.

"Pantages, is it? The Captain says that will be *your* area. Don't worry, my dear, live theater audiences are in our scope of responsibilities; dead people are not."

Alice's words did nothing to blur the dreadful picture forming in Margaret's mind. Somewhere between the captain's office and the front door, she fainted.

CHAPTER SIX

Burly arms caught Margaret and pulled her over to a long wooden bench. The red-faced Hibernian fanned and splashed her face with water and blurted out an apology.

"May all the saints preserve you. Forgive my wild tongue, lass. I'm not used to polite company in the station."

"I'm sure the saints forgive you and so must I, if I'm to be a proper policewoman."

Margaret smoothed her dress, retied her bonnet, and tried to ignore the smirks on the faces of all the men in the room, save her rescuer.

"So, you're the new one," he exclaimed without a trace of mockery. "Captain Clarke's told us all about your work with young ladies in trouble. We could use a fine woman like you in this investigation."

"I doubt the Captain had murder in mind when he commissioned me. Neither I nor, I dare say, Mrs. Wells have enough experience to become directly involved. I'd probably run the other way if I came across a killer or dead body. Are you sure this victim isn't another one of those poor Parlor House girls?

"I think not. Beggin' your pardon, but in my experience, fiends like the Horror never change the way they kill. That fellow splits his victims open like chickens and scoops them out. This woman's death was not the result of his *modus operandi*."

Margaret retched slightly and rose to leave. He gently placed a hand on her arm.

"My words never come out the way they should when I'm around ladies. Let me say this a better way. The coroner's report states she still had all her organs inside."

Although his description scarcely improved her initial reaction, Margaret appreciated the effort and sat back down. His words might be clumsy but she suspected he had more respect for women than any other man in the room.

"We were never assigned the Parlor House cases, but since we found this body, she's ours. Somewhere, someone must be worrying about her. There may be dozens of young dancers or singers at Pantages who would know if anyone in their troupe was missing or in trouble. Their boss has been herding them in by the trainload, he has, and it's my guess they're far from home and the wise counsel only a mother, or, I should say, older sister, could give."

Margaret smiled at his clumsy if well-intentioned reference to her maturity.

"I'm not yet thirty."

"When you smile like that, you look no more than twenty."

He reached for her hand and then thought better of it. His blushed slightly and his tone became serious.

"They'll confide in you, Mrs. Morehouse. Meanwhile, my partner and I shall go about finding the responsible party."

"You have me at a disadvantage, sir; you know my name, but I don't know yours."

"Seamus McManus at your service, Ma'am. Detective McManus if you wish."

"And this partner you mentioned?"

"Charles Tyson, also at your service."

A lean ginger, half a head shorter than McManus, stepped forward. The two made an odd couple. Tyson radiated brash energy while his partner conveyed strength and competence.

"I couldn't help overhearing your discussion with my friend here," the new arrival announced. "No offense, Ma'am, I'm not at all sure how I feel about working with a woman."

He tilted his head awaiting her response, like a hawk trying to determine if the morsel in front of him were a pebble or a crumb.

She managed a weak smile.

"None taken. I'm not sure I could handle cases of such a violent nature, but, since this one involves a theater, why not grant me an audition?"

Tyson's grimace turned into a lopsided grin.

"Well said, Ma'am, but how could we be sure you wouldn't go off on a wild goose chase of your own?"

"I'm a minister's wife, Detective. I not only know how to follow directions but give them, when appropriate and necessary."

"Would you be willing to talk to these young females my friend McManus feels so sorry for? Actresses are rarely ladylike."

"More than willing if the chief approves. I've held unwed mothers' hands during childbirth. I doubt any actress's language would be coarser than the cries of those fallen angels in labor."

"How did a proper lady like you find herself in such situations, Mrs. Morehouse?" asked McManus.

"We have a well-organized ladies' group at St. Paul's. As Pastor's wife, I was duty-bound to join but it didn't work out. Perhaps I was too young and eager to please. I collected more coats, scarves, and galoshes for their annual clothing drive than anyone in the group."

"Let me guess you got more jealousy than approval," ventured McManus.

"Right you are, sir. It came to such a point I finally asked Reverend Morehouse for a meaningful project of my own."

"What did he say to that all that?"

"To my relief, he agreed! In fact, he said the ladies would just have to find another dedicated soul willing to collect overcoats for all those heretofore happily unclothed natives on a tropical island somewhere in the South Pacific."

The men laughed and Margaret grimaced.

"I'd put up with their petty squabbles for over two years because I always wanted to live up to their expectations. My husband had to remind me the only thing they had over me was years."

"I wonder if any of those snooty ladies had their fancy hats set for Reverend Morehouse before you came along," speculated McManus.

"He claims to have resigned himself to bachelorhood until I waltzed into his life."

Margaret tried to avoid sharing personal moments with strangers, but something about them made her feel part of a team already. The men were cut from the same ethnic stone but shaped by different circumstances. McManus appeared to be methodical and Tyson more a man of action. Her own unique life experiences could give them another perspective.

"My project fell into place when a wealthy man willed his mansion to the church. It was a huge white clapboard structure. As my poetic husband uttered when we first laid eyes on it, 'Tis set in an orchard thick with blossoms and bees.'"

"How long had it been empty?"

"Hard to tell. Edmund and I swept away cobwebs, opened doors, and evicted hosts of winged intruders. Even in such a wretched state, the place was beautiful. There were bas-relief fruits bordering the parlor and dining room ceilings. Every window opened on a landscape worthy of a John Constable or, after a few glasses of wine, Claude Monet."

"Monet? Isn't he that painter fella who does all the fuzzy pictures?" asked Tyson.

His partner groaned.

"He's a leading impressionist. Those short thick brush strokes make the pictures brighter, which I only wish was the way you sounded right now."

"Oh, I get it," Tyson retorted. "You *paint* quite the picture, Ma'am, but not one where I'd ever feel welcome."

"Cut it out, Tyson. Let the lady tell the story her own way."

Margaret smiled her thanks. The slender detective would need more convincing. How could someone who'd likely climbed his way out of poverty ever believe a woman like her shared his views?

She looked her challenger straight in his bright blue eyes and continued.

"I'll get to the point. The house came with enough cast-iron pots and skillets to prepare food for a small army. We'd just been handed twelve bedrooms, four bathrooms, two parlors, and countless storage closets. The beauty of that place was a way to lift the women's spirits and point them towards a brighter future."

"And just what kind of female were you hoping to help?" asked Tyson.

"From the minute I set foot inside, I knew the place should be a sanctuary for unwed women in the family way, especially if there was no one to support them. I suggested calling it the Violet Morehouse Home in honor of my husband's mother!"

"And the good Reverend agreed to all this?" asked McManus, raising skeptical eyebrows nearly up to his hairline.

"Unwed mothers fall into a pit of disgrace and can't climb out, unless there's a supportive family, which is rare. Edmund tried to help these poor girls, but there were few resources available. Still aren't, for that matter. So yes, the good Reverend agreed to this. In fact, he cracked a smile so wide I knew this was what he'd been planning for us all along."

Margaret didn't share how they'd sealed the deal with a passionate kiss and tarried a bit longer than society might deem proper in one of the upstairs bedrooms.

"Unwed mothers?" Tyson sniggered. "Anyone else in your congregation think that was a good idea?"

Margaret shook her head. The biggest objectors still avoided her and did little to hide their feelings unless Edmund was around.

"It took six weeks to draft our proposal for staffing and renovations and three months of debate before the elders gave their approval.

"Word got out to the community. Posters condemning us appeared on lampposts throughout town. Flyers mysteriously turned up folded and tucked into hymnals. A dozen more, attached to rocks and shredded by window glass, landed on our living room floor."

McManus bristled.

"Narrow-minded fools who can't think beyond their own lives! How did you change their minds?"

"It was entirely Edmund's doing. Threats continued until he preached from the pulpit about casting the first stone and suffering little children. In a matter of weeks, he won over most of our parishioners.

"We celebrated Thanksgiving Day 1903 at the Violet Morehouse Home with a doctor, two volunteer nurses, and our first four mothers-to-be. There were tragic losses over the next few years, but the amount of survival rates and reshaped lives far surpassed my expectations."

As Margaret finished the tale, Tyson snorted slightly, a sign, she soon learned, he was ready to change his mind. The three marched into the Captain's office where McManus presented their case in eloquent tones.

The Captain turned his attention to Margaret.

"Are you a bookish woman, Mrs. Morehouse? Have you read the works of Sir Arthur Conan Doyle?"

"Oh yes!" she answered delightedly. "My husband and I enjoy following Sherlock Holmes and his lines of deductive reasoning, but why do you ask?"

"Too many of your fair sex cannot separate fact from fiction. If I agree to this unusual partnership, you must limit your activities to questioning the female vaudevillians. Relay any information they divulge, no matter how insignificant, directly to these detectives. I'll write a letter for you to take home to your husband."

"Why on earth would you need to do that?"

"To allay his fears, naturally. You of all people should know how much convincing I had to do before he sanctioned my hiring you in the first place. He needs to know you will be providing support for good, moral men. I cannot emphasize the word *support* enough. Do not, and, and I repeat NOT, investigate anything on your own."

Margaret agreed, first of many promises easily made and hastily broken in her new-found career.

CHAPTER SEVEN

In dreams that night, Margaret flew above the city, dipping down from time to time to rescue lost children and recover stolen jewels.

The twin brass bells atop her alarm clock rang before dawn. She went straight to her closet to find an outfit along the lines of Alice's classic elegance. Trouble was, Margaret didn't have one. Any style a pastor's wife maintained was determined by a mishmash of hand-me-downs from well-meaning parishioners and her own skill with a needle.

A dark blue lightweight wool skirt and pinstriped blouse went together well. She topped off the ensemble with a modestly brimmed hat fastened with navy and white ribbons.

The chill morning air required an outer layer. Capes and shawls were all Margaret could find until she remembered the maroon riding jacket a women's society member had given her. As the lady hadn't included a horse, it languished in the back of Margaret's closet for over a year. She put it on, pulled the nine tautly sewn buttons through their corresponding holes, and heaved a sigh of relief. It fit like the proverbial glove.

Margaret spritzed the lining with light cologne and ran downstairs to put the kettle on. She stood on a footstool, holding the jacket over the steam for a full five minutes. It shook out tolerably well. Any stubborn wrinkles could always be blamed on weather.

With little time to spare, she peeked in on a restless Edmund, mumbling words of caution in his sleep. Margaret kissed him lightly on the forehead and ran out to catch the trolley.

The conductor shrugged when she flashed Alice's badge and let her board free of charge. Once seated by a window, Margaret watched the city flash by and pondered the forces reshaping society during this first decade of the new century. For months, the whole world seemed to be teetering on the brink of unprecedented change, heralded by the massive plume of Halley's Comet.

As Mark Twain predicted, the celestial wanderer who brought him into this world in 1835 carried him away on April 21st, 1910, one day past its closest approach to the Sun. Telescope sales soared. President Taft was roused from his slumber to view the silver spectacle and went back to bed duly impressed. An ocean away, Pope Pius the Tenth, similarly awakened, returned to bed uninspired.

Charlatans warned the public about poisonous cyanogen gasses, a term they conveniently invented, and how they would curdle clouds and smother every living thing. Householders boarded their windows and stuffed blankets into door jambs. Street vendors hawked comet pills to the gullible. Farmers let fields lie fallow.

Worldwide floods and unseasonable weather supported naysayers' claims, while rooftop viewing parties and tunes such as "Halley's Comet Rag," played counterpoint to their warnings. By midyear, predictions of the world's end proved false. For women, the comet symbolized the end of one era and the dawn of a new one.

Surprised to be hanging onto its tail in a most unorthodox fashion, Margaret hopped off and headed straight for the station. The detectives were waiting for her outside. Less than twenty feet away, she saw one of their fellow officers wipe away false tears and overheard his condolences for their bad luck getting saddled with a woman.

"She's a smart one, I tell you," McManus roared loudly enough for Margaret to hear, "and 'twas by our own choosing she joins us."

After making rude but appropriate gestures towards their jeering brethren, McManus and Tyson rushed to Margaret's side.

The trio proceeded to Broadway and Spring Street where the beautiful Pantages Theater would soon open its doors. Gilded concrete letters spelled out "PANTAGES" above the marquee. It was hard to conceive how anything grim as a dead body could have been found just outside those ornate walls.

Tyson pounded so hard on one of the massive doors Margaret feared the bevel-edged glass would shatter until a strange, bespectacled face appeared. He was a bit too tall for a gnome, but that's the only description that came to her mind.

His features were distorted by reflected light but Margaret recognized his head the minute it turned to profile view. The high forehead and smashed Roman statue of a nose belonged to the same man she'd raced after the day before.

What to do? She wanted to arrest him there and then but had no earthly idea how to proceed.

What good are my arrest powers? Margaret thought. *No one's showed me how to use them. If I were a man, I'd just pommel him.*

The thought of poor little Eleanor having to confront this deviant again sickened Margaret. If questioned, his version of events might well be given more credence than her own. In the end, fear of undermining a murder investigation sealed her lips.

CHAPTER EIGHT

The man in question unlocked the door with all the enthusiasm of a miser forced to open a vault. Either he didn't recognize Margaret or was too devious to give himself away.

"No one allowed in here during rehearsal!" he snarled.

McManus pointed to his badge and forced the door open.

"We are Los Angeles Police Department detectives, here to investigate a murder that likely took place just outside your building."

The surly sentinel regarded the detectives with caution, if not respect, while giving Margaret no more than an impertinent glance.

"You mean that tart they found in the back alley? Nothing to do with us."

He pivoted abruptly and ushered them into the theater. Tyson followed briskly while McManus dropped slightly behind to assist Margaret through the dark lobby.

"How did he know the body was female?" she whispered.

"Good question. I mentioned her possible gender in my report. The story wasn't front page news, but it did make the paper. He and his boss must keep a watchful eye on the dailies for good or bad publicity."

"Why did he call her a tart? I wonder if that nasty creature talks about all women that way!"

Their conversation ended abruptly as they entered the opulent interior and turned into insignificant baubles inside an immense treasure chest. Exquisite murals and tapestries lined the walls. Margaret feared one false move would part the inlaid marble floor tiles and drop them all down into a pit.

"Supposed to look English. Can't say for sure, since I've never been to London and don't want to go there," muttered Tyson.

"The architectural team of Octavius Morgan and J. A. Walls

designed our theater in the English music hall tradition. This theater seats 1400," came a booming, Mediterranean-accented voice from the back. "Soon every major city across America will brag about their Pantages Theaters; some bigger, some smaller than this one, but all splendid."

Wavy dark hair, Brilliantine-coated mustache, and bright black eyes more than offset the short stature of the man approaching them.

"Back to work, Walters," he bellowed, shooing his lackey off as briskly as he would have flicked a gnat from his well-tailored suit. He bowed expansively.

"Alexander Pantages, at your service."

He looked surprised when McManus introduced *Policewoman* Morehouse but shook the men's hands and lightly brushed his lips across the back of her glove. Margaret tried to subdue the color rising in her cheeks. It was the first time any man had introduced himself to her in such a Continental manner.

McManus handed him a search warrant and his back stiffened.

"First, sir, we are required to tell you the purpose of our visit is to identify the woman found last week in your back alley."

"And find out who did it and why," added Tyson.

His partner shot him a warning look.

"All in good time, I assure you. Detective Tyson and I will inspect your backstage, talk to male performers and crew, and, if time allows, take another look at the alleyway. The coroner identified the body as female; therefore, Policewoman Morehouse will conduct private interviews with the women involved in your theater. I trust you can find our colleague an appropriate, *private* place to work."

Pantages nodded.

"I would know if my girls were in trouble and I tell you, every one of them is thrilled to be opening in this palace."

Tyson eyed him skeptically.

"Women have been known to keep secrets from the man in charge."

Ignoring the remark, the impresario escorted them all to a windowless office. His mahogany desk and silk-covered chairs glistened amidst a profusion of kerosene lamps. Row upon row of burgundy, green, and brown leather-bound books sporting gilt titles, chosen more for effect than content, lined the walls.

He lifted a Georgian crystal decanter from his desk and offered the men a brandy. When they refused, he took them all backstage to meet the head flyman, a strapping fellow in charge of the pulleys used for lifting and lowering scenery. Taking one set at a time, the trio examined drop-down panels and rearranged props. McManus drew out a thin leather-bound notebook from his vest pocket and began to scribble notes with a small enamel pencil.

Tyson rolled his eyes. He would never resort to note-taking, probably couldn't for that matter.

Pantages took his leave of the men and escorted Margaret past dancing dogs and juggling cyclists to his office.

"My inner sanctum, Madam, I turn over to you!" Pantages declared with a flourish and bow. "Make it your headquarters this afternoon. I'll fetch the young ladies in one at a time and they can tell you all their little secrets, maybe their big ones, too."

He smirked, perhaps thinking Margaret might find his comment clever. She chose not to react.

"The interviews will be done in private. You must leave after each lady enters and close the door behind you."

His deep-set onyx eyes regarded her with combined curiosity and respect. Although issuing an order to a man for the first time in her life felt a bit overwhelming, Margaret maintained her composure.

"Your wish is my command," he uttered, and his behavior remained as good as his word.

The women he brought to the office were tiny, tall, buxom, small, and, for the most part, terribly young. Those who weren't relied on curls, lip rouge, and distance to create the illusion of youth. Up close, even the gas light by which Margaret was scribbling notes couldn't soften their worn features.

The interviews yielded suspiciously consistent responses.

"We are all one big, happy family!" declared Lorelei the tightrope walker, without once meeting Margaret's eyes.

"Uncle Alexander takes good care of us," insisted Rowena the snake dancer, biting her lip as if there might be more to say.

If Margaret were to believe all they told her, no jealousies existed amongst the variety acts and headliners slated to perform for the opening. They vouched for everyone except the Asian tumblers who kept to themselves when not practicing contortions.

Two unproductive hours later, Margaret gathered her belongings and decided to tell the ever-solicitous Pantages interviews were done for the day.

As she opened the door, in rushed Amy Wetherby, a songstress she'd spoken to earlier. Pantages had introduced her as the "American Nightingale," thereby inviting comparison to Jenny Lind, the "Swedish Nightingale" opera singer who toured America with P. T. Barnum more than fifty years earlier.

The woman lurched inside and pressed her back against the door. Hairdo, dress, and manner looked slightly askew and her earlier poise was gone.

She unfurled an artfully crafted poster of *Marco the Mesmerizing Magician,* compelling in profile as he loomed over a fainting blonde beauty. His dark velvet cape accentuated the folds of her diaphanous gown as well as her vulnerability.

"This is Marco, I think his last name is Andreoni. He always went by 'the Mesmerizing Magician' or, more recently, 'the Magnificent'. He was about to become the lead act here at Pantages. I'm so afraid your dead girl might be Marie Levecque, the nearest thing to a friend I had here. Last time I saw her was just before Marco was offered a job on another circuit.

"Were Marie and Marco romantically involved?"

"Marie was crazy about her magician, but I know they were having problems, chief one being our boss always had his eye on her, barging in when we were half dressed and whispering things that made her blush. Marco sure didn't like it. That's the real reason he left, just as much as the money. Maybe she was afraid to join him."

Outside the door, the sound of heavy footsteps grew louder and nearer. A terrified gasp escaped Amy Wetherby's lips. Margaret pushed her aside and opened the door just wide enough to stick out her head.

"May I please have a few more minutes to myself? I'd like to review my notes while everything is still fresh in my mind."

Pantages shrugged and walked away, barking commands to performers and stage crew. While her misgivings about him remained, Margaret couldn't help admiring the ease with which he controlled every detail of his bustling theater.

She turned her attention back to the room. Half-hidden in one dark corner, the young woman crouched wide-eyed with fear.

"Tell me more."

"I've said too much already," Miss Wetherby sighed and slid out the door.

Fear of scuttling a second interview forced Margaret to let her go. However intriguing the information might be, it was not enough to solve a murder mystery.

※

Margaret found McManus and Tyson out in the alley, leaning on packing crates and comparing observations. Their questioning of actors and crew had yielded nothing.

Knowing she'd uncovered useful information but uncomfortable about taking credit, Margaret shared her interview notes. Both men listened attentively.

McManus offered congratulations.

"We can't identify the body from what the girl told you, but you've come up with a likely lead. Face it, Charlie, this is what a woman does best. That girl would not have whispered so much as a syllable to the likes of us."

Tyson flashed one on of his rare smiles.

"We need to know more about this magician and the beautiful Marie. Pantages is the kind of man who's used to getting his way, whether with business or the ladies. Might be upset with anyone who didn't return his affections. Or maybe she did and it got her into more trouble."

"Maybe nine months' worth of trouble?" speculated his partner.

They turned to Margaret in unison, somewhat horrified to have voiced such a carnal idea out loud to a woman.

She took it in stride. They'd admitted her to an intriguing game and she was eager to take her turn.

"Alexander Pantages strikes me as being too brash to cover up a crime. On the other hand, a jealous magician might be far more capable of deception."

The men nodded in agreement.

"It'll take all three of us to get little Miss American Nightingale to give us an encore."

Margaret beamed, finally convinced a woman like her could indeed be effective in a man's world.

"And if we proceed discreetly, Seamus and Charlie, perhaps she'll sing all the words," she added brightly.

"Well said, Mrs. Margaret," McManus answered playfully.

It seemed natural for Margaret to use their first names by then, even though they would continue to use *Mrs.* before hers. Hadn't she called her husband Reverend Morehouse until a week before they were married? This was a new century; she was a New Woman; and no one seemed to mind.

The trio turned their attention to the infamous carpet left propped against the back wall of the theater. Every bird flying overhead or dog needing to relieve itself had christened it. Still, the remaining pile was thick enough to warrant closer inspection.

Brushing her hand across the tight weave, Margaret noticed a curious lack of wear. The stench McManus wrote about in his initial report was nearly gone.

"I can still make out a Persian border."

She pushed her hand deeply through the fibers. At the center was a matted black clump, not the typical bold pattern found on most fine carpets. The realization of what it must be made her recoil in horror.

McManus produced a small vial from his vest pocket and asked her to step aside. He released several drops of clear liquid on the murky stain. White foam bubbled up to the surface.

"What was that?" Margaret gasped.

"Hydrogen peroxide," he explained. "Good for cleaning wounds and testing for blood. It's blood alright."

McManus recapped his vial.

"This just confirms what we already know," he added. "but I'll get you a bottle of your own, if you like."

"You'll have to show me how to use it," Margaret answered.

Hearing herself sound more like a wide-eyed girl than a member of the Los Angeles police force, Margaret tried to change the subject.

"What else do you carry around in that vest of yours?"

"Pincers, magnifying glass, and dusting powder for fingerprints."

"Don't forget all those sticks of chewing gum and too much blubber to keep up with the likes of me," Tyson grumbled.

Margaret was puzzled.

"Why do you need powder to find fingerprints? How could that be useful? We all leave fingerprints if we don't wear gloves."

"They're identifiers. We all leave different marks, as wise folk have known for over a thousand years."

"How could anyone know for sure?" Tyson snarled.

"It's a science. *I* read up on it all the time. In France, they have what's called a forensic laboratory. In Los Angeles, all we have right now is ridin' around in my vest."

"And your excellent mind, I'm certain," Margaret added before returning her attention to the rug.

"Could it come from Pantages's office?" Tyson asked, recalling the deep pile they had all sunk into earlier in the day. "Let's look and feel for flat areas made by a heavy desk and furniture."

Margaret's eyes widened in agreement. They examined the fibers carefully but found no sharp grooves or indentations.

"It still might belong to him," Tyson insisted.

"You're undoubtedly right," Margaret added, patting his shoulder. "Maybe he planned to use it in a show or some other part of the theater".

Margaret mystified Tyson. What was it about this woman that made him feel better about himself, son of a son of an Irisher who could barely write his own name? The nuns had given up on him, but he hadn't, not quite. Still needed a drop of whiskey sometimes to make him feel better.

They went back into the auditorium and paused to watch rehearsals still going on in the auditorium. Acrobats were forming a human pyramid, then hopping down to cavort all over the stage. They looked like painted figures on a Chinese vase, too perfect to be real.

When they were done, the Harrolds, European whirlwind dancers, twirled across the stage. A busty woman dressed like a Viking warrior came out last, adjusting the horns on her head.

"I never interviewed that one ...," Margaret began.

She paused a moment and looked more closely. This Brunhilda's mustache and squeaky falsetto voice would have made Wagner spin in his grave.

"That's because *she's* a *he*," Tyson explained.

Just at that moment, one of the woman warrior's melon breasts escaped its harness and rolled into the orchestra pit. The two tired detectives, along with a rookie policewoman who just might turn into one, laughed all the way to the trolley.

CHAPTER NINE

Hoping a small libation would lighten Edmund's mood, Margaret filled two footed crystal mugs with cocoa and sherry and topped them off with mounds of whipped cream. Sweetness, spirits, and a roaring fire might be all she'd need before sharing a full account of the day.

Her efforts were rewarded by a warm smile, made even more endearing by speckles of cream left behind on his mustache.

"What an adventure you're having and how lucky the good detectives are to have you by their side! Clark endorses them as honorable men. I trust they'll drop by soon so I might have the opportunity to introduce myself."

He turned his back momentarily. If Margaret had glimpsed his tightly clenched teeth, the evening might have ended earlier.

Perhaps, Edmund thought, *there's not much difference between pulpit and stage after all. I won't ask her to abandon the case. Not now.*

He took a deep breath before she continued. They were chuckling over her Valkyrie description when Leland Morehouse, Edmund's wealthy nephew, appeared at the front door carrying a thick leather valise. Cushman, their faithful manservant, ushered the young man into the parlor.

Edmund and Margaret hadn't laid eyes on him since January, when, along with throngs of flight enthusiasts, they'd boarded the red Pacific Electric trains headed for the nation's first air show at Dominguez Field, a mesa fifteen miles southeast of Los Angeles.

Such a mindboggling experience it had been! A slight wind from the west had swept the skies clear. From the highest tier of the grandstand, they'd set their eyes on the horizon and a remarkable city on the rise, energized by rail and real estate beyond all expectations. Down below, the score of aviators threading their way through rows of enormous white tents paused only to tinker with engines.

In their usual grand style, Edmund's nephew and his wife Yvette drove up in a brand-new Stanley Steamer. It must have taken Leland fifteen minutes to build up enough steam for the drive, yet they emerged at the meet looking as if they had just left home, she in a powder blue gored skirt, flared jacket, and wide-brimmed hat; he in a long canvas duster, elbow-length gloves, goggles, and French chauffeur's cap with leather visor. Too much perfection for Edmund's taste, and all on the surface.

With no more than a passing nod, the young couple swept past them, the judges' booth, and boys hawking peanuts and crackerjack for five cents a bag. Yvette slipped her arm through Leland's as they climbed to the best seats in the grandstand.

"That is the most public display of affection I've ever seen between them," Margaret whispered to Edmund.

"More display than affection," he whispered back.

The sight of famed pilot Glenn Curtiss distracted them as he wheeled the Golden Flyer, his trademark yellow-winged biplane, to its starting point. Five months earlier, he'd been the only American to enter the first international air meet in Rheims, France, where he'd set the speed record, flying a ten-kilometer course at nearly forty-five miles per hour in sixteen minutes. His triumph earned him the Gordon Bennett Trophy and made it necessary for the next competition to be held in the United States. Los Angeles was the most logical location during the winter season.

At a signal from the craggy-faced aviator, his crew cleared the area of black-capped photographers. The crowd hushed. One assistant yanked the propeller clockwise; the engine sputtered, then roared. All eyes followed the minute-and-a-half long flight as it gracefully arced through a zenith of fifty feet to an easy landing five-eighths of a mile from the starting point. As one, the crowd cheered and rose to its feet.

Edmund was gratified when Glenn Curtiss outdid his former speed record by ten miles per hour. "Close as any man alive can physically get to heaven," he declared, too enthralled by the spectacle to give the younger Morehouses another thought.

Over the next week, Edmund followed newspaper accounts of the contestants' progress with zeal he normally reserved for the pulpit. Louis Paulson had traveled all the way from France to set world records and took home most of the prize money by achieving an altitude of over three-fourths of a mile and carrying a passenger almost 110 miles. Edmund grudgingly pronounced the Frenchman "deserving."

Perched on the edge of an easy chair more than ten months later, Leland disclosed that Yvette had run away on the day of the air meet and hadn't been heard from since. He'd told friends and family she was off touring the Continent.

"Your excuse must be wearing thin, Leland. Liners cross the Atlantic in a matter of days and she's been gone for an awfully long time. Is that what brings you here today? Or is it my ties to the church or your aunt's to the law?"

"Both, Uncle. My failure to report the situation to authorities until two weeks ago has compounded the predicament. She told me she was leaving just before Glenn Curtiss was about to take off."

"Leaving?" Margaret asked. "Did she mean for a while or for good?"

"At the time I thought she was going down to a lower level of the grandstand to find shade or purchase a lemonade. She has a delicate nature, you know. It was windy, noisy, and well, smelly. She's not used to all those..."

He stopped himself short. Edmund was poking the fire furiously.

"Working-class people?" he growled.

God's voice banishing Adam and Eve from Eden couldn't have been more disapproving.

Margaret beamed at her husband's implied reprimand and added one of her own.

"If Yvette thought she wasn't feeling well, why didn't you go with her?"

"She always claimed to have a weak constitution. Despite family expectations for us to start a family, we'd been sleeping in separate bedrooms from the very beginning."

Margaret looked uncomfortable. The younger couple's sleeping arrangements hit too close to home.

"Over breakfast a few months ago, I told her about Curtis's exploits, starting with his winning the Scientific American Cup back east to up to the point when he flew an aircraft of his own design at the French competition. She seemed excited at the prospect of seeing the great aviator in person."

"Then at last you had an interest in common!" Margaret interjected.

Leland shrugged.

"Attending the meet seemed to be as much her idea as mine. I didn't find anything odd about her sudden departure until afterwards when I couldn't find her. At the time, I was only irritated she would choose to miss such an historic moment."

"What did you do once the historic moment was over?" Edmund asked icily.

"Yvette has many talents but driving isn't one of them. Thinking there was no way for her to go back home without me, I stayed in my seat and scanned the field through binoculars. The aviators and their crew came from all four corners of the world! Louis Paulhan — did you know he brought two monoplanes, two biplanes, and apparently half of France with him? There were dirigibles and ..."

Margaret groaned.

"We were there, Leland! What did you do after the meet was over? Give us as much detail as you can remember."

Edmund handed Margaret a sheet of parchment and his prized fountain pen, normally reserved for writing sermons. Compared to the dip and drip of steel pens, he knew she'd be astonished by the speed with which she could record Leland's words.

"I thought it would be easier to find her after the crowds thinned. Most of all, I wanted to savor the moment, undistracted by her constant primping. She was another part of my lockstep life, bought and paid for by my mother."

Edmund shuddered at the mention of his tyrannical sister-in-law but didn't soften his tone.

"Did you even try to look for your wife before cranking up that contraption and heading home?"

Leland stood his ground.

"I questioned anyone on the field who would listen and searched behind the grandstand. That's where I came upon a group of scavengers trying to open this valise, one I recognized all too well. There was nothing I could do except pay them off, go home, and wait."

Unbuckling the valise's leather straps, he pulled out the skirt, jacket, boots, and hat Yvette had worn that day. A lightweight corset and pair of bloomers lay underneath.

"I found this message on my nightstand."

He handed Margaret a piece of folded foolscap, previously used, with his name written clearly on top of old writing. She read aloud.

Cher Leland, though only dear for form's sake. I told you I was leaving. You'll get more pleasure watching your heroes through binoculars than seeing me up close. Someday, if you find the courage, let your mother know what I have done. You are free now, and so am I.

~ Au revoir, Yvette

Margaret was stunned.

"Has any word arrived?"

"No, and Mother's asking questions. I couldn't tell her what really happened, so I came up with a story about my homesick wife going to Paris. Mother made me contact Yvette's family. They said she'd never arrived and professed ignorance of any planned visit. I suggested hiring detectives, but Mother insisted on handling the matter privately. She has a rogues' gallery of thugs in her service, all beholden to her."

Margaret shook out Yvette's garments and fold them into a neat pile.

"Her clothing wouldn't take up much room in my closet. Why don't you let me keep them here for a while, along with the letter?"

"Could you? I worry one of Mother's lackeys will find them. I can't move forward until I know the truth about what happened."

Edmund's frustration mounted. Hearing his nephew whine was pathetic. Leland's mother controlled him as tightly as the bank her father had founded. Like a queen bee, Elvira Gibbons Morehouse hired male drones to represent her interests in their world. Her penchant for politicos was unseemly; her lust for grabbing every dollar she could lay her calf skinned-gloved hands on an embarrassment. She had built a comfortable life for Leland and, for the most part, he hated her for it.

Margaret took it upon herself to accompany Leland to the door and made sure he buttoned up against the cool night air.

"We need more time. Maintain your story a little while longer and we'll do whatever we can."

When Margaret returned to Edmund's side, he was downing another sherry, this time without the cocoa.

"If Leland's upbringing had been warmer and more physically challenging, he might have joined these new heroes who defy gravity," he mused.

"He's tall and well-built, just like an adventurer should look. Did you notice his mustache is trimmed to the same length as Mr. Curtiss's?"

They held hands and gazed at the fire.

"If I'd ever found a way to treat Leland more like a son," Edmund murmured, "we might not be facing such a disappointing outcome."

"Your nephew lacks daring. You told me he's sole heir to a fortune founded before the Civil War. He must have the wherewithal to do as he pleases."

"That fortune grew through shrewd investments on both sides of the Mason-Dixon Line, with no loyalties attached. His ogress mother holds the purse strings. Behind the turquoise eyes my poor brother found so captivating lies a heart, mind, and soul molded by deceitful cunning."

"Dearest, I've long known you disapproved of Elvira, but I had no idea your feelings were that intense."

Edmund pounded his fist into the chair arm.

"Servants and a constant stream of tutors surrounded Leland from crib to boarding school. Many of them came up with excuses to leave at the first hint of the little tyrant's displeasure. They were terrified Elvira would blackball them with bad references.

"Do you think she spent much time with him?"

"The servants told my brother Mummy might march into the nursery from time to time, mostly to quiz and pat Leland on the head if he came up with the right answers. She treated him almost as well as her lap dogs."

"I doubt Leland spent much time on her lap."

"Only for the occasional family portrait, when my brother came home from another world adventure."

Until that moment, Edmund had never shared details of his brother's family life. Margaret was eager to hear the whole story. Something in that hidden history might explain their current situation, bookends holding a world between them, unable to see each other for the work they had to do.

"What about Jack? You always speak of him in glowing terms."

"My brother made me feel anything was possible when I was a little boy and restored my self-respect when I lost it later. Elvira was his spiritual blockade. Too late, he recognized the demon within the damsel but feared Elvira would find a way to deny him access to their son. It was his only cowardly act in an otherwise exemplary life. He always saw his boy first when he came home laden with foreign coins, toys, and treats. He died just three days before Leland's sixth birthday."

"How did Elvira handle the situation?"

"She didn't. A butler probably broke the news to Leland. We'd buried Jack at sea. A few weeks later, Elvira shipped the lad off to St. Alban's School for Boys in New York."

"Didn't he graduate from Yale?"

"Barely. Money admitted him to the best schools and kept him there despite mediocre grades and a disdain for authority. He reminded me of my more dissolute younger self, but his behavior was rooted in childhood. Whenever I tried to communicate, he treated me like an intruder. Once he came of age, I decided my travel expense was not worth the effort. He came back home with as much education as a man could get without discovering his true vocation."

"You're saying he became vice president at his mother's bank because he never found anything he wanted to do?"

"Or if he did, he was unwilling to try."

"So that's why he agreed to an arranged marriage! I doubt he ever gets the chance to make a single financial decision on his own."

Edmund shook his head sadly.

"I'm surprised she doesn't try to pick out his wardrobe. Who knows, maybe she does. Leland never had the kind of male chums his father and I always had around us. Jack wanted much more for his boy. Leland has his father's good looks and stature but that's where the resemblance ends.

"All I see when I look at him now is no more than an outline of the brother I loved. Elvira took away any sense of self-worth and filled him with an internal litany: *I am unworthy and incapable*."

Unworthy and incapable he'll remain, Margaret thought, *unless he can set himself free as his wife has apparently done.*

CHAPTER TEN

They climbed the stairs to separate bedrooms. Margaret stepped out of her clothes and let her hair cascade below her waist. She glanced in the mirror. Her reflection was lithe, she thought, almost pretty. Her hands fluttered to cover nudity for God-knows-what reason, then pulled a flannel nightshift over her head.

She fell into the bed they'd shared until Edmund moved a rock-hard mattress into his study, claiming he needed to strengthen his back and didn't want her to lose a wink of sleep. Wondering why he no longer found her attractive, she closed her eyes, hoping no nightmares of dead women and devious showmen awaited.

Dreams of Pantages lovelies dancing on wings of biplanes were mild enough and faded when she rose to face the new day's challenges.

She crossed the hall, blew a kiss to drowsy Edmund, donned a waist-length bottle-green cape to fend off the chill air, and ran outside.

She thought an imp must have hopped on board that morning or perhaps she was pushed; no woman in her right mind would jump off a moving trolley. Hurrying down Broadway past shopkeepers cranking up their awnings and drunkards weaving their way home, there was no other explanation for such rash behavior. She had nothing to fear. No one paid any attention to a woman whose appearance displayed neither wealth nor loose morals.

Hoping to avoid flamboyant Greek or his crony, Margaret approached the Pantages Theater by way of an alley extending to the street. Crouching in garbage near the back door, she overheard the unmistakable high to low exchange of a woman and man arguing. Their volume grew louder with each accusation.

"You mucked it up, you stupid strumpet!"

"I gave it to her just as you told me, and now it's time to pay," demanded someone sounding exactly like the American Nightingale.

"I was hiding in the closet while Mrs. Prim-and-Proper Policewoman talked to the girls. Could barely hold my water but heard every word. I told you to tell her who must have done it outright, but oh, no, first you made one man look bad as the other, and then made matters worse by running off."

The harsh whining voice could only belong to the Alexander Pantages right-hand man. Walters, Margaret believed he had called him.

The door swung open and an infuriated woman flew out. Amy Wetherby's eyes widened at the sight of Margaret nonchalantly plucking weeds and bits of broken glass off the hem of her skirt.

"Are you all right, my dear?" Margaret asked.

"What are you doing here?"

"Just passing by," Margaret responded, grateful the lying hadn't been listed in the Ten Commandments. "You seemed so upset yesterday. I had to make sure you're all right."

The sound of approaching footsteps made Amy scamper off. When Walters walked out seconds later and confronted Margaret with a vicious "You again!", she too took flight.

Margaret's brisk walk to the police station shook off any grime. She tucked a few wayward strands of hair back under her hat and began to make up a story about an accident to explain the delay.

She needn't have bothered. Policemen clustered around Captain Clarke nearly blocked the station door. Lewd laughs and whistles met her ears.

What do you think she's like under the covers? queried one. *Only one way to tell if she's a natural blonde,* sniggered another.

Unaccustomed to such vulgarity, Margaret retreated. Several minutes passed before she mustered sufficient courage to make her way back inside. A ring of patrolmen surrounded Tyson, cheeks red with humiliation, and McManus, nearly purple with anger. Margaret could not have felt more uncomfortable had she wandered into a saloon.

Arms firmly folded, Captain Clarke allowed the bawdy talk to continue, knowing his men were either letting off steam or grateful not to have caught the new assignment. One penetrating glare from

Alice was all it took to change his mind. He praised McManus and Tyson for taking on a difficult case and ordered everyone back to work.

Doubly mortified to catch sight of Margaret near the doorway, the detectives quickly crossed the room to explain their predicament.

"Captain Clarke's made the capture and arrest of the Boyle Heights Fiend this precinct's top priority, even more important than the Pantages case," began McManus.

"Rape Fiend, you mean," added Tyson.

McManus scowled. "You're speaking obscenities in front of a lady."

Margaret was at a loss for words until Alice Wells rushed over to join them.

"Please gentlemen, you're discussing a crime in front of a policewoman, which should be a different matter entirely," she began in her usual non-nonsense way. "May I suggest you tone it down unless you want half of Los Angeles to hear? We've all read the newspaper accounts about this brazen villain. Doesn't he stalk and capture couples out for an evening stroll, tying up the man and uh ... uh ..."

McManus finished her sentence.

"'Assaulting the woman' is the polite term journalists use. Or 'taken unawares,' as in the *Times* headline 'COUPLE TAKEN UNAWARES BY BOLD ASSAILANT' two days ago. Ten times in recent weeks these poor ladies have been violated, accosted, molested, or whatever you want to call it."

"The captain's making us bait the trap for this fiend," Tyson added. "We hate getting sidetracked from the Pantages investigation, but refusing a direct order would cost us our jobs."

Alice looked skeptical.

"Surely there are men on the force with less seniority who could track down the Fiend and free you up to solve your murder case."

"In the scheme of things, the Pantages girl doesn't matter very much. No one even knows her name. They're not going to raise a hue and cry if the investigation gets postponed. We may have been here longer than most of the fellows but like that poor Pantages lass, we lack family connections," responded McManus.

"Do you think the captain plays favorites?" Margaret asked.

Alice spoke before he could answer.

"The press and public get riled up very time the Fiend strikes. The Captain's a fair man with keen political instincts. For everyone's sake, he must be."

As Margaret learned much later, Captain Clarke had assigned these men based on their backgrounds. McManus's renown as a wrestler made headlines until his competitors became younger, suppler, and luckier. He was a self-taught man whose depth of knowledge on subjects practical and arcane equaled those of any academic.

Tyson's running abilities had taken him to the 1904 St. Louis Summer Olympics, where he nearly earned a bronze medal. What he lacked in height he made up for in sheer tenacity.

Neither man possessed all the skills required to be a detective, but together they were an unbeatable team. The Captain could not have found two more dedicated or talented men under his command.

Although Margaret considered herself a worldly woman, the plight of the Boyle Heights couples sickened her. Alice tapped her on the shoulder.

"Margaret Morehouse, I've never been more proud or worried sick about anyone in a very long time. Let me know the moment these two formerly self-reliant men manage to give you some time off for tea and talk."

She patted Margaret's hand and took off in a straight trajectory toward the theater district, leaving McManus and Tyson a bit chagrined. Margaret lightened their mood with a brief description of her morning's encounter with Amy Wetherby.

"Sounds like that Walters fellow might have thrown us a bone," grumbled Tyson.

"You think so? I may have run into him only hours before I first met you. On my first day working with the police department, Mrs. Wells took me along to patrol the Clune where we rescued a little girl who said he, or someone very much like him, was touching her in an unfitting way. I have every reason to believe her."

Neither man reacted strongly to the shocking news. Right then, Margaret silently vowed never to develop the kind of detachment that derives from recurring contact with evil.

"He's more than capable of acting on his own," she insisted.

"His mean spirit doesn't make him a murderer," said Tyson.

"Maybe he made all the arrangements!" muttered McManus.

He took out his notebook and pencil stub and began making notes and diagrams. Margaret glanced over his shoulder. Lines connecting the names *Marco the Magician* and *Pantages*, with *Walters* in parentheses, spidered off in several directions.

"We can't jump to conclusions. If the body belonged to Marie Levecque, we should narrow our suspects down to Marco and his former employer. Jealousy is a powerful motive. Pantages has an unsavory reputation with the ladies. Walters's role might include finding hoodlums capable of covering up his employer's indiscretions. My guess is he wanted Miss Wetherby to tell you more about the jealous boyfriend than the lecherous boss. She probably forgot her lines."

"Well of course, *that's* why he was so mad at her!" crowed Tyson triumphantly.

Margaret could not resist playing devil's advocate.

"Wouldn't Alexander Pantages's daily associations with beautiful women make him a frequent target for slander?"

"First of all, his name isn't Alexander, it's Pericles," said Tyson, derisively, "and I never heard tell of a more dandified name than that one. They say he styled himself after Alexander the Great."

McManus began to share more anecdotes.

"He wasn't all that great in the Nineties when he was a wrestler in the prize ring. My Da' favored the top welterweight Mysterious Billy Smith and took me to all the preliminary bouts between Smith and Pantages. Da' made a bit of money on his wagers that night and Pantages hung up his gloves.

"Next, we heard he was in the Yukon, hunting for Klondike gold. Found it easier to extract the stuff from miners than the ground, so he tended bar. Met a dance hall girl named Klondike Kate and convinced her to buy him a theater where she would be the star and he would bring in other acts. When the gold strike played out, Kate went on the road and he moved to Seattle, where he met and married the present Mrs. Pantages and opened another showplace. Kate caught up with him, sued for breach of promise, and settled for an ungodly amount."

Margaret shook her head in dismay.

"Then there is a Mrs. Pantages after all."

"He'd have never come this far without both ladies' backing. You'd think by now he might have learned to be more careful around women. The way they flock to him for fame and fortune makes him a target for accusations. Still, there's nothing to link him directly to the murdered girl, at least for now."

"Sounds like even detectives with experience like yours can be misled. It must take time to learn how to sort things out and trust your gut feelings."

McManus nodded.

"That reminds me. Gut feelings need proof. Here's the forensics kit I promised."

He handed her a grey, slightly padded drawstring bag containing a small magnifying glass, tweezers, and dropper-topped bottle of peroxide.

Tyson remained unconvinced.

"All I can say is Pantages acts like a rooster in the henhouse around them chorus girls. That's what makes him worth watching. Don't you take it upon yourself to do the watching, at least not until we're done with Boyle Heights."

Tyson looked at me almost meekly.

"Now, that's a case we could use your help on."

"Confront a fiend like that? Never!"

"Confrontations will not be necessary, Ma'am. You simply need to find me a dress."

CHAPTER ELEVEN

Tyson was forced to wear the wig, black veil, and amethyst skirt that night because they wouldn't look good on his partner. McManus was the handsomer of the two, but no disguise could conceal those broad shoulders, wide enough to carry a steamer trunk, and belly paunched by schooners of beer.

They'd been ordered to stroll arm in arm along the streets of Boyle Heights, Tyson in taffeta and McManus in tweed. Once accosted, they were to capture the Rapist, although how they were to bind and haul him off to jail with only a single trolley running late at night was beyond anyone's understanding.

With Margaret and McManus standing by, Mary Ellen Tyson assembled an outfit from a trunkful of clothing once worn by her deceased grandmother. Her husband would have preferred wearing long johns in public, but, as they all kept reminding him, time was of the essence.

Margaret rummaged through their pantry to make an early meal. Limp onions and potatoes with rotten parts cut out would have barely stretched the family of five's leftover stew for another evening, let alone feed two more adults. McManus and Margaret left Charlie in Mary Ellen's capable hands and went out to purchase a capon, bread, and apples at a nearby grocer.

After dinner, Mary Ellen laced her husband into an S-bend corset and covered it with a long-sleeved top, which she called a chemise, to hide his chest and arm hair. She tucked folded linen napkins underneath to give him a more feminine upper chest. It was hard to tell which Tyson found more annoying: his lopsided bust or the stiff lace collar rubbing against his Adam's apple.

"I can loosen it at the back, dear," Mary Ellen said, trying to make him feel better. "Grandma's wig will cover the gap."

A few snips of her sewing shears eased the tightness while

preserving what she insisted was a more stylish neckline. Grandma must have been a short, sizable woman. He stepped into the skirt; with a few inches let out at the waist and a ruffle tacked onto the length, it worked passably well.

Next came a pair of calfskin boots with dainty heels designed to make a big footed woman appear elegant. Tyson squeezed his toes together and clenched his teeth when Margaret laced him up. Cursing with every step, he lumbered about the room.

"Women take shorter strides," Mary Ellen advised. "Lift the hem of your skirt when you come to a puddle or step off the curb."

"Don't you think he should wear his own boots?" McManus asked. "His skirt touches the ground anyway."

"Our rapi …," Margaret couldn't let herself finish the word. "The villain would spot the way he walks right away. Once our Charlie's used to those shoes, he'll move more daintily."

"The suspect would probably notice him wobbling along and wonder what a fine-looking chap like me is doing with such an ugly girl."

"Bloke big as you would be lucky to be out walking with any girl," Tyson grumbled before plopping down in front of the mirror for Mary Ellen's final ministrations.

After a ten-minute application of powder and paste, it seemed he might pass for a homely woman under a streetlight at night. At a distance.

Mary Ellen rubbed the bristle under his chin.

"Too much stubble. Would you like a quick shave, dear?"

McManus checked his timepiece and reached for his hat and bowler.

"We must be on our way. Put the veil on our Gibson Girl, two if you have 'em."

Mary Ellen pinned a thick swath of black lace to the underside of the bonnet and tied it firmly to keep the wig in place.

From the bottom of the trunk, Margaret picked up Grandma's last contribution to the disguise: a black three-quarter length coat.

"Please put this on. It completes the outfit and covers up all the strained seams."

"Have her home at a respectable hour," Mary Ellen teased from the porch.

The men walked towards the streetcar, pretending not to notice the neighbor squinting through her lace curtains.

Tyson grunted low and loudly to remind everyone the hobbling frump they were laughing at was no one else but a proud member of LAPD's finest. Dress or no dress, when the night was over, he might end up a hero.

CHAPTER TWELVE

Margaret put the children to bed and yearned to stay longer. Nicks and scratches throughout the home bore witness to youthful shenanigans, yet everything was dusted and polished. Mary Ellen's loving common sense had been handed down through generations. Hers was the wisdom of the hearth, necessary skills to care for her brood.

Holding on to wriggling baby Michael proved a challenge until he stopped protesting that Margaret wasn't his mother. She stroked his plump cheeks, relishing the satin skin most ladies desire and can only mimic with lotions. His skin would toughen over time and those sparkling eyes might see success or failure.

"They are blessings all," Mary Ellen murmured, taking Michael from Margaret's arms, "as well as beautiful burdens. I drew my last calm breath when Charlie Jr. was born but would not trade these children for all the world's riches. Do you have children, Mrs. Morehouse?"

"Not yet, and after almost a decade of marriage, probably never."

"Forgive me for asking. It's the number one topic of discussion for us Irish women. Our only choices are the nun's wimple or bridal veil. Be thankful you have other ways to go."

At long last, Margaret began to understand the enormous responsibility of motherhood. It was one thing to bring children into the world, quite another to raise them. She could take a day off and no one would think lesser of her.

Mary Ellen tucked the older children into bed while Margaret rocked Michael in the cradle until he fell asleep. Kissing the nape of his little neck, she tiptoed out of the nursery and left for home, carrying a vision of what might have been, hoping to come back for more.

The autumn air stiffened her resolve. Walking to Third and Hill

Streets, her mind hopscotched across the mysteries she'd recently encountered.

The Pantages problem was rooted in depravity. Until they pierced the conspiracy in that tight vaudevillian world, the victim would remain faceless and the culprit free. By comparison, Leland's dilemma was a mere misstep, no matter how baffling Yvette's means of escape from a loveless marriage might seem.

Margaret's usual ride did not run past sundown. She headed west towards Third and Hill where two years earlier the Benevolent and Protective Order of Elks had built a decorative arch to commemorate their convention.

The structure marked the lower access to the Los Angeles Incline Railway, better known as Angels Flight. Connected to a single cable, two small white carriages, named Sinai and Olivet after biblical mountains far higher but possibly not much steeper than the 315-foot Bunker Hill she needed to climb, counterbalanced each other. When one car reached the top of the hill, the other could be boarded down below.

Those who'd rather climb than ride could always take a flight of stairs. Margaret was in no such mood. Her late-night wanderings might well test Edmund's patience to the limit. She boarded the Olivet and showed her badge to the surly conductor.

Worried the creak of hardwood floors would awaken Edmund and Cushman, she unlaced and removed her shoes when she reached the doorstep. From faraway came a distinct *pop!* Less than a second later, something buzzed overhead, bounced off the upper brass door hinge, ricocheted against the jamb, and clattered to the porch so loudly she barely heard sounds of feet and hooves running off into the night.

Peeling off a glove to feel around, Margaret half expected to find a dazed bird or bat. Her fingers came upon a metallic object, cylindrical and burning hot. She picked it up gingerly and went inside. Under the dim light of the lamp Cushman had left by the window, she saw it was a large leaden bullet.

CHAPTER THIRTEEN

Edmund and Cushman were too absorbed in the *Times* the next morning to acknowledge Margaret's presence.

Clamping her left hand around the bullet, she wondered why neither had responded to the disturbance and if it was worth mentioning at all.

Too much candor might halt her career. Tucking the bullet securely in her waistband, Margaret put on a bland smile and acted as if nothing unusual had happened.

The look on both men's faces, however, told her something else already had.

She buttered a biscuit and poured out some tea.

"Wonderful to see you up in time for breakfast, dear," Margaret ventured.

"I went to bed early. Bit of a cough coming on. Cushman poured me a small libation last night and now I feel quite fine."

A wave of relief passed over her. She launched into a description of the Boyle Heights case and how worried she was it might disrupt the Pantages investigation.

Edmund handed her the morning paper.

"Your friends' new assignment must have been deucedly difficult, but I fear they are in for much worse. Read on..."

Emblazoned across the front page in bold Cheltenham type, three-inches tall, L. A. TIMES EXPLOSION! headlined a horrific account.

Margaret read how, while she lay shaken but safe in bed, the Los Angeles Times Building fell like the walls of Jericho, trapping pressmen working overnight to churn out an extra edition. The south wall caved in first, taking printing presses with it and creating a pit through which the dead or injured fell to the floor below.

Then the first floor collapsed into the basement, destroying the heating plant and gas mains. Flames erupted from every level. Terrified workers leapt out any available window and plummeted to death on the pavement. Those who followed viewed the carnage, teetered on the ledges, and fell back into the growing inferno.

"Dear God, the detectives had to be out late on their new assignment. They must have been on their way back when the explosion occurred. I pray they are safe."

"Knowing you won't rest until you've seen for yourself, I've asked Cushman to bring round the horse and buggy and take you wherever you need to go. I can work on my sermon, and you'll have a ride at your disposal."

Margaret gasped. For Edmund, giving up Cushman was an unprecedented sacrifice.

On a rainy evening nearly seven years earlier, that tall, wooden-faced man had sprung from the gutter onto their carriage to rein in a runaway horse Edmund could not control. Once the crisis had been averted, the Morehouses took note of the stranger's grimy skin, emaciated form, and a slight hand tremor suggesting an ongoing thirst for liquor.

Owing their wellbeing and possibly lives to this scarecrow, they offered the only compensation they could afford: a tub, change of clothes, and bedroom. Within days, Cushman had sobered up sufficiently to become their self-appointed servant. He cooked, cleaned, and gardened for them. He scrutinized guests and drove for them. When they were ill, he cared for them. They scrimped to pay him accordingly.

"You've become almost as indispensable to your colleagues as you are to me. This morning Cushman suggested dedicating Daisy, the carriage, and his services to you for the next month. Considering all the dangerous situations you seem to be getting involved in lately, I've agreed."

And neither of you bothered to consult me, Margaret almost said aloud, then stopped herself short. Ready transportation was an unexpected gift, one she could not ignore.

"How will you make home and hospital visits?"

"Several parishioners are willing to help. All I ask is of you is to keep the Sabbath and wrap up these dangerous activities."

"Just don't make me resign!"

"Of course not. I'm the proud husband of a pioneer woman. All I ask is once you and your valiant partners resolve this murder, please return to more safe, routine tasks, like the ones we first agreed upon."

Margaret appreciated how much more enlightened Edmund was than his peers but resented anyone questioning her right to take on new responsibilities. Her husband's control tactics were out of character and might simply reflect a desire to return their lives to the way they'd been. Whatever his motives, he'd given her purpose if not progeny, and she did not refuse.

CHAPTER FOURTEEN

Cushman brought round the modest carriage drawn by Daisy, the dappled gray he'd found to replace the runaway horse so many years before. The Morehouses' support had been his salvation. He would do anything to protect them.

He helped Margaret climb aboard. For the first time since fate thrust them together, she felt ill at ease in his presence.

Did you hear me come in so late? she wanted to ask, but what came out was "Would it be possible to take me all the way to the police station?"

"I'll do my best. The L. A. Times building is nearby and the streets may be barricaded."

With a flick of the buggy whip, they were off.

Cushman's predictions were accurate. He tethered Daisy to a store railing three blocks away and they proceeded on foot towards the smoldering ruins, a scene as close to Armageddon as either could have imagine. Margaret felt trapped in a demon's glass globe filled with soot instead of snow. One shake might rekindle the conflagration.

The roast-pork reek of burned bodies overlaid with the scorched brimstone of melted asphalt was almost unbearable, despite the fire brigade's successful efforts to overcome the flames. Only the building's slightly blackened bronze eagle loomed unscathed atop the remaining stone walls. One disgruntled voice in the crowd said it should fall from its perch.

They found the detectives working tirelessly, as they had been since returning from Boyle Street. Few of their fellow policemen had been on duty that early.

McManus and Tyson thought an earthquake was shaking the ground until the night erupted in flames and pandemonium. Tyson forgot all about his female attire. Covering their heads with dampened coats to shield against the searing heat, the men dragged inert bodies to safer ground and brought many victims up First Street to the Receiving Hospital. More often than not, they carried corpses, making every effort to keep them intact and recognizable for families to identify. Whenever officers from the morning watch appeared at the scene, no one dared ridicule the barefoot man in a dress and his partner.

Police and firemen rolled away smoldering timbers and righted printing presses until no more bodies could be found. Cushman and Margaret joined them and scores of volunteers sifting through the ashes to uncover glasses, pocket watches, and occasional body parts. Death and destruction curbed conversation, though many laid blame for the gas explosion on faulty furnaces.

Cushman stayed with the volunteers while Margaret followed the detectives to the back of the building. Sickened by the carnage and choking from smoke, the trio made their way down Ink Alley, the narrow road between First and Broadway named for its proximity to the *Times* building.

The detectives tore up weeds and ripped open crates in search of anything that might have caused the conflagration. Margaret tried to help but Tyson shooed her off like a pesty child.

"Find someone out front who has paper and something to write with, and while you're at it round up a street boy to carry a note to my wife."

"We came by carriage. We'll take her anything, including you, when you're ready."

An extra pair of eyes would help bring their wretched night's work to an earlier end. Tyson snorted in surprise and beckoned her to join them.

They discovered a dozen suitcases with dangling straps, broken clasps, and leather remnants still clinging to their scorched husks. Strewn in and around the metal frames, spent sticks of dynamite released an acrid smell.

Hoarse from soot and shaken by this discovery, McManus yelled for help. Those who came running stopped in their tracks at the sight of the treachery. Cushman was amongst them.

As others joined the crowd, they sharedf news about another dynamite-filled suitcase exploding under the bedroom window of General Harrison Gray Otis, owner and publisher of the *Los Angeles Times*. A third bomb was discovered at the home of the secretary of the Merchants and Manufacturers Association. No injuries were reported at either site, but twenty-one people had leapt or fallen to their deaths and scores were seriously injured.

Timing clearly indicated all three devices were parts of a coordinated effort. Colonel Otis's militant anti-union attitude was public knowledge; vitriolic editorials and deteriorating employee relations only deepened the divide.

Perfidy! Murderers! came a voice in the crowd. *The unions are in on this, I tell ya'!*

Someone set them up and my money's on Old Man Otis! boomed another.

Fists swung and arguments volleyed back and forth with no one declared a winner. Cushman's mind raced back to earlier times when he'd witnessed death deal out an uneven hand. Everyone was right or everyone was wrong, and there was no room for compromise.

The day's exertions loosened Margaret's waistband. No one noticed the bullet drop and roll away. Taking it as a sign the violence would soon be ending, she chose not to run after it.

∿∿

By early afternoon, both detectives were dizzy with fatigue and more than grateful for a ride. McManus lived in a nearby boarding house. Cushman calculated the buggy's capacity against the Irishman's bulk and took him home first. An hour later, he returned for Margaret and Tyson. They squeezed into the carriage tightly as sardines, although Tyson smelled worse. Margaret resorted to breathing through her mouth. Getting away from the catastrophic scene was worth any inconvenience.

Dozens of newsboys lined the streets waving rolled copies of the morning paper.

Tyson hissed through clenched teeth.

"How did they manage to publish *The Times* right on schedule?"

"Colonel Otis owns another building on College Street between Main and Alameda. They even put out a second edition."

"How convenient."

Tyson's tone left little doubt about his suspicions or attitude towards the rich and powerful. Margaret tried to change the subject.

"Did things go well in Boyle Heights?"

"News about the rapist kept most people home. Only couples I saw at first were wrestling drunkards rolling out from under barroom doors into the street. There were a few Mexicans and Chinamen running around, more than I've ever seen on night patrol."

"No wonder. Their real homes are borders or oceans away. Boyle Heights is the only section of Los Angeles where there are no housing restrictions."

"Hmm, never knew that. Still, it's a terrible place to start a new life. My folks came over because they were starving. They stayed hungry for a long time raising us kids. Think it helped we were the same color as the folks in power, 'cause most of us who lost the brogue and scrubbed up good found jobs, although we're still not where we should be. Hope things go better for my family."

Sound social commentary from the lips of an exhausted man surprised Margaret. Gender and social norms were the barriers she hoped to overcome. Race, nationality, and poverty never stood in her way.

She wanted to continue the discussion, but curiosity got the better of her.

"How did you manage with your dress, er, I should say, disguise?"

"If it isn't the worst thing I've ever been made to wear, I'll add a mask and save it for Halloween. No matter if it costs me my job, the children will never see me in that get up again. Even worse, my feet are at least a size bigger than those infernal boots and I got slower with each block we passed."

Margaret took off her shawl and began wrapping it around his bloody stocking-covered feet.

"When did you take off Grandma's shoes?"

"Not until we reached First Street. McManus helped me hobble along to the library steps where I plopped myself down and threw them into the bushes. Even pulled off my socks to show him my oozing blisters. That hardhearted Mick told me the only reason the Rapist didn't show himself was because I looked like an ugly girl wobbling in my first pair of dress shoes. Then we saw the others."

"What others?"

"A pair of likely victims across the street, big as life. One of them was primping in the store windows by the light of the streetlamps. Never saw anything stupider.

"McManus yelled out no more women would be ravished or men disgraced. He was bound and determined to escort the foolish couple home, no matter what excuse they gave him."

"Did you try to help?"

"He told me to stay put, then crossed the street calling out *I say there! Halt!* next shouts of *Cur!* and *Thug!* come sailing back. After that I heard flesh hit flesh and a breaking window. I limped across the street. McManus stepped out of the shadows with a black eye.

"Turned out to be only O'Hara and Johnson, who'd been told we were working the other end of town and took him for the Rapist."

"I thought you were the only ones handed this awful assignment."

"We thought so, too; no one in their right mind would have volunteered. The captain must have worried we couldn't cover the whole neighborhood. Since it was past midnight, we decided to leave O'Hara and Johnson on their own, though how that fat-faced Johnson could fool anyone into believing he was a girl is beyond me."

Margaret suppressed a smile. Jealousy between two manly men over who played the better girl was a concept quite foreign to her and rather amusing.

"How on earth did you manage to make it back to the streetcar?"

"In my bare feet, holding on to McManus's arm."

"What did the conductor have to say?"

"Not a word. Maybe my beard or McManus's muscles were showing. We got off at First and Spring, saw the time on the public street clock was 1:10 a.m., and proceeded towards Central Station. You know what happened next."

CHAPTER FIFTEEN

Twenty hours of nonstop rescue work had taken their toll. Tyson's legs buckled when Mary Ellen opened the door. Cushman dragged him over to the fireplace where he would doubtless awaken stiffer than the boards beneath him. Margaret draped him with a quilt.

The children hovered wide-eyed with worry until Margaret gathered them around and told an epic story about their father and his faithful crew on an odyssey to Boyle Heights and back to end a terrible fire.

The picture she painted was so vivid Charlie Jr. and Mary Catherine began pretending they were police and firemen. They tried to save their baby brother, a vocal victim who did not want rescuing. Despite the ruckus, their father remained inert. Mary Ellen, hoping he could stay that way for a while, shooed them outside.

Cushman and Margaret followed suit and climbed back aboard the carriage. It was too late to report to the station and too early to go home. Margaret hoped the captain might not expect her to come in at all, given the unusual situation.

The current crisis might force them to abandon their original investigation but without an order, she still had time. Cushman agreed to drive her to over to Pantages Theater. With him by her side, she might be able to confront Walters in front of Pantages and demand an explanation for the back-alley scheming.

The lobby doors were propped open, but no rehearsal was in progress. They padded over muslin runners laid across recently polished floors. Pantages was center stage, gesticulating wildly and shouting profanities toward a dark room high in the back of the theater until he spotted them.

"*La belle* policewoman!" he exclaimed, rushing towards Margaret with enthusiasm. "To what do I owe this great honor?"

Walters was nowhere in sight. Margaret came to the theater half convinced Alexander Pantages was capable of murder, either directly or by hire. She suspected he was the one who'd directed Walters to bribe Miss Wetherby into bringing her the poster.

His smile seemed genuine and her suspicions, flighty as a schoolgirl's crush, shifted once again to the jilted magician. She'd never met anyone like the gregarious Greek who laced lust with power and charm. It was not sensual attraction, at least not on her part. She extended her hand for the customary kiss and began her inquiry without mention of Amy Wetherby.

"You signed Marco the Magnificent as a star attraction, yet I see neither he nor his female assistant is on the opening bill."

"No mystery to that, Madam. Marco deserted me for the Grimaldi brothers, pirates who pay more but lack a true sense of art. When their poor excuse of a theater closes, he'll come crawling back to me. I was once a struggling young man myself. My heart is so big I might even let the prodigal son return."

"Would this offer include Marie Levecque?"

"Madam is becoming quite the investigator. Miss Levecque jilted that poor fellow before he left the show. Perhaps that is why he acted like an imbecile."

His eyes suddenly widened.

"He was crazy in love with her. You don't think ...?"

"That the body in your alley was his missing assistant? I hope not, though it's possible. The question is, where can I find this magician before he disappears again?"

"My sources tell me he is working solo and things are not working out. His sleight of hand is quite good, but all audiences want are gorgeous gowns and lovely limbs of damsels in distress climbing in and out of Chinese boxes. I've heard he's holding auditions for an assistant tonight."

"Should I talk to him before or after?"

Pantages stroked his pomaded moustache and gazed into space with the same intensity with which he envisioned his shows.

"I think, no, I *know* you must try out for the part yourself. You're beautiful, elegant, and perhaps a better actress than you think."

"I don't know what you mean, sir."

Margaret dared not look back at his admiring eyes. Only Edmund had ever praised her looks.

"You turned up a lot of information in a very short time. It takes a man like me to see how smart and pretty you are. If you let that auburn hair down and put on a bit of lip rouge, you'd be the equal of any woman on the circuit. Don't you agree, Officer Cushman?"

As blood rose in Margaret's cheeks, Pantages turned to Cushman, who played right along with the Greek's assumption.

"I'd say you're right, sir, but first I must remind you my colleague is a married woman of high moral standards. You will make no more mention of the way she looks to her or to me, for that matter."

"Then you don't think she should do this..." began Pantages.

"Oh, but I do. The part you suggest she play would be no more than an act. Also, since this magician may be a blackguard, I will accompany her for safety's sake. Don't you agree, Officer Morehouse?"

"I must remind you, *Officer* Cushman, I'm a minister's wife. I might be capable of imitating a show girl's appearance, but I don't know how to act like one."

Margaret took several deep breaths and weighed the possibilities. What forces had brought her to this point? Why had fate, the Almighty, or whatever was out there steered her along this path?

"All right, I'll do it, and yes, you probably should stay close by. The magical Marco might well see through my disguise. Mr. Pantages, may I consult with one of your dancers?"

"As long as you promise to tell me what illusions you see Marco practicing," the maestro replied.

She agreed, seeing no harm. Pantages put her under the care of a young woman named Nellie Hargrove whose sprinkling of freckles and generous smile softened her classic blonde beauty. Margaret liked her at once.

They were of similar height and build. Nellie loaned Margaret her sumptuous emerald satin dress with a forest green velvet bodice. She secured most of Margaret's hair into a half bun caught up with ribbons and let the rest, shining under the makeup lights, fall past her shoulders. Margaret watched her rouge her lips then sparingly did the same.

What Margaret admired most about Nellie was her friendliness and the ease, neither prim nor vulgar, with which she moved. The stranger looking back at her from the mirror would have to emulate that grace for as long as the masquerade lasted.

Nellie completed Margaret's transformation with a pearl choker and matching drop earrings.

"Not the real thing, of course, Mrs. Morehouse," she whispered in her ear. "Take it from one who's been on the circuit since the age of ten, they look good enough. On the other hand, if you're trying to impress a society bloke, you might be in trouble."

"I'm trying to catch a bad man," Margaret whispered back.

"There's no end to the men you can catch looking like that."

Catching sight of her full form in the nearby cheval glass, Margaret gasped involuntarily and her cheeks turned scarlet.

"Genteel young ladies," she recalled one of her mother's friends whispering on the eve of her wedding, "have a duty to please their husbands, yet never display their charms in public."

Her charms, to use that archaic phrase, were very much on display. She was a hairsbreadth away from telling Nellie she couldn't possibly appear like this in public, then changed her mind. The outlandish plan might be the best way to expose either a jilted Marco or lascivious Pantages as a criminal. More importantly, the suspension of disbelief the stage demanded permitted dress and deportment unacceptable elsewhere. Even in the intimacy of the marriage bed, drawn curtains and extinguished lights let few husbands see as much of their wives as she was about to expose to strangers.

Nellie patted the hand Margaret was using to tug up her neckline and covered the modest décolletage with a fringed shawl.

Margaret thanked her and left, passing Pantages as he bowed deeply and followed her exit with appreciatively raised eyebrows.

The inscrutable Cushman helped her into the carriage with a touch more care than he'd shown before. As they drove towards the Grimaldi Theater, Margaret silently prayed the trouble for which she might be headed would be no worse than getting caught wearing fake pearls.

CHAPTER SIXTEEN

The gilt proscenium arch and cerulean velvet drapes at the Grimaldi Theatre rivaled, but did not eclipse, Pantages.

Marco the Magnificent, handsome in person as in Amy Wetherby's poster, was rehearsing onstage. Flowers and playing cards sprouted from his gloved fingertips, vanished, and reappeared out of thin air.

Four women wearing elaborate costumes and hopeful expressions watched his every move. Two sported the modified turbans and harem pants popularized by the recent Parisian debut of the ballet *Scheherazade*. Three rows back, another woman wrapped in a ruby red kimono swayed to the strains of mandolin music playing offstage.

The fourth appeared to be a demure Gibson Girl. On closer inspection, the gauze of her high-necked blouse exposed more than the most plunging of necklines. Her whole bodice jiggled when a newcomer in emerald green tapped her on the shoulder to ask if she were waiting for an audition. The Gibson Girl sniffed and nodded warily. Margaret took the seat behind her while Cushman settled in the back row.

"No good," snarled a large, Italian-sounding manager entering from the wings. "You are the opening act. I'm not giving you a half hour to do card tricks no one can see from the back rows."

Marco turned his black, compelling eyes on him and spoke, voice resonant and bristling with anger.

"These Egyptian props and sets demand a well-trained assistant. My former partner mastered my methods, then vanished. I can only hope my secrets are safe. Sleight of hand I can perform without her; I learned the technique from no lesser light than the Great Thurston."

"When you can take any card someone in your audience

picks, put it back in a deck, and make it rise into the air so people can see the full effect the way Thurston does, I'll build an entire show around you. Until then, find a girl quickly and make sure she's good looking."

Rage rippled across Marco's well-developed shoulders. His jaw was taut with tension as he spoke.

"I am not one of your cheap dumb opening acts, you fool. Why don't you trot out the dancing dogs instead? After all, you chose to give me top billing."

"We gave you and your beautiful young lady top billing because she's such a looker no one would notice if you dropped a card or two. Dumb acts open the show, and that's all you are without her. Pick an assistant and train her by next week or you'll be performing with the Chinese acrobats, if we keep you on at all."

Dumb acts? Margaret wondered to herself. *Why would anyone hire stupid performers?*

She would later learn the term applied to acrobats and jugglers or any act that did not rely on speech. In vaudeville hierarchy, dumb acts ranked at the bottom.

Marco reacted to the insult by placing the tip of his right thumb underneath his front teeth and flicking it in the manager's direction. From the manager's mottled expression, one could only assume this gesture symbolized great contempt, possibly close to obscenity.

Marco pointed at the five women waiting to audition.

"No one in that group could replace Marie. Before we were together, my solo performances dazzled many aristocrats. I can entertain the bourgeoisie of Los Angeles just as easily on my own."

The implacable manager folded his arms across his chest. Once more, Marco glanced in Margaret's direction, but this time he *saw* her, and his gaze lingered.

"She'll do."

Cold panic poured over Margaret as she stepped up to the stage. His compelling voice made her wonder if he might not be using some form of Mesmer's animal magnetism.

She gave him her maiden name, Margaret Ellison. He asked if he could call her Meg, and then, without waiting for a response, ordered stagehands to bring up the cabinet illusion.

It took four men mere moments to fill the stage with the trappings of faux antiquity: potted palms, sphinx, and pyramid cutouts, along with three chairs padded thickly enough for the most indolent of Egyptian princesses. At center stage set an assembly of perpendicular gold-painted pipes joined on top by a square of short rods and secured to an elevated base on casters. Marco deftly flung a large dark blue velvet drape embroidered with glittering stars over the framework, completely covering the four open sides.

"Put these on," he commanded, handing her a bundle of cloth and jewelry.

The manager gestured towards a sturdy screen in the right wing where Margaret could hide from view and complete her second transformation of the day.

A bejeweled vest and collar necklace provided a degree of modesty above, while below a sheer gauze skirt flaring out from the thick band of fringed deep blue satin wound around the abdomen displayed quite a bit of her. She pulled half a dozen bracelets onto each arm and crowned herself with an ornate gold circlet.

Margaret slithered back on stage as what she hoped Marco would think was a fair facsimile of a dancing girl.

"Cleopatra may have been a redhead after all! All I ask is you try to move in a more stylized manner."

Marco walked around her slowly, holding his arms in the birdlike positions Margaret and her brother used as children to make shadow pictures on their parlor wall.

Thankful Cushman's gaze could not penetrate the curtain, she followed Marco's example and added a wiggle or two. He nodded approvingly, then brought out a well-worn edition of the King James Bible and swore her to secrecy.

Marco uncovered the cabinet to prove the oversized chair placed immediately behind it was not merely ornamental. Built atop four carefully crafted doors, the throne, as Margaret learned to call it, hid an interior chamber.

Crouched on a padded cushion inside this cleverly constructed box, she awaited her cue. To the rumble of pulleys parting the curtains and mystical music from reedy pipes and a lone tambourine, she made her debut.

Marco's voice resounded throughout the auditorium.

"Ladies and gentlemen, follow me now through the portal of time through which only the most spiritually advanced souls may pass. The great comet soaring through the skies has wreaked havoc amongst the living and resurrected ancient spirits whose earthly tasks are incomplete. They wander homeless across the astral plane and are sensitive to my summoning. May the wisdom they have guarded through the ages now guide and protect us."

He waved his arms in the air and spun the open cabinet around four times. Once it stopped, he thrust an ivory-tipped wand through the open spaces.

"Soor kabaj! Hamare ghali ana, accha din! Soor Kabaj!" he chanted.

His wand struck the box with a heavy thud.

"Homage to thee, oh Nut, goddess of heavens and sky," daughter of Shu and Tednut. Mother of Ra, the sun god born from you each morning and swallowed by you each night. You hold the balance between chaos and the cosmos. Resurrect and incarnate for us tonight!"

By the time he uttered *Tednut*, Margaret passed through the material covering the back and emerge from her chair. Marveling at the silence of the spring hinges, she struck an artful pose. Marco pulled away the drape with a flourish, revealing her limbs barely covered in flimsy finery.

The manager applauded, as did stagehands, musicians, and a scattering of hangers-on. Slouched somewhere in the back row, Margaret knew Cushman must be watching in total disapproval. Immersed in a new identity, she took Marco's extended hand and danced onto the stage, caring not a fig for anyone else's opinion.

"Abide with us, oh goddess!" he implored her quietly. His face remained impassive, but his eyes were smiling. Margaret could only assume she had done well enough.

"Dismiss the other women with my thanks," he told the manager, who nodded in agreement.

Marco turned his attention back to me.

"Go home. Come back rested and lightly fed tomorrow morning, no later than ten."

"Lightly fed ... what do you mean?"

"Tea and toast, perhaps a poached egg, no more. A full stomach will only slow you down. For illusions to succeed, you must move like the spirit you're pretending to be. If you're even five minutes late, our relationship is over.

"We have terms to discuss and at least a dozen illusions for you to learn, some more complicated but none as theatrical as the one you've just mastered. We'll rehearse long hours. If you continue to make progress, I promise to make it worth your while and, if all goes according to plan, we'll be headlining the bill next week."

He circled Margaret, eyes riveted on her form, cautious as a collector appraising a potential purchase.

"You have the all the skills and appearance of a star performer. Tell me, Meg Ellison, can you handle multiple demands?"

Margaret Morehouse, pastor's wife, would have wilted under such scrutiny but those strange incantations had worked their magic. She nodded, feeling the stirrings of desire for the first time in years and nodded eagerly as a child offered sweets, all the while trying to silence an inner warning voice.

"I knew you were capable, but not of *that*," Cushman uttered gruffly as they left the theater.

It wasn't quite praise, but was it censure? She couldn't be sure.

They returned home in a silence woven from threads of fatigue and disapproval.

CHAPTER SEVENTEEN

The sun glinted bright through the chill morning air. Margaret was shivering in the old woolen coat pulled over her gossamer costume, but ready to meet the day.

She gave two notes to a passing street urchin and a coin to insure their delivery to the police station. The Captain's stated she'd inhaled too much smoke after the L.A. Times fire and her doctor advised her to stay home for a while. The same excuse went to McManus and Tyson, but she pledged to meet up with them when fully recovered.

The buggy stood ready, Cushman was on the driver's seat, barely flicking Daisy's reins.

Why doesn't he look me in the eye? she wondered. *After all, it was he who told Mr. Pantages my behavior would be only an act. And it was, for the most part.*

Cushman maneuvered through morning traffic without his usual weather commentary. They reached the theater fifteen minutes early.

Marco waited in the wings, seated on a small Persian rug in a yoga position. He was bare-chested except for a cotton vest and wore loose iridescent trousers. Eyes closed, face frozen, he appeared completely detached from reality.

Margaret would have not been surprised had he'd floated away as Aladdin had done in Sir Richard Burton's salacious *The Book of a Thousand Nights and a Night*. Edmund and she had found the translation rather titillating in their earlier days.

She took off her coat and sat down in front of him, mirroring his pose. Sensing her presence or perhaps heeding an internal clock, Marco opened his eyes.

"Timely as well as beautiful!" he proclaimed. "I have chosen wisely after all."

He smiled, pulled on a voluminous cape, and resumed

Margaret's education in magic.

What lessons they were! Marco spoke in an accented baritone voice, not as distinct as those bandied about in Little Italy, but vaguely European. He declared the only way to convince the audience was to believe in the magic herself. Margaret was sure it would not be difficult since she was already under his spell.

From the first moment he demonstrated the mechanics behind the illusions, she convinced herself the fingers used to loosen latches were not appendages, but wands. Slender cords for maneuvering objects did not exist; they were simply magical currents responding to one's will.

During the rare times they talked of matters outside the theater, Margaret made up a story about a wealthy aunt and uncle who'd taken her in after her parents, lesser lights of the international stage, died in a shipwreck after touring Europe.

The more farfetched the story, the easier Margaret found it to make believe. She explained away Cushman's presence as a condition laid down by her benefactors to indulge creative whims while preserving reputation. In the real world, no guardians in their right minds would have allowed a young woman to go about in the company of an unmarried man, a fact apparently foreign to theater people.

On their second day together, after a particularly good rehearsal, Marco began to share a bit more about himself.

"I was seventeen when I came to New York harbor in steerage. I vowed never to return until I could go first class. I'm not there yet. One day, mark my words, I'll perform before the crowned heads of Europe."

"Where did you learn magic?"

"Hawking newspapers on the streets of New York when the famous magician, Howard Thurston, came to town. His posters were all over town and the *Sun* and *Tribune* ran his story with picture on their front pages.

"Passers-by said I looked like him, so I softened my accent and learned a few tricks. I could pull a quarter out of someone's ear and end up with a ten-dollar tip. All the ladies, and even a few gentlemen, said I was good-looking. If I only had Thurston's white ties and tails, I might attract even more money and admirers."

"Did you ever meet him in person?"

"Thurston was performing his Wonder Show of the Universe at the New Amsterdam. Tickets were expensive and my rent was overdue. I moved my newsstand next to the theater hoping to catch his eye and maybe make myself useful."

"Were you successful?"

"Not until the run was almost over. One night, Thurston was late and rushed through the main doors. His assistant dropped a cage full of pigeons. The bamboo door flew open and released the birds into the night. Most were too dazed to get very far and landed on ledges and windowsills."

"Don't tell me you were able to recapture them!"

"My boyhood herding sheep served me well. I grabbed the cage, climbed a tree, and cooed most of them back in before making my way back down covered in feathers and pigeon filth.

"Thurston came back outside and saw everything. He let me wash up in his dressing room and gave me a ticket to the next night's show. By the end of the week, I was under his wing and learning his craft."

"Did he take you on tour?"

"For the next two years. He was at my side when I was inducted into the Society of American Magicians. Now it's time for me to become a star on my own."

"What a splendid coincidence! It took a chance sighting of your poster with Marie Levecque to spark my interest in magic."

Margaret immediately wanted to retract her words. Marie's name was not on the poster and there was no way in this new magical universe she should have known it.

"I asked someone who she was because I'd never seen a prettier woman in all my life. With practice, I hope to be just like her before too long."

The longing in his Marco's face revealed how much he wanted to make that happen.

Back to rehearsal they went. With each incantation - *Soor Kabaj! Hamare ghali ana, accha din! Soor Kabaj!* - he beguiled her. She sauntered on stage carrying a tray of tissue paper blossoms strung with nearly invisible threads. When Marco flipped his cape, Margaret attached one end of the thread to the lining underneath. The challenge was to do this swiftly and precisely while keeping the audience's attention focused on his waving wand.

When he chanted, "All hail, Repnet, Goddess of Spring," the flowers levitated and danced through the air like fairies while Margaret and Marco bowed low in pretend astonishment.

Once Marco gave his approval and a farewell wave, she departed.

Cushman's dubious demeanor had seemingly mellowed during the day. Before taking up the reins, he extended an arm to assist her into the carriage and let out a torrent of words, more than he usually spoke at any one time.

"You are doing rather well. I do not approve of your costume or the way you've placed yourself in jeopardy, yet I must admit only a woman could pull off what you've managed thus far.

"Therefore, I've resolved to be with you every step of the way. I'll let the detectives know what we're doing. We must talk to them soon. As far as your husband goes, if you let me do the talking, I'm sure he'll support our investigation."

Our investigation? Margaret grumbled inwardly.

Once again, she silenced her thoughts before they escaped her lips. The past few weeks had been the experience of a lifetime. Any support on the road to equality would be welcome.

Her head swirled. She might be steering her own ship into the straits of disaster. There was no mother, sister, or friend to turn to for guidance. Her father would have understood the interest in police work but never her unseemly emotions. Truth be told, she didn't, either.

A thought occurred.

Perhaps Alice Wells might be able to advise me.

Broaching the subject with a woman so certain of her path was frightening, but perhaps she should try.

CHAPTER EIGHTEEN

A week later, at the stroke of noon, Alice knocked on the rectory door. Margaret greeted her with the most elegant spread a pastor's wife could devise: poached eggs, cold salmon, and banana muffins slathered with strawberry jam.

"The berries came from our own vines," she declared proudly.

Alice clucked appreciatively and sampled each item. They washed down the meal with Typhoo tea before proceeding to the parlor.

"Tell me, my dear, how did you manage to prepare such a lovely repast when I understand you've been feeling unwell?"

"It was nothing, really. I took over the kitchen when my mother passed away and learned from every dish and disaster I made. We've simply had a later-in-the day version of Reverend Morehouse's standard Sunday breakfast, although for him I throw in a sausage or two."

Alice patted her tummy.

"I'm honored and oh so full. Also glad for a chance to get to know you better. I'm curious about what brought you to the Mayor's attention in the first place. I've heard you founded a home for unwed mothers, admirable indeed, but how did that lead to police work? Surely you must have done something more?"

"Yes and no. The controversy surrounding the home would have put me at the bottom of any candidate list, but once has a way of testing our mettle. *My* test happened there."

She wondered how much to reveal. Sensing Alice's genuine interest and eager to strengthen their bond, Margaret settled back in her chair and relayed a tale only Edmund and a few trusted others had ever shared.

"I was determined none of the infants born, often into my arms, would be flung onto the dung heap of foundling homes. If a mother decided to give up her child, I tried to place the newborn with a financially stable childless couple. Whenever I proposed taking one of the newborns home, Edmund rejected the idea, first citing his desire to have children of our own and later, flatly refusing."

Alice put an admonishing finger to her lips.

"Careful not to reveal so much, my dear."

"It's part of the story and I know I can trust you."

Alice nodded but maintained a slight warning look over the rim of her teacup.

"I might have continued along this path indefinitely, but the recommendation only came about because of my work with one *wed* mother."

Telling the tale felt like unlocking a cedar chest and airing out the contents. Everything was still intact but a certain stench remained.

"One spring evening back in 1909, a woman dressed in elegant clothes appeared on the Morehouse Home doorstep. Even under lantern light I could see green discolorations beneath the powder on her cheeks.

"I took her to a small storeroom for privacy and cleared away supplies to make her comfortable. She let me lift the curls at the nape of her neck and loosen the back of her blouse, revealing more injuries."

Alice held back tears. For a woman of her background, the scene that was all too familiar.

"Bit by bit, details of her five-year marriage came out. Her name was Anna Mobley. Husband Arthur's reputation with ladies of all social classes had made their way before even to my tender ears."

"Mine too," admitted Alice. "He's sullied the lives of women and girls I've counseled but always emerged unscathed."

"Our doctor in charge, Marcus Sherman, told me later that he held Mr. Mobley accountable for more than one child born here and at least one maternal death."

Hands shaking from dredged-up anger, Margaret put down her teacup and stirred more sugar into the cooling brew.

"Anna told me she'd had four pregnancies but none lasted more than six months. The images she carried of their tiny faces in her heart made her unwilling to respond to her husband's touch. This only angered him and he repeatedly forced himself on her, the last assault happening only three weeks earlier. Her courses had just come. There was no baby.

"Nothing in all my time at Morehouse Home had prepared me for such a predicament. I searched my brain for an answer and finally asked if she thought he would temporarily leave her alone if our doctor agreed to write a letter verifying a pregnancy."

"Not a bad short-term solution," commented Alice, "but the abuse would only start all over again in a manner of months."

"In the long term, her inability to carry an infant to term would remain an affront to Albert's manhood. Moreover, his younger brother had a son. His parents might find a way around primogeniture if they didn't produce an heir. She feared he might kill her and marry someone more fertile. Hers wasn't much of a life, but she didn't want to die."

Alice moaned in dismay.

"We women have few protections under the law. If she died at her husband's hand, he could be exonerated simply by testifying how badly she'd provoked him."

"More than likely. She described her bedroom as a torture chamber but still clung to the hope of bearing a child. If she produced a son, she was certain he'd leave her alone to her dying day. The plot I began to devise was so devious it surprised even me. Not only must Anna pretend to be pregnant, but she would also have to leave Los Angeles until the due date we'd give her had passed."

Alice chuckled.

"Devious? A sweet, old-fashioned girl like you?"

"Don't tell me you've never bent the truth in the interest of public safety."

"I'll never tell, and you shouldn't either. Except for now. You've piqued my interest and my lips are sealed. Please continue."

"My plan was straightforward but everything had to fall in place. As it happened, we were extremely lucky. Dr. Sherman wrote a letter vouching for Anna's pregnancy and sent a telegram to his progressive brother and sister-in-law in Arizona. Within the week, they agreed to shelter Anna – no questions asked, no money exchanged. Albert Mobley never suspected anything amiss about his wife's pregnancy or the good doctor's insistence she travel to perpetual warmth and dryness in the desert 'to ensure a successful gestation'."

"Isn't that going against whatever oath he had to take?"

"Doctors pledge to do no harm and that was just what he was doing. Marcus Sherman takes his Hippocratic Oath seriously, caring for all who come his way, including society's outcasts. He'd been at the bedside of a parlor maid who named Albert Mobley the father of her stillborn child before she died."

Alice grimaced in disgust.

"What did Anna tell her family?"

"I advised her to keep up the pretense with her elderly mother and father but confide in her brother James, a man I knew as a trusted member from our congregation who would always have her best interest at heart.

"I also told her to start wearing shawls and, when the weather got too hot in Arizona, loose dresses with a little padding underneath. Albert was unlikely to visit but had the means to hire a private detective. She had to look convincing up close and from a distance. Anna complied and wrote to her husband regularly."

"Time away must have been a huge relief, but weren't you merely delaying the inevitable? What happened after nine months passed and there was no baby?"

Margaret broke into a triumphant smile.

"Oh, but my dear, there was! When the time arrived for her to be near term, I promised to send an envoy with the healthiest available newborn in our nursery, a boy if possible. Anna, in turn, pledged to raise the child with the all the love and care she would give her very own!"

"That's ingenious!" exclaimed Alice, slapping her forehead in mock dismay. The obvious solution, with so many babies available and needing placement at hand, had not occurred to her.

"The first of our 1910 Morehouse Home babies arrived just past midnight on January 1st with blonde hair and lusty lungs. Throughout her pregnancy, his birth mother had declared her baby would have a better life, even if she had to relinquish him. I saw no merit in that outcome and packed them both off to Arizona. Albert Mobley, Jr., and the mother who became his nursemaid returned to Los Angeles alongside our Anna, upon whom sunshine and her caretakers' kindness had bestowed a maternal glow and a few needed pounds. As you may have guessed already, Anna's brother suggested the Mayor appoint me to the force and is responsible for us becoming colleagues!"

"And friends, I hope. That was fascinating! I'll never tell another soul."

She rose to leave.

"Please stay a while longer. There's something more I need to talk about."

"No time for that today. I must be off but thank you for the lovely meal and amazing account. Your inventiveness astounds me!"

Grabbing her hat and cloak, she hurried towards the door before pivoting to look back in Margaret's direction.

"It also worries me. I've heard how you set foot in the vaudeville world of make-believe with your fine detective friends and searched for them in the aftermath of the bombing."

"They asked me to interview the female performers. The Captain and I believed that to be an appropriate function for a woman to serve. As for the morning after the explosion, I was simply worried sick about them and thought I might help."

"I'm sure you did but the glow about you does not belong on a woman who inhaled too much smoke. I do not know what or *who* has grabbed your heart, but I recognize infatuation when I see it. Take care before you split yourself in two, my dear!"

Alice bolted out the door before Margaret had a chance to say anything in her own defense.

CHAPTER NINETEEN

By opening night, Margaret's timing was flawless. With a whirl of cape and snap his fingers, Marco burst onto center stage. His patter was glib and illusions fascinating.

"Ladies and gentlemen, tonight the gods have chosen to bestow their favors on this great and noble assemblage. Secrets locked away with the pharaohs for millennia have been resurrected for your edification and amusement."

Huge papyrus scrolls crafted from long sheets of treated canvas plummeted from ceiling to floor. Projected hieroglyphs appeared on them as if drawn by demonic hands. An eight-foot ankh on one panel and an enormous eye of Horus on the other floated eerily above the stage for the rest of the performance.

Next, Marco stacked six large containers into the shape of a pyramid.

"Tombs of the pharaohs were laden with treasure. None were so flawless as the jewel we shall uncover tonight."

One at a time, he opened and shut drop-down doors on the boxes to prove they were empty. He spun the stack around and pulled on a hidden lever. All doors opened at the same time. After Margaret popped out of the center box, she made a full, graceful circle around the stage.

Marco extended his caped arm and entwined her jeweled fingers in his own. Flinging open an ornate sarcophagus, they tilted it steeply to display a shrouded figure inside.

"Behold the mummy of King Ramses the Fourth," he announced while unwinding long strips of muslin starched just enough to hold a corporeal shape.

Marco looked astonished to uncover a body.

"As you all can see, there is no human, shriveled or otherwise. Floating high above your heads or underneath your seats, his *ka* or mystical spirit awaits my bidding."

Thunderous applause filled the air although a few audience members recoiled in fear. Marco stooped to the floor to retrieve the mummy's flail and crook, then juggled them so high they vanished into the proscenium.

"Ka of Ramses, return the symbols of your authority to my control. You still rule the hearts and minds of men and can rest for all eternity."

Gold glitter rained down. Margaret gyrated, using a huge ostrich feather fan to dust Marco off and sweep up the shiny flecks before tossing them into the sarcophagus.

Proclaiming *"Hamare ghali ana, achna din!"* he solemnly closed the lid, opened it, and pulled out the fully restored flail and crook.

The greatest feat came in their final moments when, in less than two minutes, Margaret transformed from lightly clad handmaiden to powerful Nut, goddess of heavens and sky.

To appear as two different women, Margaret changed from a severely styled brown wig to a bejeweled headdress and pulled a golden tunic over her simple white shift. Marco timed her moves with a stopwatch. After a few tries, she managed to change in the overstuffed chair and make her way to the cabinet without a glimpse of red hair showing in fifty-two seconds flat.

She often asked if his former partner had done things a particular way or had a favorite illusion. Marco answered all her questions until she mentioned Marie while swooning in his arms, much like the pose struck in the poster. In a cold, calm voice, he warned her never to mention that name again.

At every performance, Cushman stationed himself in the wings, maintaining his vigil from the time the curtain parted until they left for home. Marco's skill and respectful attitude impressed him so much he suggested they might be able to drop that part of their investigation in the very near future.

Margaret agreed but asked for a little more time. She didn't want to take her eyes off Marco the Magician.

CHAPTER TWENTY

A week after the magic act opened at the Grimaldi, Cushman and Margaret met with McManus and Tyson outside the police station. Captain Clarke walked by, too preoccupied with outside pressures to acknowledge their presence.

The Boyle Heights Fiend had not struck again but another poor girl's body was found brutalized in the same manner used by the Parlor House Horror. Learning this homicide had transpired hours after she first auditioned in the skimpy dancer's costume chilled Margaret to the bone.

Instead of investigative work, both men had been assigned to keep watch on "The Bivouac," Colonel Otis's massive home on Wilshire Boulevard.

"Mayor's offering a ten-thousand-dollar reward for anyone who has knowledge of a conspiracy, no conditions attached. Wish it could be me."

Tears welled in his eyes at the thought of what such a sum could do for his family.

"The unions added another eight thousand," chimed in Cushman.

McManus cleared his throat.

"That money's no better than a pig in a poke. The unions want to avoid suspicion and cast it instead on folks who could profit in the long run, like Colonel Otis and his cronies."

Tyson shushed him.

"Keep that notion to yourself or we'll all be out looking for work. Even if we caught the bomber tomorrow and locked up all his equipment, no one would give us a dime. I hear tell the Mayor's hiring a fancy private investigator so he can arrest someone convenient."

"Haven't we forgotten about our Pantages girl in all this speculation?" Margaret asked.

McManus sighed.

"Well, now, *forgotten* isn't quite the right word. More like *postponed*, and we'll get back to the investigation in good time. This bombing took twenty-one lives, after all, and that poor girl's not going anywhere."

"Her killer might," Margaret insisted, "and with Cushman's help, I've continued the investigation."

McManus and Tyson stiffened in surprise.

She began to describe every detail of the clandestine operation, except for her growing attraction to Marco. The claim he had on her defied polite description and was making her a stranger unto herself.

"I believe the Pantages corpse is none other than Marie Levecque!" she concluded, gratified to see both men nodding in interest and Seamus taking notes.

"That's what the American Nightingale told you and could well explain what we found in the back alley," McManus summarized. "If Marie Levecque's dead, maybe your magician murdered her in a fit of jealousy and left the body to implicate Pantages."

Before she could offer an alternative theory, Tyson chimed in with his own.

"Don't rule out the Greek himself although it's beyond me why a rich man like him would kill a girl when he could have any one of 'em he wanted."

"Might have wanted to rid himself of an embarrassing entanglement before the wife found out," McManus responded.

Cushman finally broke his silence.

"Both had motives. If you ask me, only Pantages and his lackey have the means."

McManus was intrigued.

"Sound conclusion, Mr. Cushman. Have you ever been an investigator?"

"Perhaps I read too many detective stories late at night."

"Don't sell yourself short, sir. My only counter to your argument is I don't think Pantages would leave the girl out in the open like that, right next to his theater."

Before the men had a chance to monopolize the conversation, Margaret added a speculation of her own.

"Maybe Alexander Pantages hired an assassin to do the dreadful deed and didn't pay up. A villain like that might want his revenge. We can't rule anyone out."

Tyson turned to her with worried eyes.

"Right now, we're too busy to help and may be on the bombing investigation for a long time. I guess you'll be safe with Cushman close by. Just in case, better learn one of those vanishing acts real soon."

"Meg Ellison can get away at a moment's notice. A week ago, Edmund gave me as close to a blessing as he could bestow: his buggy and Mr. Cushman at my disposal for the coming month."

"An uncommon gentleman he is," added McManus. "I'll join his congregation if we catch the killer."

"I took you for a Papist, sir, coming from the Auld Sod and all."

Tyson almost choked on his laughter.

"The Pope himself would step down if this guy set foot in church, for that would mean the Apocalypse was comin' soon."

McManus ignored him and turned his attention back to Margaret.

"Report new developments soon as you can, and we'll try to lend a hand. Don't worry about being right or wrong; we can sort that out later. Run if you even think you might be in danger, and don't let the Captain find out what you're up to or we'll all be fired."

Cushman took out his pocket watch.

"Best be off. Our magician is a perfectionist. We can't keep him waiting."

Cushman and Margaret arrived in time for rehearsal. That evening, Marco the Magnificent and his beautiful assistant played to their usual full house.

The stale, fetid air of the bottom pyramid box made Margaret lightheaded. She reached out to steady herself. At the seam where the right and back walls met, she pulled out a swatch of silky fabric scrap. Worried it might have come from her costume, she tucked it into her bodice for future repairs.

Following the thunderous applause, Marco complimented her performance. She returned to the dressing room and examined the material by the flickering light. It turned out to be a large square of turquoise silk, the same hue Marie was wearing in the poster. An ominous rust-colored smudge stained nearly one third of it.

Seamus's forensic kit was always in her bag. She loosened the bottle dropper and squeezed a few drops of peroxide on the material. Bubbles formed instantly. Shoving the one piece of evidence she never wanted to find in a drawer, Margaret staggered out the door.

Marco sprang to her side. He pressed a thick volume by the magician and mechanical genius, Jean Robert-Houdin, into her hands.

"Read this!" he insisted. "It holds the key to our success!"

A fringed leather bookmark protruded from a page containing an illustrated description of the sawing-a-woman-in-two illusion. Margaret was rather horrified by the sketches of complicated, lethal-looking devices and skimpy costumes for the girl about to be dismembered.

Houdin referred to the make-believe victim as a Zig Zag girl. At the time, the term sounded silly. Looking back, it was oddly prophetic.

"I've never seen such a thing," Margaret remarked, barely concealing her disgust.

"Until now, it has been no more than a theory, my dear, one fully discussed by the author but never attempted. Less than a year ago, an Italian designed a scaled-down model. From what I've read, the design is ingenious, although any competent magician could safely perform the illusion. He wants to sell it to me for a reasonable price and charge royalties for the next five years. At the end of the contract, it will be mine alone."

"If others bid against you, the price could become astronomical!"

"This inventor is loyal to me. Because other magicians and theater company representatives have seen me use his props, and most effectively, I must add, they tend to use him exclusively. He designed the Egyptian sets we've been using and is willing to show me the box first. If he has done his usual superb job, we shall be making so much money entertaining on the top circuits, dazzling all the kings and queens of Europe!"

"We?"

"Of course, *we*, which means we must both test his wares."

"We cannot take time to travel while our show has just begun its run. Surely the Grimaldis will refuse to let you go!"

"Even those rank amateurs recognize the opportunity of a lifetime. They've given me two weeks and a thousand dollars to test, buy, and bring back the device to this stage. They've signed a pair of comedians who'll be passing through to fill in during our absence. In return, I'll sign a year's contract as a guaranteed headliner!"

He took Margaret by the hand and looked deeply into her eyes.

"After that, there will be no limit to what I can do with you by my side. I need your skill and beauty."

He looked hesitantly at Cushman.

"Do you think her guardians might let her travel to Chicago if you come along as chaperone?"

The bloody silk square was still in the dressing room and there, Margaret decided, it would stay. Rationalization ruled. A large splinter could easily protrude from unfinished wood to pierce an assistant's skin! Hadn't she herself experienced a few such scrapes?

Suspicion vanished, along with her poster image memory of the missing magician's assistant. Once again, more than anything, Margaret needed to prove Marco's innocence.

Cushman looked oddly intrigued.

"I'll clear *our* way, or try to," he stated as he briskly escorted her outside.

CHAPTER TWENTY-ONE

The Chicago Plan, as Cushman came to call it, met with some resistance. The mere mention of train travel turned Edmund an unbecoming shade of apoplectic purple, but Cushman worked his own kind of magic. In less than five minutes he'd convinced the good reverend their mission would restore law and order.

Cushman retrieved a box of maps and train timetables from his room. Margaret wondered why a man who never left town would have such a collection until she recalled all the recipes she'd written down but never tried.

Edmund agreed Marco was a likely suspect and urged caution. Margaret was relieved to see his change of attitude. She was also annoyed. He was putting more stock in Cushman's opinions than her own.

At least it will no longer be too much of an exaggeration to claim I have my family's blessing, she thought, sealing her frustration with a smile.

∿∿
∿∿

When Cushman and Margaret returned to the theater, Marco was nowhere to be found. One of the Grimaldi brothers informed them he'd taken the magician to La Grande station before dawn. He'd left on a train to Chicago, and they expected him to return within a fortnight.

They went back home. Margaret moped about for five days, anxiously waiting for word. She baked enough for a small army but couldn't eat a bite. She visited Morehouse Home every morning but never stayed more than an hour. She went to bed early but barely slept.

Cushman dropped by the theater and picked up a telegram addressed to Margaret: "DEVICE PERFECT. ALL I NEED IS YOU."

Edmund's face clouded as she read the words aloud. The realization of how he might interpret the words took Margaret by surprise.

"All he *needs* me for is to test the illusion. I am the only person he trusts to follow his directions."

Edmund appeared to accept her explanation. By the next day, he was playing Watson to Cushman's Holmes.

Their collaboration relegated Margaret to minor character status, but she didn't mind. She'd cast herself as a female detective character in a mystery motion picture of her own.

If Edmund had any misgivings about Margaret's welfare, he didn't reveal them, although he gave her extra money to purchase warm outerwear to withstand Chicago's winter air. It became Cushman's duty, though not his pleasure, to accompany her on shopping excursions. The woman he was with, the one for whom he had to fetch and carry, was acting nothing like the woman he'd known.

♒

For the next week, Margaret rehearsed the role of the rich, adventurous, self-indulgent woman Marco thought her to be. Cushman simply rolled his eyes and tried to distract Edmund with train schedules.

The generous outlay of money Edmund proposed spending on their travel and lodgings astonished Margaret, given the fact she had maintained many of her wardrobe items season after season until repairs were no longer possible.

They shared more decisions than most couples but Edmund controlled finances and doled out funds as needed. Margaret could not keep herself from asking about the source of this sudden largesse.

"You are!" he beamed.

"I am barely an heiress!" she insisted.

Indeed, her father had been wealthy until the New York-based Knickerbocker Trust went bankrupt in 1907, spreading panic from coast to coast. Before J. P. Morgan and his cronies invested their own resources and saved the country's banking system, Peter Ellison, too long retired from the world of business to properly supervise his accounts, was near financial ruin.

Shame compounded heart problems and led to his death. The house and all its elaborate furnishings were auctioned off soon afterwards. When all debts were settled, Margaret and her brother divided what little was left.

"Your father never lost sight of your welfare. Before we wed, he gave me a substantial sum to provide for emergencies or occasional luxuries. Although I balked at his generosity, I respected the spirit in which it was given. I kept my pride intact by banking the entire amount!"

"Wouldn't it have been better to give it back to him during his last terrible year?"

"I offered but he refused. We've earned considerable interest on your nest egg over the past ten years. Because you've been an admirable helpmeet, we've lived well if prudently within our means. Consider this a reward for your good efforts."

Margaret bit her tongue and tried to look happy. Of all the deceptions she had practiced of late, this was the easiest to maintain.

Preparing a wardrobe diverted her frustration. The sheer magician's assistant costumes she would wear on stage packed easily, but even her alter ego preferred a degree of modesty. She settled on a velvet vest with a bottom hem barely reaching her sternum and pants cut high on her thighs underneath sheer puffy leggings.

From her drab pastor's wife wardrobe, Margaret assembled three smart traveling outfits, softening their exteriors with a sparkle of jewelry on the bodice, a touch of lace at the collar, and a soft sash at the waist. With each embellishment, she imagined being with Marco in Chicago as they met with important people, went to the theater, and dined out. Cushman never took part in those daydreams.

The fantasies grew so vivid she forced herself to keep the bloody material from the pyramid box on her person to remind her of their mission. Truth must prevail, whatever the outcome.

Marco returned to Los Angeles ten days before their scheduled departure. They gave one final performance at the Grimaldi theater. Margaret emerged unscathed and triumphant from the sarcophagus. Marco beamed his approval. They took bow after bow as the audience rose to its feet.

The Grimaldi brothers embraced them both in the wings and expressed concern for a safe return, a sure sign the act was successful. Marco publicly acknowledged Margaret's assistance. Privately, the meaningful looks he bestowed upon her felt dangerously close to caresses.

She kept the next Sabbath as best she could, although the mischief brewing in her soul was more difficult to contain than a bottled genii. After the service, dozens of dowagers, taking note of her beaming face, clustered around and glanced covertly at her waistline. She smiled at their transparency and wished her inner glow could be attributed to something as wholesome as pregnancy.

Two evenings before the trip, Margaret countered the chill air seeping in through the window glass with a hearty roast pork and applesauce dinner. Afterwards, seated peacefully before a crackling fire, Edmund dozed peacefully. Margaret's misgivings began to waft up the chimney until, once again, Leland Morehouse came knocking on their door.

CHAPTER TWENTY-TWO

Leland's stiff movements and sunken eyes made them fear the worst. He brushed aside Cushman's offer to hang up his greatcoat reached into his pocket and took out and opened a small lacquer box.

A silver ring inside shone dully against a soft golden cushion. Margaret recognized the filigree setting. It looked identical to Yvette's engagement ring, but the oversized stone was missing.

Margaret recalled complimenting the couple on their engagement and the brilliant sapphire. In truth, she'd thought it garish, but hoped to soften the remarks Edmund had just made about the price Leland must have paid and how it could have fed a family of four for a year.

Without hesitation, Margaret removed the ring. She shook the box to make sure the stone was missing and squeezed the cushion. What she thought was silken fabric began to unravel in her fingers. The strands she pulled up curled into a lock of hair. Long, golden, and very possibly Yvette's.

Margaret covered her mouth, barely suppressing a scream.

Edmund was indignant.

"How dare you upset my wife?"

"He has no one else to turn to, dear..."

"You two the only ones who know the delicacy of my position," Leland stammered. "I discovered this box inside a bag outside my front door last night. Along with another note, far more frightening than Yvette's."

He pulled out a gold-colored bag secured with purple cord from his coat and handed his uncle a piece of paper. Edmund unfolded and read from it aloud. The message was written in a forceful if uneducated script.

TO THE RIGHT HONORABLE LELAND MOREHOUSE, DEARE SIR, WE HAS YER WIFE. FIGRING SHE HAS NO NEED FOR A RING NO LONGER, WE BE SENDIN IT TO YOU AS A GOOD WILL GESTER. WE'S ALSO SENDIN A CURL FROM HER PRETTY HEAD SO YOU KNOWS WE HAVE HER STILL. ALL YOU NEEDS TO DO TO GET THE REST OF HER BACK SAFE AND SOUND IS PUT FIVE HUNDERD DOLLARS IN GOLD COINS IN THIS VERY SAME BAG AND BRING IT TO THE HOTEL NADEAU AT 1ST AND SPRING ON THE MORNING OF MARCH 20 AT 10 O'CLOCK SHARP. STAND OUTSIDE BY THE FRONT DOOR. WE KNOWS WHAT YOU LOOK LIKE AND A YOUNG LADY WILL COME YER WAY, REDDY TO PICK UP THE BAG. GIVE IT TO HER AND DON'T DARE GO TO THE POLICE. IF YOU DO, WE'LL BE SENDIN' THE MISSUS BACK BIT BY BIT UNTIL THERE AIN'T NO MORE LITTLE WIFE OF YERS LEFT.

"The twentieth? That's a week from tomorrow!" Margaret cried. "What a large sum, even for you! Can you get the money together by then? Have you notified the police?"

"The ransom is not the problem; I can afford to pay it many times over. You may recall I told everyone she was touring the Continent and would spend much of her time in France visiting relatives. To keep up the charade, three months ago I wrote to Yvette in care of her parents."

"Wise move, for once!" Edmund snarled.

"Her mother wrote back. Yvette never arrived home. She suspected her daughter might have run off with the globe-trotting adventurer she'd been engaged to before my mother and her desperate father ruined their plans.

"I went straight off to the police. If they confirmed my suspicions about her flying off with some man, I'd have grounds for divorce. They turned up nothing. Now I'm afraid talking to them would only put her in more danger."

"You might be the one in danger. The police tend to treat family members like suspects, so be careful," Margaret cautioned. "Are you telling us her former fiancé was waiting at the airfield last January?"

"Either him or an associate. That show-off Louis Paulhan brought his dirigible and a crowd of his countrymen with him to Dominguez. Whoever it turns out to be, I bet they'd been planning her escape all along. I can almost understand her desire to retaliate against mother and me."

"Let me guess you said nothing to your mother," Edmund interrupted.

"No, Uncle, I didn't. She would blame me, as always."

"Are you familiar with the Hotel Nadeau?" Margaret asked.

"Who isn't? It's the only four-story building in that part of town. I often patronize the barber shop on the lowest level."

Edmund picked up the ring and held it to the light.

"The police must see this first thing tomorrow morning," Edmund declared in a detached tone.

"Maybe, maybe not," murmured Margaret. "Curls can be cut; rings can be left behind on purpose."

"You mean to say my wife might be behind this?"

Margaret eyed him like a stern school marm. "We can't jump to conclusions, my dear. Just because they haven't chopped her to pieces *yet*, doesn't mean someone sinister doesn't have her."

Leland's anxiety level heightened visibly.

"What if everything they say is true and these extortionists carry out the threat? I may not love Yvette, but I can't bear the thought of her being tortured."

"Might tarnish your sterling reputation," Edmund growled. "If you did not love her, why did you marry her?"

"You know the answer to that, Uncle. It was all Mother's doing."

"What possible motive could she have to force you to marry a Frenchwoman? And why must you always yield to her demands? There are plenty of beautiful homegrown heiresses available; Lord knows she was once one of them."

"The same sort your brother pursued," Leland responded a bit testily. "Banking is my only skill; that and waiting for her to r-retire."

"Don't you mean d-die?" Edmund retorted.

"Mother needed a French collaborator to secure her European

holdings. Yvette's father had a title and position. His bank was on the brink of disaster. Mother proposed a merger, maintaining him as titular head of La Banque de Lyons while she, with the help of handpicked subordinates, would oversee everything."

"Your marriage sealed the deal," Margaret commented.

Leland nodded. "It made great sense at the time. Yvette was beautiful and titled, though we were incompatible. Both of us resented being forced into the match. We tested each other with tardiness, inattentiveness, and insults. She accused me of being my mother's puppet in public. I called her a spoiled brat in front of our wedding party. By the time we went on our honeymoon, we detested each other."

Edmund reached for and unclasped a hinged brass picture frame. Inside a portrait of him in younger days faced one of his brother.

"Your mother has compromised many lives, including yours," he said solemnly.

A long, painful silence followed. Margaret did not want to go to Chicago without leaving a plan of action in place.

"You've already told the police Yvette is missing; the note gives you another week. If the culprits were able to get past your gates and leave this ring on your doorstep, they'll have no trouble tracking you to the police station."

"What should I do?"

"Let me handle it, Leland. Do whatever it takes to meet their demands. I work with two fine detectives who may be able to intervene."

"You put much faith in their abilities, my dear," Edmund interjected, "though I'm sure it's well deserved."

Margaret ignored his slightly patronizing tone.

"I have been assigned to an important case and will be away for a week, at the very least. There will be no way for us to keep in touch. No matter what happens between now and next Tuesday, get yourself to the Hotel Nadeau on time with the ransom they're demanding inside the bag they gave you. With luck, my associates will be nearby, ready to help if necessary."

Leland murmured his thanks and walked away with a steadier stride.

CHAPTER TWENTY-THREE

Margaret knocked on Cushman's door but he did not answer. She ventured out to their small stable where he was currying Daisy's coat to a soft pewter sheen.

"You always take wonderful care of all of us...but does she really need all this grooming so late at night?"

"I must remind you, Madam, we'll be gone for a while and no one else will be around to give our girl the attention she needs. A few minutes daily brushing a horse is time well spent. Aside from giving her a clean, glossy appearance, it stimulates circulation. As for the lateness of the hour, I was too busy finishing up all your last-minute shopping to take care of Daisy at the usual time of day."

Ignoring the implied disapproval, Margaret quickly changed the subject to Leland's perilous situation and swore him to secrecy.

Cushman's demeanor shifted from resentment to genuine interest. Solving a mystery wiped ten years off his face. Adding one more twist to the tale seemed to only make him happier.

"I agree. Enlisting McManus and Tyson to follow your nephew while we are gone only way to help him. Time is our biggest obstacle. We have a train to catch."

"If we start out early, we might be able to talk to them before they report for duty."

Cushman nodded in agreement. Margaret went back to the house. Everything was tidy and her clothes were packed, but no amount of preparation could calm her pounding heart. She read by candlelight into the early morning and fell, at last, into a fitful slumber.

Edmund's snores woke her early. She dressed in haste, went across the hall, kissed him lightly on the cheek, and pulled the cover up to his whiskers. When he did not stir, she recalled the delight of their early days and shed a silent tear. The love they'd pledged each other still bound them. When and why had they started leading parallel lives?

Margaret tiptoed downstairs, sipped some tea, and went outside. By pale lamplight, she could make out their valises lashed to the back of the buggy. Cushman was nowhere to be seen.

A stream of curse words clearly not meant for her ears alerted Margaret to his location. Cushman was chasing a small gang of street urchins. He turned when she called out his name and trudged back up the hill.

"Can't drop your guard for a moment, these days. I turned my back briefly to close the stable door. Caught those rascals crawling all over the carriage. Bet they were after our luggage. Where in blazes are their parents this time of the morning?"

Margaret wondered silently if he'd ever experienced poverty before John Barleycorn dropped him off at their doorstep.

"Their parents may be incapable of looking after them. Maybe they must steal to survive. Whatever the case, it wasn't your fault, and no harm was done."

Cushman tugged on the leather straps. The luggage was still secure. Satisfied nothing else was amiss, he assisted Margaret to her seat and drove off on the first leg of their adventure.

Even at an early hour, the police station brimmed with activity. Tyson and McManus were front and center in the crowded main room, looking fully recovered from recent ordeals. They greeted Margaret and Cushman warmly and caught them up on the *Times* investigation.

"Technically we're still assigned to the case," said Tyson. "They've brought in college-boy detectives and private investigators to find the murderous rascals. We got lots of thanks for all the fetching and carrying we did that night and a fortnight after, without a cent of extra pay."

McManus nodded.

"The bigwigs put more stock in brains than brawn. Trouble is, the brains they're willing to pay for fall short on common sense. We spent three nights last week staking out the home of a union labor leader who disappeared the night of the bombing. Whether we were supposed to nab him as he was sneaking back or save his hide from

Colonel Otis and his cronies in the Merchants and Manufacturers Association, no one took the time to say."

"Either outcome would make you heroes to one faction or the other," grumbled Cushman. "This city has enough troubles without vigilante justice further damaging its reputation."

McManus laughed.

"Los Angeles is too deeply corrupt for anyone to think our actions would ever amount to much."

Bitter words from such a dedicated man took Margaret by surprise.

"If you're so jaded, why did you join the police force in the first place?"

"Because once in a very short while, we do make a difference, if only in the short run: catch some crooks, save some lives. And it's an honorable living."

Tyson nodded.

"Yeah, and one of the few lines of work open to us Irishers. Got too many kids to enter the priesthood and no wish to go to blazes with the fire department. It's a copper I am and proud of it."

They were running short on time. Margaret gave a brief description of her new investigative tactic, keeping her voice cool and detached to conceal a hidden objective: clearing the name of a man whose mere presence had reawakened her passion for life and adventure.

The detectives commended her determination. She was grateful for their supportive words but doubted they would have said them without Cushman by her side.

Margaret handed McManus a note addressed to the Captain. In it, she attributed past and future absences to family illness and promised to return when the situations improved.

Before McManus and Tyson rose to leave, Margaret asked for a few more minutes of their time. She gave them a brief overview of Leland's predicament and pulled out a daguerreotype of his handsome face, along with the box containing the ring and hair. She made no mention of her suspicions about Yvette's complicity.

"Quite the situation your nephew's in," said Tyson. "Way too much for us to take on right now."

McManus raised some objections.

"I think it's high time we provide all the support this woman deserves. First and foremost, a lady's life is in danger, doubly so if the criminals think police are involved. Second, she's Mrs. Margaret's kin, if only by marriage, reason enough for us to pretend we're merely passing by the Nadeau next week and just happen to see Leland Morehouse give away his gold."

Tyson nodded reluctantly.

"At least Mrs. Yvette Morehouse is a society lady, not some Pantages showgirl, so we won't get in quite so much trouble if that story doesn't hold up."

"We'll let him complete the transaction and see where the girl goes. If we try to nab her before she returns to the other conspirators, who knows what they will do to the poor hostage?"

"Assuming they still have her," murmured Cushman.

"We must assume so for now. That time of morning, there are always men lined up outside the hotel to visit the bootblacks on First. No one will notice us," added McManus.

"Stay away from high heels or hoopskirts, Charlie," Margaret whispered, "or you'll never catch the culprits."

Tyson ignored her teasing. McManus promised to lock up the box and its contents in the station evidence room. Confident Leland would have hidden help, Margaret and Cushman set out for the train station.

The ride was uneventful until the carriage started to shimmy. They pitched back and forth. The left back wheel detached just before they toppled over. Cushman and the carriage canopy provided Margaret her only protection from the jagged paving stones.

She crawled away and righted herself. Cushman rose stiffly out of the wreckage, shaking his limbs to test for sprains and breaks. Finding themselves unharmed, they turned their attention to Daisy. She whinnied softly when Cushman patted her down from withers to knees but otherwise appeared intact.

Cushman paced furiously around the ruined coach. Their bags were none the worse for wear nor, as Margaret discovered when looking through hers for hairpins and brush, were the contents.

"Those little devils must have loosened the axle bolts. How did they get hold of a monkey wrench? We wouldn't have made it as far as the police station if I hadn't surprised them. Tell me, Mrs. Morehouse, do you have any enemies?"

"Many people disapproved of my involvement with the Morehouse home, but our work has continued uninterrupted for years and no one, to my knowledge, has ever directly threatened my life."

"What about Leland's mother?"

"Elvira Morehouse? She's not said more than ten words to me the entire time I've known her. Her primary concerns are banking and power and not a single part of her life, except for the relationship to Edmund, involves mine. I've yet to hear about her attending church anywhere or assisting the poor. The only mean things I've ever said about her were for Edmund's ears alone."

Cushman was about to ask more when Providence intervened. Edmund had enlisted a parishioner named Thomas Warren to meet them at the train station and drive the buggy back home. Noise from the crash brought that fine gentleman and half a dozen other Good Samaritans to the rescue.

After moving carriage remains to the side of the road and tethering Daisy to a hitching post, Mr. Warren escorted Margaret and Cushman to the station platform. He handed them a hamper of sandwiches, boiled eggs, potato salad, cake, and lemonade to consume while waiting to board the Los Angeles Limited, ready for its return trip to Chicago.

"Cushman, what makes you think I might have enemies?" Margaret asked between mouthfuls.

"You're in an unorthodox line of work for a woman, Madam. There may be those in the community who may think you're getting too good at it. Who knows what you might have uncovered without fully understanding its implications? Last month, I thought I heard a pistol shot when you came home so late."

Of all the day's twists and turns, this one surprised Margaret the most.

"So, you were awake, after all! Why didn't you come out to help?"

"It was so dark. I might have gone out to look for you before the libation I shared with your husband took hold. Should never touch a drop again. The urge was far too powerful after I took one whiff of that fine brandy. Dozed off in my chair, fully dressed except for my coat and bowler.

"I could barely move when the gunfire rang out but knew you were safe once the door closed and I heard your footsteps tread softly up the stairs. That's when I decided to approach Mr. Edmund about dedicating myself to your service. Although my presence might make matters worse, I have some, shall we say, *competencies* that could protect you."

His words baffled Margaret.

"How could you make matters worse?"

Cushman looked up at the ceiling, down at the floor, and then, directly at her.

"At the time, I thought any bullets directed at your doorstep could only be intended for me."

CHAPTER TWENTY-FOUR

Margaret choked so hard her last sip of lemonade sprayed across her bodice and down Cushman's tie.

"Why would anyone want to shoot you?" she gasped.

The Los Angeles Limited's unrelenting cacophony muffled his response.

Margaret regarded the waiting train with growing trepidation. She might be headed into the dark unknown in the company of a man with a dangerous past. They never asked for references. Whatever had possessed them to open their home to Cushman on mere faith?

Her first impulse was to return home, preferably alone. Before she could act, a porter, glistening in a dark uniform with gleaming brass buttons and a red, black-brimmed hat, placed a wooden block before the entry stairs. She climbed up to the narrow doorway, fascinated by his dignified bearing and the luster of his rich, dark skin. It was the first time she had closely encountered a man with ancestors from the African continent. She felt honored by his attentiveness.

The interior combined opulence and practicality in a manner most inviting. The porter led them down the aisle to a pair of facing velvet wine-colored seats that at nightfall converted to curtained upper and lower berths. Twinkling lights from a dozen small crystal chandeliers illuminated mahogany walls, silver fittings, and cut-glass vases filled with bouquets. Inlaid card tables and a small library of books with gold-tooled bindings offered many diversions.

Margaret had anticipated some degree of luxury but never to be surrounded by it. George Pullman publicly claimed to be running the world's largest hotel, based on the fact his cars had carried over twenty-one million people across the United States during the previous year. If all his trains running through Christmas were as full as this one, they would break the twenty-two million mark before New Year's Day.

"It must require extraordinary effort to keep these cars clean with passengers coming in and out!" she observed, trying to make conversation.

The porter must have been unaccustomed to having a passenger, especially a woman, speak to him directly. He smiled faintly, looking back not *at* her but a point over her head.

"I'm but one of many, Ma'am. Once we reach Chicago, this car goes to a storage yard. We take out all the pillows, blankets, mattresses, and seat covers and air them on racks, preferably in sunshine. Next, we roll up the carpeting, take it outside, and unroll it on the platforms. We'll blast it clean with compressed air shot through rubber hoses, then lay it back down in the cars and repeat the process for good measure. Seats and cushions go back in their proper place, and we polish all the crystal, woodwork, and silverware."

Cushman's gruff voice cut through the porter's explanation.

"All the lady needs to know from *you* is how to adjust the metal footrests on our seats."

The porter complied as rancor rose in Margaret's cheeks.

"Obviously there are a few things even a man like you can't handle," she muttered, scooting herself as far from Cushman as possible to get in their adjoining seats.

The perceptive porter gestured towards the car behind them.

"If Madam wishes to move about, may I suggest visiting the observation car. She will find the seats more comfortable and widely spaced. The windows extending around the back provide a panoramic view."

The porter tipped his hat ever so slightly and proceeded down the aisle.

"I'm not sure I can move about very well in a moving train," Margaret mused aloud.

Cushman stirred.

"The secret is to proceed slowly and wait until we've left the station and are progressing at a steady rate. Rather like a sailor getting his sea legs or rail legs, in our case."

Margaret shot him a withering look.

"I'm not going anywhere for the moment."

Cushman slouched, doffed his hat, and twisted it around by the brim. After several awkward minutes, he broke the silence.

"Forgive me for having spoken out of turn."

"Seven years living under our roof without mentioning someone was out to shoot you is hardly too soon."

"You're right. Long ago, I was a professional investigator before I fell into the morass where you found me."

"That's why you've given me all this support! Seamus and Charlie were right all along. What happened? Did it take whiskey or women to drive you to the gutter?"

"Both, I fear. Too much for one telling."

"Thirty-six hours is more than enough time to tell many tales, and I'm more than willing to listen. Let's go to the observation car for privacy's sake."

Cushman nodded and helped Margaret to her feet. When she lurched a bit, he took her arm. They wended their way down the aisle and through the sliding doors.

The observation car was every bit as sumptuous as the porter had described. Other than the small group of gentlemen congregated around cards and brandy snifters, they were alone.

"We may find sufficient privacy outside," Cushman suggested as he gestured toward the car's large rear glass-and-wood-paneled door.

They walked silently past the gamers out onto a platform covered with black-and-white checkered tiles. Once the door shut behind them, Cushman and Margaret could not be overheard, although they managed, with difficulty, to understand each other.

"Please share your history, in complete and accurate detail." Margaret shouted. "I alone shall decide whether we proceed or I go back home alone at the earliest opportunity."

He directed his gaze towards a distant time and space.

"Do you mind if I smoke?"

"I can brave this deck and railing for as long as it takes if you don't exhale in my face."

CHAPTER TWENTY-FIVE

"Very well. I grew up in Chicago, only son of English immigrants. They decided I would become a doctor before I could walk. My father earned a decent living as a tailor and, with scrimping, sent me to Rush Medical College.

"Before I entered the second term, a wealthy classmate introduced me to firearms, horses, and liquor. My accuracy at the pistol range attracted a gentleman's attention, and he recruited me for the Pinkerton Agency."

"Your parents must have been deeply disappointed."

Cushman shook his head.

"Since Allan Pinkerton had foiled an early plot to assassinate Lincoln when he was a candidate and continued to provide his security during the Civil War, they came to regard this line of work as a noble calling."

"My father always said Lincoln would have survived if a Pinkerton had been on duty that night at Ford's Theater."

"An opinion Pinkerton himself shared. You may recall he designed that unblinking eye logo and their motto, 'We never sleep.' Be that as it may, I found success in the first year of my new calling, foiling a bank robbery and recovering a kidnapped heiress. By 1891, my superiors considered me one of the organization's most promising undercover agents. That reputation, along with my marksmanship and familiarity with common folk, made me Pinkerton's own choice to infiltrate a labor union."

"Were you involved in the Homestead Strike?" Margaret asked.

"How did you know about that? You must have still been playing with dolls."

"My father discussed everything newsworthy with me, even as a child."

"A singular father raises a singular daughter," Cushman noted without a trace of sarcasm in his voice.

The clatter of train and track grew even more deafening. Cushman opened the door behind them and stuck his head back inside.

"The game is over, and the drinks have been cleared away."

"Are all the players gone?"

"Oh yes, let's find a corner table. If I'm about to bare my soul, you need to hear every word."

They shooed away a bevy of anxious waiters and sat themselves down.

"It's difficult to revisit that time in my life," he began. "To answer your question, Pinkerton dispatched me to Homestead, Pennsylvania, under the name Harold Cooper, to infiltrate the Amalgamated Association of Iron and Steel Workers who were at odds with Carnegie Steel Company. Old man Carnegie professed to favor unions, even said no mill was worth spilling blood. Union membership and its treasury had grown over the years. Many, including me, thought the workers had gotten greedy."

"Did you change your mind?"

He frowned in reflection.

"Sharing meals and attending meetings with these men for over three months convinced me their hard-won benefits might vanish if negotiations were unsuccessful. Henry Frick, the man Carnegie put in charge, vowed to break us.

"Such a contradictory decision by an otherwise hard-headed Scots businessman made little sense to me, then as now, still there's no way I'll ever understand a millionaire's thinking. Union leaders had already started negotiations when I arrived. A day before the contract expired, Frick barricaded the plant with barbed wire fences, high-power water cannons, and snipers."

"Didn't Mr. Frick bring in outside workers?"

"Tried to, but he wasn't successful. Our mechanics and drivers stayed away; even workers at other Carnegie plants struck in sympathy. We set up picket lines and escorted suspicious strangers beyond city limits. State-dispatched deputies posted scores of handbills demanding we stop all interference with plant operations.

We tore them down, herded the men onto a boat, and sent them downriver to Pittsburgh."

"You sound quite the union man."

"By then I had aligned with them. It was the first time I ever felt the power of a common cause, and my identity fused with its purpose.

"My Pinkerton contacts got word to me they would leave from Pittsburgh on July 5th, floating down the Monongahela at night to break through the strikers. I passed this information to union colleagues, who acted swiftly, summoning thousands of men, women, and children to tear down the barbed wire fence and create a human wall around the mill. They, I guess I should say we, also sent our own flotilla downstream to halt the barges."

"You put me in mind of the Roman god Janus: two heads facing in opposite directions."

"Judas is the name many would use. There was no bloodshed until the Pinkertons attempted to land. Witnesses swore we fired first but sure as we're sitting here, I say it was the Pinkertons who shot into the crowd, killing two and wounding nearly a dozen. I was one of many who responded in kind.

"From rowboats, we took potshots at the barges. Men on shore fired on them with brass cannon. We didn't scuttle 'em and when they attempted to disembark at eight A.M., another violent exchange killed four strikers. Scores of us took rifles and headed for higher ground. We fired steadily at the barges, but it was I, responding to suspicious movement on the hillside, who shot a Pinkerton dead."

"Had you worked with him?" Margaret asked gently.

"When I heard his dying curse, I knew I'd hit Sam Renner, an old friend, perhaps the only agent foolhardy enough to leave the safety of the barges.

"The nightmare continued through the heat of day. Once Sam fell, I stopped shooting. Had it been possible, I would have turned the weapon on myself or walked into the line of fire to quiet my guilt. My fellow strikers abandoned me. They tried to burn down the barges with lit oil slicks, blazing rafts, and a flaming rail car loaded with oil drums rolled toward the wharf. They failed, but their anger would not be extinguished."

"As I recall, the Pinkertons surrendered."

"Yes. When a small army of armed mill hands from nearby towns arrived, the agents raised a white flag and were granted safe passage. They were forced through town to the Opera House through a torrent of verbal and physical abuse. One of them saw me walking around half-dazed and yelled out my true identity.

"My striker friends dragged me through a gauntlet of enraged men, women, and children who beat me unconscious. A special train removed my battered body and all remaining agents to Pittsburgh where I ended up in a hospital."

"At least you were safe."

"Not at all. The strikers told them how they'd acted on information I'd given them. Even in my fragmented awareness, I knew the policeman posted at my bedside was not there for my protection. He was careless, never questioning my pretended stupor. Little by little, my wits returned. A month later in the dead of night, I whacked him over the head with his own billy club, stole his trousers, and escaped out the window."

"Where did you go?"

"Chicago and the home of my betrothed."

"You never mentioned an engagement."

"It's difficult, even now, to think about Tess. I've heard Edmund call you a New Woman; she was, too, one of the first and finest lady detectives Pinkerton hired."

"I had no idea Pinkerton had women in his employ."

"It's not common knowledge. I know for a fact he observed your gender's communication skills and keen eye for detail — qualities Detectives Tyson and McManus value, as well.

"It took me two weeks to reach her door. Tess let me in for a moment but sent me packing with a satchel full of food and warned me never to return. She lashed out mercilessly, salting my wounds with news the strike was broken and the mill back at full capacity. To the best of my knowledge, she never alerted the authorities.

"Whisky became my new companion; somehow, we made our way to California. I never saw warrants for my arrest. They might still exist. No matter how much drink has wasted my frame and changed my appearance, I anticipate a day of reckoning."

He folded his arms, awaiting Margaret's response. The train's relentless cadence allayed the awkward silence.

Margaret returned to the passenger car on her own. Cushman followed close behind. Overwhelmed by his story, she picked up a book and did not look up. Cushman returned to his assigned seat and calmly awaited her verdict.

At dinnertime, he stood and extended an arm to escort Margaret to the dining car.

"Is your first name really Harold?" she asked.

"Yes; Harold, after my mother's father."

"Doesn't suit you. I'll continue to call you Cushman."

"Continue?" he asked, with a note of skepticism.

"It seems there are two things I cannot do without for travel: Pullman accommodations and a former Pinkerton agent by my side."

CHAPTER TWENTY-SIX

After indulging in a superb four-course dinner, they waited for porters to convert their seats into sleeping quarters and draw curtains around the lower berth to shut out ambient light. Engine noise and a comfortable mattress lulled Margaret to sleep despite the drone of Cushman's snores coming from above.

Past mountains, ranches, and fields they rode until Chicago's relentlessly perpendicular skyline came onto view. A looming clocktower bell rang midnight. A day and a half after leaving Los Angeles, the train finally pulled into the Wells Street Station.

Margaret and Cushman made their way through a lofty colonnade of Corinthian marble pillars to a carriage waiting on Harrison Street. She still harbored misgivings. Could she ever fully trust Cushman? Might his early years in Chicago prove useful? Or, perish the thought, would someone recognize him?

Their destination, the twenty-two story Hotel Lasalle, dominated the financial district through a chiaroscuro of streetlights and shadows. Courteous staff welcomed them into a city within a city, replete with a multitude of eateries. From floor to ceiling, every aspect was perfectly maintained, befitting an establishment touted to be one of the safest and modern hotels outside of New York City.

After they registered, a bellhop, too young to fill out his brass button-studded uniform or keep the gold-trimmed hat and its visor from falling over his eyes, accompanied them to a passenger elevator. With a knowing smirk on his face, he ushered "Uncle" Cushman to a well-appointed single room on the ninth floor and Margaret across the hall to a suite overlooking LaSalle and Madison Streets. Cushman dispatched the young man with curt thanks and a few coins, then carried Margaret's travel case into her room, peered behind the drapes, checked the closets, and looked under the bed.

What does he expect to find? Margaret wondered, worried her attraction to Marco had not gone unnoticed.

She did not want to prolong his presence with debate. The moment he left, Margaret caught the scent of fresh-cut flowers. *Roses in January?* she wondered. Spinning slowly before the dark vistas outside her windows, she shed her clothes Salome-style and dropped on the down-filled comforter, naked on a bed for the first time since childhood.

Seven hours later, she rushed to prepare for the new day, Marco's name resonating in her brain. Never had she seen such an exquisite bathroom, painted pale aqua with white and brass fixtures. The claw-footed porcelain tub was quite the distraction; if the purpose for travel had not been investigative, she could have soaked in its deep waters all day.

Margaret descended the staircase on Cushman's arm, demure though daring in a refurbished gown cinched with a sash the same pale pink as the blush she'd pinched into her cheeks.

The green-and-gold lobby décor looked even more lavish by daylight. The comings and goings of the small throng they joined made the trembling chandeliers scatter rainbows across the walls. Not a single uncouth syllable spoiled this ornate universe. Cushman said LaSalle's management was striving to shed the smoke-filled, male-oriented image of yesteryear and cater to modern women.

The glitter ended at the colossal fronds and dark jade pots of the Palm Room, where lantern lights hung from the ceiling on sturdy chains cast a softer glow. Water from the fifteen-foot, centrally located Donatello fountain cascaded down the statue of a cherub, then tumbled into tiered marble receptacles stacked below. Fine china and linen covered the tables clustered around its base, but Margaret was oblivious to the perfection, for walking toward her with a wave and warm expression was Marco.

"Beautiful and breathtaking," he whispered in her ear, brushing his lips lightly across the lobe until he caught Cushman's reproving look.

He introduced her to his associate Giacomo Conti, who had arrived two days earlier with equipment to saw Margaret in half. On the strength of both men's patronage and a few extra dollars, the hotel allowed them to set up the illusion in the grand ballroom. Mr.

Conti played the gallant every bit as well as Alexander Pantages.

"Ze young lady siete magnifici, my friend," he told Marco. "Perfetto in every way."

Margaret felt anything but *perfetto* that morning. Nervous butterflies had set her stomach a-flutter and she could only pick at her food.

"Perhaps the lady about to be sawed in half doesn't want anyone to see what she what she had for breakfast," Cushman remarked as they were leaving.

She ignored the men's laughter on their way to the ballroom. In one corner loomed the device, part thick platform table and part cabinet. Despite openings for head, hands, and feet, it was shaped like a casket. Margaret visibly recoiled.

"This looks far too realistic. Sawing a woman in half for amusement is barbaric, even if it's only an illusion."

Giacomo bristled defensively.

"But surely the satisfactory ending reassures and enchants the audience!"

Marco hushed them before the argument grew heated and introduced Margaret to a twelve-year-old kitchen hand he'd just recruited.

"The key to the deception is, there are two ladies!"

"Although this young man may not yet have reached his full height, he is no lady," Margaret responded, feeling sorry for the blushing lad.

"He'll do until we find one. We'll be using your lovely head; he'll supply the feet."

They withdrew to the opposite side of the room where Marco swore the boy to secrecy and described various positions and actions.

"Where is your costume?" he asked impatiently as they returned to the others.

"Underneath," Margaret answered, grateful her slender figure could conceal another layer.

She shed her outer garments.

"Not easy to fool an illusionist," Marco murmured appreciatively.

Zig Zag Woman

Margaret slowly removed elbow-length gloves and began ever so discreetly to unbutton the top buttons of her bodice. Marco was riveted. If he could have conjured a magical curtain around them, there's no telling where her movements might have led.

Instead, Giacomo had set up a row of chairs and cajoled several passersby to fill them. The magician bowed as deeply to this group as he would a paying audience.

"Welcome to this historic moment, ladies and gentlemen. I, Marco the Magnificent, having wrested the secrets of the pharaohs' physicians from their ancient crypts, am here today to perform a feat no one has dared to attempt in the current age: I shall sever my lovely assistant in two. Rest assured the operation will be painless, and afterwards I will fully restore this brave young woman to her normal condition."

Gasps arose from the uninitiated audience. After waving his hands in front of Margaret's eyes, she pretended to fall into a wide-eyed trance and swooned into his arms. He gently lowered her limp form onto the table. Giacomo helped him position the cabinet in such a way her hands stuck out through the top holes and head extended beyond the semicircular neck opening. Two feet jutted out the opposite side. They weren't hers, although the shoes were identical.

She drew her knees up to her chest. Secreted in the lower half of the table below, the kitchen lad extended his stockinged feet in ladies' shoes through the opposite end. There was enough space between his head and her bottom for two audience volunteers to pull an enormous saw through the soft wood without injuring either of them. The men looked horrified; whether from the wink and smile her head gave them or the grisly deed they might have performed, she would never know.

Marco turned the cleanly-cut cabinet halves towards the audience. Taut black interior curtains created an illusion of emptiness. When he returned the cabinet to its former position, his lovely assistant stretched out full length. The boy retracted his feet into the table and Margaret's took their place. With his usual *Soor kabaj! Ya, huzzor! Soor kabaj!*, Marco unlocked the top cover and released her intact. She paraded triumphantly on his arm, surprised so small an audience could produce thunderous applause.

Triumph buoyed them through the rest of that fateful day. One of the men who'd witnessed the rehearsal turned out to be the hotel manager. He offered Marco a substantial sum to repeat the performance the next day for more guests.

Marco suggested Margaret run back to her room for a winter coat, bonnet, and muff. She was heady with success. Had she gone outside in nothing more than the flimsy costume, sensuality alone would have warmed her body.

Back in the lobby, no prince could have been more noble than Marco leading his new lady-in-waiting to the coach he'd hired. Cushman, their dour duenna, remained close while they toured the city's fashionable lakefront district resplendent with new homes built in various architectural styles from Gothic Revival to Queen Anne.

They rode past the new Blackstone Theatre, preparing to open on New Year's Eve with Chicago playwright George Ade's comedy, *U. S. Minister Bledsoe*.

"Beautiful venue," whispered Marco, his hand gently squeezing hers, "built for shows far grander than vaudeville. I hear it's equipped with every theatrical device. One day I'll design a three-act magic play for that stage, and you will be my star!"

Margaret glowed; Cushman glowered.

"Unless your name is Harry Houdini, you can't turn a two-minute trick into a full-length production," he muttered.

"That's where you're wrong, sir," Marco replied stiffly. "Houdini claims to be a magician but in my opinion he's little more than an overblown escape artist. Now my mentor Howard Thurston is a master illusionist. He gave me his blessing when I set out on my own and is currently touring the nation.

"He manages to keep audiences in thrall for over two-and-a-half hours making animals, girls, and even automobiles disappear. Waterfalls tumble out of thin air and glowing orbs dance across the stage at his beck and call.

"I have not achieved his standing but my skills improve every day. Our new device should attract the attention and income we need to become his equals."

They passed a brick structure too massive for a home, too plain for a hotel. The signage said Hull House, a haven for newly arrived European immigrants. Founder Jane Addams had been Margaret's role model ever since she'd read of that reformer and author's work with unwed mothers. Unfortunately, the hour was too late to pay a formal visit to that worthy woman.

They headed back to the LaSalle where Marco had dinner reservations. It must have been a wonderful meal, but after Margaret's third glass of claret, only vague impressions of a perfectly done roast followed by a moist chocolate cloud sliding softly down her throat remained.

A string quartet struck up sprightly tunes. Margaret danced with Marco, their bodies a hair's breadth from embrace, until Cushman abruptly cut in. He placed one hand firmly on her waist. Rather than waltz, he maneuvered Margaret off the dance floor.

"Madam has been up too late," he growled through clenched teeth.

The room moved in and out of focus. Margaret tried to keep time with the music while turning her head left and right, desperately scanning the crowd for Marco.

Using the hand that should have been holding hers, Cushman cinched Margaret's neck in a vise-like grip and jerked her head around. He looked her in the eye.

"Madam does not wish to make a fool of herself."

No pilloried Pilgrim maiden could ever have felt more shame. Cushman propelled Margaret back to her room. He took the key from her bag, unlocked the door, and shoved her inside.

As the tumbler clicked back into place again, she fell on the bed, sobbing. Through a haze of humiliation, her mother's voice warned she would pay tomorrow for tonight's folly. As she stood back up to undress, her clothes dropped off too effortlessly. The gentle lips caressing her burning shoulder were no illusion. Margaret stepped out of her undergarments and into the arms of a magician.

CHAPTER TWENTY-SEVEN

And then out. A whiff of sandalwood and brush of satin cape left no doubt whose arms were trying to claim her. And still would have had she not reacted quickly. The force rising within her as she shook loose from the embrace surprised them both. She wanted, and God knows needed, to set herself adrift on a sea of passion, but this conjurer did not possess the map to her heart.

The face was wrong; the place was wrong. It had all been staged, nothing more than an act. The only man she wanted was miles away, languishing over some sermon or agonizing over a parishioner's plight. He was not facile, he was not elegant, but he was true and predictable as the sunrise. He was Edmund.

Marco did not persist; she had to give him that. With a flourish and bow, he blew her a kiss and left like a night wind that had suddenly blown in, tousled her hair, and changed direction.

Margaret sank back upon the mattress where she stayed until a shaft of sunlight woke her from wine-induced slumber. Marco was gone, leaving behind a single long-stemmed red rose. She stroked the barely opened petals and laid it down on the pillow, where it remained like a ruby-tipped arrow.

Cushman came to her door at nine. Eyes forward and head held high, Margaret walked past him without acknowledging his presence. They maintained their silence all the way down the elevator, through the lobby, to the first available café. She hurried through breakfast and looked anxiously for Marco.

He must be practicing in the ballroom without me, she thought.

As she predicted, he was in the ballroom, but not alone. A woman with an all-too familiar classic profile and abundance of golden curls had taken Margaret's place in the cabinet.

Marco flashed his most winning smile.

"Now we are complete! Meg Ellison, meet Marie Levecque!"

He unlatched the cabinet. The blonde rose to her full height. Her beauty surpassed the face depicted on that infamous Pantages poster.

Weeks of artful deception, both on and off stage, made it possible for Margaret to shake her hand.

"Miss Levecque? Aren't you the partner Marco chose me to replace?"

The newcomer smiled condescendingly.

"I was the first woman Marco trusted to take part in his illusions. He tells me you're almost my equal."

"Marie has come back to us!" Marco called out. "That rat Pantages almost had her in his clutches, but she escaped."

Marie grabbed his arm to steady herself.

"It was too awful, my dear. Alexander Pantages told me to come to his office on the pretense of meeting an agent from the London Palladium. Neither Marco nor the agent was there, only that dreadful letch wearing nothing more than a black satin robe. I flung one of his Ming vases at him and escaped before he could trap me."

The picture she painted was all too vivid. Marco put one arm around Marie's waist and pulled her towards him as if they'd never been apart. Head spinning, knees rubbery, Margaret almost collapsed until Cushman sidled up close enough to brace her with his arm.

"At least you ruled him out as a suspect and her as a body, er, a dead one," he murmured in her ear.

He flicked his eyes the way most men would across Marie's ample proportions and left abruptly.

"So, tell me, Miss Levecque, why didn't you send word to Marco and let him know you were safe?"

Margaret spat out the words, infuriated Yvette's disappearance had cost them precious time locating a murderer. No matter how embarrassed she felt, Margaret could never give voice to sordid emotions.

"I feared for us both. You have been working with this man long enough to witness his dark temper. If unleashed, that anger would only hurt him professionally."

"And, perhaps, physically, given the thugs Mr. Pantages may have on his payroll," Margaret conceded.

"You're a good judge of character. Neither Marco nor I would be safe until he was successful in his own right."

"I was already well established long before I met either of you," Marco stated loftily.

Marie suppressed an indulgent smile.

"How did you let Miss Levecque know we were coming to Chicago?" Margaret asked.

Marie answered for them both.

"Our reunion was sheer coincidence. My family lives here and, as you may have guessed, our last name is not Levecque. Chicago was the logical place to hide. The prodigal daughter was allowed to return home under strict conditions, including renouncing the stage, church every Sunday, and introductions to eligible bachelors.

"I overheard talk about Marco's grand new venture while having tea with my aunty and one of those gentlemen in the hotel lobby yesterday. This morning, I decided to come by on my own to make amends and offer congratulations."

"And, it appears, your services," Margaret whispered, lowering her head. "What will your family say?"

"I'm not going back to them. Marco is my heart and only true family," she replied simply.

She loves him after all, Margaret thought, *and Marco surely looks smitten with her, if he's even capable of true affection.*

The magician regarded Margaret with what might have passed for sympathy in one not so self-obsessed. He grabbed her by the shoulders.

"We could be an unstoppable team. No scruffy boys to look after, just two beautiful women similar in grace and form. Our illusions will baffle the world. Who cares if one's a blonde and the other a redhead?"

He glanced at Margaret's less voluptuous shape.

"With wigs and a bit of padding, you'll appear identical, and richer than anyone you know or read about in the papers."

The only wealth Margaret needed was constancy of heart, and she had almost squandered what little she'd had left of that on desire. It was clear that unless Marie was indisposed, Margaret would always be the feet to her head, a pale reflection of her sumptuous reality.

She was about to respond when Cushman rushed back into the room, waving a telegram.

"Madam, your uncle is dying. We must return to Los Angeles at once."

His words stiffened her spine. Marco and Marie offered a few words of sympathy as they stood there holding hands. Margaret realized his interest in her was never more than an illusion, one he could easily replicate with anyone he beguiled.

"I will write to you once my uncle's affairs are settled," she said, showing no outward resentment. "Meanwhile, get your show on the road, as I've heard stagehands say."

Marco might have tried to saw her in half, but in the end, it was Margaret who performed the ultimate disappearing act. She pivoted and marched out of the ballroom a few steps ahead of Cushman.

"Well done," he said. "Are all of your belongings packed?"

She nodded.

"Please forgive me; I should have served you better. I have no idea if that weaselly wizard found access to your room. Shortly after escorting you to your door, I heard footsteps in the hall. I caught a glimpse of his red-lined cape rounding the corner. At least he was leaving."

He hesitated, pursed his lips, narrowed his eyes, and instantly turned inquisitor.

"There wasn't very much time for anything to happen, I hope, but if he tried to force himself upon you, there is an excellent chance he will have a serious accident."

Margaret looked downward, shaking her head, afraid of what her scarlet cheeks would disclose.

"He did find a way into my room. I don't know what his intentions were, nor can I understand how he gained entry. He left the moment I insisted he go."

Rage and a shadow of doubt played across Cushman's face before he pronounced his conditions.

"Without you, I would not be alive. Last night, you acted in an unseemly manner that could very well have encouraged Marco's passions. I'm glad your good sense and values deflected that

Lothario's attentions.

"Swear he didn't touch you and promise never again to threaten your reputation, and I won't breathe a word to your husband. He will hear about how adeptly you closed this part of the case, however."

"Marco did me no harm." Margaret gulped, then added in tearful tones, "On my honor, I pledge not to drink so much wine in the future."

She almost choked on the words but would have said anything to drive the searing shame from her soul. In the end, gratitude saved the day. This rough-hewn man believed her and swore to keep his own counsel.

They took the elevator up to Margaret's room one last time. Cushman picked up her bags while she, astounded by his loyalty as much as Marco's seeming ability to walk through walls, tossed the wilting red rose out the window.

Cushman anticipated her unasked questions.

"Pinkertons learn to read people," he said. "If I were a woman, I'd probably find that fellow deucedly attractive."

She laughed for the first time that day. The idea of Cushman pining after Marco was almost as silly as a pastor's wife thinking she could turn herself into a showgirl. She continued to giggle until rage and embarrassment took over, howling out of her body like demons escaping Pandora's Box.

Cushman let her tears splash onto his vest and ignored curious passersby. Once the tirade ended, a smile cracked his cigar-store Indian face, and he shouldered his carpet bag.

"Suppose we save the bellhop a trip. You're a modern woman; carry your own belongings," he said with sardonic glee, "and let's head for the stairs."

Margaret offered no objections. Taking the stairway would avoid having to traipse through the ballroom where Marco and Marie were no doubt dazzling onlookers.

A swift carriage ride brought them to Grand Central Station. Cushman puffed on his pipe. Perhaps he needed to steady his nerves or no longer felt a need to observe the niceties.

"You can't blame yourself entirely for getting us into this situation," he growled.

Something in his patronizing tone was unbearable.

"Whom do you suggest I blame?" she snapped. "Marco, who mesmerized both of us into wanting to clear his name? What about Edmund, for his emotional inattentiveness?"

Cushman scowled. His knowledge of their lack of marital relations was as clear as his distaste for her mentioning it.

"What about you?" she continued, "for — what is the term lawyers use? — oh, yes, *aiding and abetting* my thirst for adventure?"

Cushman folded his arms and pulled his bowler over his eyes.

"Blame yourself, why don't you. There is no way the actions of three insignificant men could compete with the force of your feminine will."

Before reaching the station, they achieved an uneasy truce. A trip cancellation sent them back to respectability on the 11:30 A.M. train for Los Angeles. The panorama streaming past her window played Margaret's misadventures in reverse.

"He is a learned man, isn't he?" Margaret mused out loud. "How else would Marco have known so many Egyptian words?"

"Like most performers, Marco is little more than a fraud, educated by the world rather than institutions of learning. He has smatterings of various languages, but no living soul has any idea what ancient Egyptian sounded like. 'Soor kabaj,' is Hindi for 'son of a swine,' the foulest insult a Muslim can use. 'Hamare ghali ana, accha din' is Pushtu for 'Good day, come into my street'."

"That's polite enough," she remarked, not wanting to admit she'd never heard of Pushtu.

"Only on the surface, much like the man in question," Cushman asserted. "Those are the words Afghan prostitutes use to entice their patrons."

"Where would he have heard such phrases? For that matter, where did you?"

"Magicians gather in disreputable places all over the world. As for me, I read."

The Cushman Margaret came to Chicago with would never have used the word *prostitute* in front of her. She opened a copy of Mark Twain's *Eve's Diary* and to conceal her flushed face. Worried she might be seen leafing through illustrations of their unclothed ancestors, Cushman snatched it away and wrapped his kerchief round the cover before handing it back.

Before easing into the deep leather seat and losing herself in witty words, she asked the question looming over them from the moment he'd stormed into the ballroom.

"What did the telegram really say?"

He took the message from his vest pocket.

"About time you asked. Those fine fellows Tyson and McManus are going to need your help, as does your whole family."

His slow sonorous voice suited the big block letters:

YVETTE STILL MISSING. LELAND ARRESTED. COME HOME SOON. ALL MY LOVE, EDMUND.

CHAPTER TWENTY-EIGHT

They pulled into Los Angeles station twelve hours later. Thomas Warren drove up in a new deluxe Maxwell touring motor car painted a blue so bright it put the sky to shame. Brow furrowed, bowler in place, Edmund sat beside him,

Cushman hopped off the train and brought round a yellow metal stepstool to help passengers descend to the platform. Edmund ran to their side. Safe in her husband's arms, Margaret silently cursed herself for being a fool.

Cushman's attitude continued to fluctuate between civil and surly. She felt his gaze drill through the nape of her neck.

Does he still have suspicions about me? she wondered.

"My darling, my angel," Edmund whispered in her ear.

His eyes were brimming with tears. She gave him a reassuring smile and climbed into the automobile.

The ride home would have been exciting had it not been so uncomfortable. Cushman straddled the bags they had piled in the back. Margaret and Edmund squeezed into the one passenger seat.

The incessant forward motion made Margaret feel she was leaving her troubles behind. Gravel pinged against the undercarriage. The sputtering motor made her miss the clop-clop of horse's hooves and the swish of their flickering tails. Still, it was a relief to think nothing could ever startle a metal beast.

The front door of the rectory gleamed brighter than heaven's gate. Up the stairs Margaret raced to reclaim sanctuary. No secret spaces lurked within their cushioned furniture; no hidden panels lay beneath the parquet floor. Every picture, pillow, and vase remained where she'd left them; no magic wand could make them disappear.

The staid man beside Margaret might not grasp her unfulfilled longings, but he tried. Clearly, she was the love of his life, narrowly surpassed by God and the church. She vowed to remain Edmund's perfect partner and redouble her efforts on Leland's behalf.

Within the hour, Margaret unpacked her belongings, leaving bits of finery tacked onto the traveling clothes and shoving the gauzy costumes into her charity basket. If she did not find a use for them, one day they might turn into window curtains. For the moment, she only wanted them out of her sight.

On her way downstairs, Margaret paused at the landing to catch an overhead view of Cushman pacing around the parlor. Edmund hung on his every word. No thespian could have performed a more theatrical retelling.

In Cushman's version, it was he who spotted Marie Levecque amid the hotel crowd and Margaret who persuaded her to come forward. His lavish oratory ended with a grand upward gesture in my direction.

"By using her powers of observation and deduction, the estimable Mrs. Morehouse eliminated Marco the Magician as a suspect in the Pantages Theatre Alley murder!"

Edmund clapped his hands, springing to his feet when she entered the room.

"Bravo, Margaret! You reunited a couple forced apart by cruel circumstance, though destined to be together. Even theater people have been known to be happily wed. May they choose to enter that blessed sacrament and be as happy as we are! A toast!"

They clicked brandy snifters as Margaret studied her toes. Edmund cupped his hand under her chin.

"Without you, my life is eternal winter. I must force myself to share your brilliant mind with the good people of Los Angeles. Just promise me you'll never again take that beautiful face away from me so long."

His ardent embrace almost took her breath away.

"Nothing could please me more," she gasped, then look hard over his shoulder at skeptical Cushman, who shrugged and looked away.

Edmund burrowed his head in her shoulder, possibly to fend off tears. A shudder of emotion passed between them. The old connection, frayed by time and inattention, felt restored.

"There's little I can add to Cushman's account. Nevertheless, your telegram and my womanly intuition tell me you have much to share."

Edmund settled onto the sofa, and Margaret sidled up next to him. Back at home where she belonged, it was time to reclaim her rightful authority.

"Cushman, could you kindly check on dinner?"

He pivoted and left, visibly insulted.

She turned to Edmund.

"Tell me what happened with Leland, dear."

"Detectives Tyson and McManus kept me informed from the time shortly after they made the arrest. They did everything you asked, down to the last detail, and stationed themselves outside the Hotel Nadeau on the morning of the 20th. Before I go on, I want you to know how grateful I am to them and you for trying to protect Leland, despite the dreadful consequences."

"Is he safe?"

"If you describe being confined to his home by Los Angeles's finest as safe, I suppose he is, at least for now. Not even his mother's influence has led to his release."

The last comment surprised Margaret more than Marie's sudden reappearance.

"Much as I hate to cast doubt on city officials, if Leland is only under house arrest, Elvira's money may be the only thing keeping her son out of prison. I would enjoy her frustration more if I weren't worried about you. Did the young lady show up to collect the ransom?"

"A few minutes late, the detectives informed me. Once she opened the bag and bit into a gold eagle, she hurried off."

"I take it they followed her?"

"All the way into the hotel, where she must have given the loot to a creature they described as a hulking oaf. They saw the man come out, bag in hand, and hop into a waiting carriage while the girl took off in a different direction."

"Hmm," Margaret mused. "Could that be where they've hidden Yvette? Revisiting the hotel might prove worthwhile."

Edmund bristled with alarm.

"Officers Tyler and McManus should do this, not you."

"Of course, not me," Margaret said quietly, all the while wondering how to strike up a conversation with someone at the front desk, or better yet, one of the housekeepers. "Did the detectives follow the man or the girl?"

"The girl was fast on her feet. They didn't catch up in time to see her meet up with accomplices. There was no mistaking the bag, however, and they followed the man with the money. Unfortunately, they were on foot. By the time they spotted the horse and carriage outside Elvira's bank, it was speeding away."

"Did they chase after the carriage or go into the bank?"

"Before the suspect reached the carriage, Tyson jumped on his back. They rolled down the cement stairs together. Tyson was unscathed but the blow knocked the fellow out cold. They had plenty of time to summon help."

"Once Tyson and his captive were on the way to jail, McManus went into the bank. The manager was more than cooperative. It didn't take too much time or effort to determine most of those gold coins had been deposited back into Leland's personal account."

The last revelation made Margaret's head reel.

"That doesn't make sense. Gold returned to Leland's, account may appear suspicious although I don't see how it would be considered incriminating."

Edmund drank two glasses of sherry in quick succession.

"If a man murdered his wife, he might fabricate her abduction," he said quietly.

"Why would he return the coins to his account so soon and in such an obvious way? Leland's too smart for that! Surely an investigator would realize someone is trying to incriminate him. You don't think he's capable of doing such a horrible thing, do you?"

"I have my misgivings. Elvira's blood runs through him too. Your friends wasted no time. After detaining the big man, they returned from the station with a warrant to search Leland's home. That evening, they put him under house arrest. If Leland weathers this storm, one day the bank will be his. If not, he could go to prison or, at the very least, tarnish his reputation."

Margaret gave Edmund a hug of support. He drew her near, stroking her hair. Eyes locked with renewed passion, they climbed up the stairs and into the same bed, together for the first time in years.

CHAPTER TWENTY-NINE

Two days later, Cushman and Margaret met the detectives at a park near the station. McManus's large frame barely left enough room for Margaret to sit on the park bench comfortably. Cushman, stiff as a lamppost, posted himself behind her. Tyson circled the trio, sniffing the air like a bloodhound, impatient to be on with the day.

Their banter wore thin after Margaret gave them an edited version of Chicago adventures but the banter soon wore thin. The detectives were focused on a more immediate matter: the guilt or innocence of Leland Morehouse.

They had followed through on their original promises, but to Margaret's mind they'd ignored truth in their eagerness to make an arrest. The knowing glances they exchanged angered her even more.

"I asked you to protect our nephew, not take him prisoner!" she shouted out suddenly in a voice shrill enough to startle pigeons.

Margaret jumped to her feet and began to pace back and forth. Nannies rushed their perambulators by, trying to spare their charges from the sound of her tirade.

McManus stood, hat in hand, and gestured her to sit back down. When she refused, he looked her squarely in the eyes.

"You'd have done the same if you were in our shoes, Mrs. Margaret. We did not inform the captain about our promise to follow Leland Morehouse because he would have never approved. I couldn't argue on your behalf without jeopardizing your privacy. Our sole purpose was to protect the young man but what transpired outside the hotel steered us in another direction."

McManus continued the tale in his deep, lilting voice.

"The weather was balmy and our Charlie's missus turned him out dapper enough to join the line of fine business gentlemen waiting for the shoeshine boys. I sat on a nearby bench with the *L. A. Times* propped up in front of me. Onlookers would have sworn my eyes were on the paper, but they were trained on Leland Morehouse, less than thirty yards away."

"How did he look?"

"Surprisingly calm, given the circumstances."

"The girl caught my eye soon as she stepped onto the green," added Tyson. "She was awful pretty, looked out of place. A bit more decked out and I would have thought her a doxy for hire. She didn't give the time of day to any man save your nephew. Her big blue eyes kept shifting back and forth until she saw young Mr. Morehouse and went up to him."

"Did he recognize her?"

"Hard to tell," McManus responded. "They spoke too quietly for us to make the words out. He did hand over the sack of coins, heavy burden for the little lady's delicate wrist. I daresay one can always find enough strength to carry extra coins."

"I warned him to use the same distinctive bag they'd sent him with the ransom note."

"That he did," responded McManus appreciatively. "Soft gold chamois cloth cinched with a thick purple cord."

"Edmund told me she bit into one of the coins."

Tyson laughed.

"She smiled so sweetly you'd have thought it was candy. Mr. Morehouse went about his way. Nothing else happened. Made McManus and me wonder if they hadn't staged the whole transaction."

"Surely you didn't expect one of the girl's cohorts to step out of the crowd with Yvette?" asked Cushman.

"Of course not, " answered McManus. "No self-respecting kidnapper would have brought his quarry that near to freedom. Too much could go wrong. Still, in an exchange like that, there should have been some form of *quid pro quo*."

Tyson grimaced. "Quid pro what?"

"Quo, my friend," explained McManus patiently. "Something for something; say, another note written by his wife or even another lock of hair. Leland Morehouse merely strolled away as if he'd given alms to the poor and was going about the business of the day."

"I prepared him for your surveillance beforehand. He was

leaving the matter in your professional hands."

"If so, he didn't show the slightest hint of curiosity."

"Yvette and he were estranged," Margaret began, then wished she hadn't. Any allusion to Leland's marital woes might only compound the evidence piling up against him.

"I went after the girl swift as a tiger, I did, but more stealthy-like," Tyson beamed in recollection, "and she never gave me a moment's notice."

Margaret glanced over at McManus.

"Did either of you stop to think the kidnappers' headquarters might be a room in the hotel?"

"Hmmm ... you mean young Mrs. Morehouse might be hidden in plain sight? Wish I'd gone back and turned up something! We didn't witness the exchange. When the huge lout came out toting the bag with the purple cord over his shoulder, we knew he was part of the plot.

"The girl probably took off immediately. I wasn't about to try to launch a search since it would take two of us to tackle the accomplice. The man hopped into a waiting carriage, bold as brass, like he was used to transporting that much loot daily. Traffic must have slowed them down. The travelin' tiger and I had to follow on foot. We caught up with him but not before he was leaving Union Bank."

"You mean to tell me this is the flimsy evidence you used to put Leland in jail? Our nephew is neither devious nor stupid."

Tyson barely restrained his anger.

"I jumped on our suspect's back and nearly gouged his eyes out. Only way I could slow him down enough for McManus to catch up and arrest him. We found a gold coin in his vest pocket, probably a reward, though he was too scared or stupid to tell us even after we hauled him off to jail. And that took quite a bit of doing, considering we weren't supposed to be on this case in the first place."

"How did you explain yourselves to the Captain?"

"I told him we'd just happened to notice the transaction between Leland and the girl while we were out patrolling and decided to see what happened next."

"Turns out our boss had suspected Leland Morehouse of foul play ever since the wife was reported missing," added McManus. "I've only spoken to your nephew while posting a guard at his door. Much as I hate to say this, he did not behave like an innocent man. He well may be but his arrogance only shows a lack of common sense."

"He was downright rude and guilty as sin," Tyson jumped in. "The note McManus pried from the big man's meat hook hand turned out to be a receipt for five hundred dollars in coin deposited to Leland Morehouse's personal account."

Margaret felt flustered as a fish on shore, convinced they weren't exaggerating, hoping they were somehow mistaken.

"A receipt is one thing, but a deposit slip is quite another. The bank would not accept the gold into that account without a deposit slip signed and dated by Leland himself!"

"The manager and a teller produced that very document, just as you described."

"What if someone was able to forge it?"

"If it was a forgery, it was damned near perfect," muttered Tyson. "We went straight off to his home. It was still early afternoon, too soon for the bank to close. The servants let us in, a little too eagerly if you ask me; made me wonder how he treats them."

Grim realization took hold of Margaret. McManus proceeded in his usual direct manner.

"His signature is an odd mix of schoolboy script and flourishes. We uncovered several signed documents in his desk. When we showed them alongside the deposit slip to the captain, he directed us to place your nephew under house arrest. A signature like that is hard to copy."

"But not impossible," Margaret asserted. "Why would Leland engage in such behavior knowing you were watching all along?"

"Maybe he had more than a little to do with his wife's disappearance and cooked up this fancy story to cover his tracks. I bet he thought we'd get as far as the hotel and leave," ventured Tyson.

"When Leland came to Edmund and me for help, he was

genuinely troubled."

McManus looked up at the sky as if looking for a gentle way to convince her of hidden motives.

"Does he fear for his wife or himself? This much I know for sure: the coins were headed for his account. People forge signatures to steal money, not give it back. If you ask me, he was trying to throw us off course."

"Or perhaps worse," Margaret said sadly, doubt undermining family loyalty. "You may be right about Leland. I hope, for both his and my husband's sake, there's a better explanation. I must pay a visit to that young man tonight. Can you help me?"

CHAPTER THIRTY

The detectives went back to the station bearing Margaret's latest message to the Captain, in which she asked to be reinstated and work on the Yvette Morehouse case. Fearing her chances for approval were slim, she cited her relationship to the young woman and the clause in her job description about locating missing persons.

Daisy transported Cushman and Margaret both ways that morning, confining her gait to a walk due to the recent injuries. They could not bear the thought of putting the dear creature out of her misery and agreed they would soon need to find a younger, stronger horse.

Back in her kitchen, Margaret threw herself into making Edmund's favorite dinner. The roast beef turned out tender, flavorful, and rosy pink throughout. Cooked in the drippings, Golden Yorkshire puddings puffed up perfectly with hollow centers in each to catch the gravy. Spices bound in layers of red cabbage, apples, and onions blended with all the meaty smells.

If only the ups and downs of life could be handled half that easily! Margaret murmured to herself, crimping crust for an apple pie.

A jubilant Cushman burst into the kitchen and asked her to come outside. Thomas Warren had just driven up in a carriage drawn by a young roan gelding. He proposed giving the horse to the Morehouses and taking Daisy to a well-earned retirement at his summer home in the country.

"What a dear man he is!" Margaret exclaimed and invited Thomas to dinner.

Edmund championed everyone in the parish, but the Warrens were a special case. Their loyalty had begun when Edmund married them.

Olivia Warren's fair skin and rich brown hair made her look

like a woman of wholly European extraction, but one of her grandparents had been born a slave and emancipated after the Civil War. When she became pregnant, the Warrens came to Edmund for counsel, which he provided with so much reassurance they also took Margaret into their confidence.

Olivia agonized throughout the months in waiting. Mary and Maximilian, the twins she bore, resembled both parents. Edmund baptized them and they quickly became everyone's darlings. The Warrens rejoiced, confident the status of their children, and most certainly their grandchildren, would no longer be determined by the color of their skin.

Olivia graced many committees with her sweetness and gift for organization. Under her leadership, St. Paul's opened a kindergarten with the twins as its first enrollees. Thomas worked hard as assistant manager at Mason's Mercantile and eventually bought the store.

Offering a wide array of fabric and clothing departments, the establishment was already unique to the West Coast. When it reopened as Warrens', the new proprietors added tailors, a children's department, furniture, and linens. Customers flocked to their doors. On the national level, commercial efficiency and mechanization were taking hold but local mercantile success was a rarity. All went well until Thomas opened a second store.

If he'd found a location other than boomtown Hollywood, still separate from Los Angeles in 1907, nothing unfortunate might have happened. They chose a vacant building near the Hollywood Hotel, hoping to catch the eyes of rich families on their way to theater, dances, and card parties. There was no way for them to know Elvira Morehouse had already set her sights on that property for future development.

Thomas Warren's ability to secure the deed was due to one of Elvira's rare lapses. He had gone to the bank with money in hand and signed on the dotted line. Elvira was in Europe at the time; upon her return, finding the property on which she planned erect a six-story office building no longer available, she began to plot revenge. Secret sources uncovered ample evidence to feed her dark suspicions.

A series of carefully worded unsigned missives disclosing Olivia and her children's mixed heritage arrived on the doorsteps of the city's notable families. Anonymous Letters to the Editor decried the Warrens' tailors as Chinese, working off-site. In that matter, Elvira, who started the rumor, was correct, although the Warrens employed workers of all ethnicities based on skills and paid appropriate wages.

Within weeks, the family sold Elvira the tract for pennies on the dollar and went into seclusion. With distracted leadership and declining patronage, their original store would have closed its doors had it not been for Edmund.

He greeted the family warmly every Sunday and played with the twins. The Morehouses patronized the store whenever they could and urged others to follow suit. They were frequent guests at the Warrens' table.

Their community embraced the store more readily than it did the stories about Olivia and the children. Unable to navigate a daily sea of verbal and nonverbal abuse, she left Thomas and took the twins back to her family in Tennessee.

His determination to provide for twins and the dream they might one day be reunited kept Thomas going. He wired them money twice a month but never heard back. He was one of the hardest working men in City, never too busy to lend the Morehouses a helping hand.

Edmund insisted the store survived because it was the best in town. His endorsement earned him Thomas Warren's unwavering support and Elvira's undying enmity.

CHAPTER THIRTY-ONE

Dinner over and stomach full, Edmund picked up a snifter of brandy and excused himself to work on the next week's sermon. Margaret and Cushman set out on their visit to Leland.

The weather was clear and the evening young. Margaret packed the last of their pie into a basket along with a bottle of sherry.

"One would think you were calling on the infirm instead of the incarcerated," Edmund declared as he helped them out the door.

Jupiter, the new horse, was larger than Daisy and brimming with youthful vigor. He barreled through the twilight streets, delighted to discover a carriage lighter than the one belonging to his former owner. It took considerable skill for Cushman to maintain control.

Jupiter allowed himself to be tethered to the hitching post outside Leland's mansion. McManus and Tyson were stationed near the doorstep and gave Margaret welcome word that the captain had approved her reinstatement.

They led her and Cushman to the second-floor library where Leland sat smoldering at his desk. Shirtsleeves rolled up and celluloid collar half detached, he was pretending to review bank records. Margaret's sudden appearance only increased his discomfort.

"To what do I owe this great honor, Aunt Margaret?" he asked, not bothering to rise to his feet.

She resisted the urge to slap him.

"I never dreamed they would have cause to take you into custody, which on the face of things they do. All I wanted was to give you a degree of protection during a dangerous negotiation."

He sneered, gesturing at the walls around us. "It seems you got your wish. I'm protected as well as any man, though not from unwanted relatives."

"See here, you pampered popinjay," growled Cushman,

bunching a fist. He might have struck the younger man if they'd been alone. "You have no idea what this woman did for you, what she's still willing to try if you maintain a civil tongue."

Leland slumped in his chair as Margaret approached the desk, towering above him more in authority than inches.

"Everything went as planned, Leland. The detectives watched you give the girl the money. She went inside the Hotel Nadeau. What none of us anticipated, except maybe you, was the girl's accomplice returning to your bank."

"Deposit slip in hand, I hear. I never signed it."

"I want to believe that. When did you last make a deposit?"

"To that account? I rarely use it. Let me check." Leland pulled a ledger out of the deepest drawer in his desk and pointed to an entry. "Last year; March 20, 1910."

Margaret scanned his neat columns as the others looked over her shoulder. "Look: same month and day, same amount, exactly $500. Someone may have been clever enough to hold onto that paperwork. With a fine, small blade they could have scraped away the ink and altered the date by changing the 1910 to 1911. Where is it now?"

"Important stuff like that gets locked up in the evidence room at the station," replied Tyson.

"Would Captain Clark to let you examine the writing and see if there were any changes?"

The men looked thunderstruck.

"We'll ask him first thing in the morning," McManus promised, then turned his attention to Leland.

"If your aunt's theories prove true, the plot against you has been brewing for over a year. You could have a serious enemy on the loose."

Cushman grabbed Leland by the shoulders and pulled him up to a standing position.

"And if you don't want one more, you need to make serious amends."

Barely suppressing smiles, McManus and Tyson left to resume what they hope would be their last night on guard duty.

Margaret simply took her leave. Standing where Cushman had put him down, Leland could not look her in the eye.

"Timely bit of reasoning on your part," Cushman commented on their way home.

The cool, moist night calmed the heady triumph coursing through Margaret. She gulped cool air and assumed a modest expression.

"I may be wrong."

"No one else came up with a version of the facts that didn't implicate your nephew. Once again, you're an exceptional woman."

She had to admit she agreed with him. After a dubious debut as magician's assistant, Margaret had recast herself in the role of a lifetime: Margaret Morehouse, Los Angeles Police Department's second female policewoman with arrest powers and first female detective. The only drawback was the last title was not, and might not ever be, official.

Even at the late an hour, she began to prepare for the coming day. They must find a reason to speak to the hotel management, possibly a church-related event. A woman could not sign a contract but might be present during negotiations for guest suites and meeting rooms. Not that it would come that. They would have to enlist someone with proper credentials.

Could she involve Edmund? Should she involve Edmund? Cushman might pass as a parishioner of some standing, but the detectives would have to keep their mouths shut or blend into the crowd. Their brogues would never suit the roles they'd need to play. A dozen strategies came to mind but scattered like playing cards dropped from sweaty palms at the corner of Spring and Main.

From the hilltop above, a motorized vehicle bore down on them, iron wheels striking sparks from the tracks they followed, screeching brakes creating a stench strong as hellish sulfur.

Jupiter reared and bounded out of the way. He would have galloped farther had not Cushman's firm hands stayed the flight and brought them back to the scene of near disaster.

A pale streetlight just below the intersection revealed the trolley on its side. The only noise came from derailed wheels whirring in

Zig Zag Woman

the air and rudely awakened residents. No human sounds came from inside.

"Brakes either gave out or weren't set right in the first place," Cushman ventured.

"What if a passenger is injured or knocked unconscious?" Margaret speculated, starting to hop down from her seat.

Cushman stopped her and handed over Jupiter's reins.

"I'll look this mess over. The situation must be stable before we tend to whatever hapless souls might still be trapped."

His logic was valid. Margaret's resourcefulness did not extend to mechanical failure, though handling a standing horse was well within her skills.

After he took fewer than ten strides, a creature emerged through a shattered window. Demonic in the half light, it flapped what looked like wings, but more likely was a cape, and ran away cackling gleefully. Cushman, the stalwart protector, fainted dead away.

〰️

Margaret tied Jupiter to a lamppost and worked her way carefully downhill. Cushman stirred. His pride was wounded but he refused assistance.

Knowing it would be well-nigh impossible to haul him to a standing position, she tackled the situation on her own. Shards of broken glass lay all around. Margaret cupped one in her black-gloved hand. When the reflection of a streetlamp appeared in it, she carefully lowered the makeshift mirror through a broken window to look for injured passengers.

The light ricocheting throughout the cab was a dim beacon at best. All Margaret made out were empty seats, although she shouted, "Is anybody here?" several times.

"It's empty," Margaret called out to Cushman, "but what in the world was that creature?"

Cushman slowly rose to his feet, shaking badly as he had with alcoholic tremors on the night she'd first met him.

"Hard to tell. Hope it was human," he answered.

Margaret attributed most of what passes for divine intervention to natural causes but thanked the Almighty aloud for the way Jupiter's wild streak had pulled them out of harm's way.

A small group of neighborhood residents began to gather around. They gave the officer who arrived on the scene as detailed a description as possible of the near crash and their efforts to determine if anyone had been hurt.

The policeman listened attentively until Margaret began to describe an elusive creature vanishing into the darkness.

"This looks more like mechanical failure. Maybe the conductor forgot to set the brakes. Quite a spill you took there, sir and lady. Might it be you saw an illusion?"

"This phantom was all too real," Margaret countered, "and we both saw it."

There was no convincing an officer near the end of his shift and in no mood to investigate. He gruffly gave them permission to leave.

Margaret reviewed the evening's events in her mind all the way home.

"Who in the world could be that quick?" she asked out loud. "Perhaps a young rowdy out for a lark?"

"We've encountered too many of those in past weeks," muttered Cushman.

Margaret caught her breath. Was this small fiend linked to the urchins who nearly thwarted the trip to Chicago? And the bullet on the doorstep; would it be necessary for a grown man to pull a trigger?

Except for his irregular breaths and an occasional flick of the riding crop, Margaret could have been riding next to a cadaver.

"The question remains," she said quietly, "which one of us were they after?"

They rode in stony silence the rest of the way home.

CHAPTER THIRTY-TWO

Morning came too soon, as did a thrum of knocking on the parish door. All hope dashed for an extra hour's sleep, Margaret forced herself out of bed and was halfway down the staircase by the time Cushman answered the door.

McManus and Tyson were the early callers. Cushman and an unusually animated Edmund were escorting them inside.

Tyson beamed caught sight of her.

"You were right as rain, young lady, right as rain!"

"About the deposit slip?"

"The captain took us to the evidence room and unlocked the box where he'd stashed the bank note. He pulled a magnifying glass out of his vest pocket. Quite fancy it was, tortoiseshell and silver case with hinges, not the kind of thing you'd expect a plain-living man to own."

"Cut to the chase, why dontcha'?" McManus cut in. "We took turns looking at the paper, even holding it up to the sunlight, and saw it to be much thinner where the numbers were. Someone had scratched out the date and written over it. Masterful job, undetectable to the naked eye."

"What does this mean for my nephew?" Edmund asked cautiously.

"It means I'm still keeping an eye on him," muttered Tyson.

McManus elbowed his partner in the ribs.

"Sir, my friend here still has his doubts. The only opinion that counts is the Captain's, and he has declared him to be a free man. As soon as we had our orders, we went straightway to your nephew's apartment, dismissed the guard, and gave him the good news. He thanked us and shared a miniature of his wife, then left for the bank to set things to rights. Even apologized about the way he'd spoken to us earlier."

Relief washed across Edmund's face but within moments

indignation surfaced once again.

"Why would anyone go to such lengths to make him look guilty! No one's the richer here that I can see. Who in the world hates him that much?"

"We don't rightly know, sir," said Tyson. "We'd like to work with Mrs. Morehouse to solve the case. The captain gave us his permission and now we'd like yours."

"The captain's permission?" Margaret gasped.

McManus beamed. "Yes, Ma'am; you might even say his blessing. We gave you due credit for the doctored deposit slip, and he's mightily impressed. Also, he admired the way you spoke up for yourself in the note you sent him and agrees locating missing persons is part of your assignment, especially in this case. No one can dispute your relationship to Yvette Morehouse or the fact she has seemingly disappeared. If along the way we manage to find out who took such extreme measures to damage her husband's reputation, so much the better."

Margaret gasped and nearly choked on her tea.

"You mean I won't have to go back to patrolling dance halls and movie shows?"

"Not now and, if we have our way, not ever," McManus announced.

"Unless some suspect we're all after ends up there," added Tyson.

Margaret waited for Edmund's objections but none came. The detectives, and, by association, her efforts, had apparently earned his endorsement.

McManus gazed up at the ceiling, searching for just the right words.

"Yesterday you suggested the criminals' headquarters might be somewhere inside the Hotel Nadeau. It got me thinking. Couldn't it be the very place to hide a kidnapped person? Even to me it seemed far-fetched, but with an accomplice, maybe someone who works there, it would be easy enough to keep her drugged and locked in a room."

Edmund looked astounded.

"Do you mean to tell me Yvette may still be alive?"

"With the suspects taking off in different directions, there was no time for a proper investigation. We must proceed on that assumption and find a reason to return."

Margaret decided not to share her suspicions about Yvette being complicit in her own disappearance. Victim or instigator, the woman could still end up dead.

"I have been giving the matter some thought. Shall we adjourn to the table, where best laid plans, in my opinion, should always be made?'

Edmund's empty stomach rumbled in agreement.

"If those plans include breakfast, I'll pitch in."

Margaret pulled on a pinafore apron and invited everyone to seat themselves. Taking eight hardboiled eggs from the oak icebox, she chipped away at the shells, minced the whites, and pushed the yolks through a sieve.

The yellow and white tidbits looked tasty enough in the bowl but Margaret was not satisfied until she'd mixed in melted butter, a dash of curry powder, and bits of grated onion.

Edmund knew the breakfast routine well. He cut a loaf of bread into thick slices and, using a long-handled fork, toasted them two at a time over the gas burner. Margaret assembled her famous curried egg sandwiches and opened two jars of canned peaches. Cushman made coffee and set the table.

Tyson was the only one at the table who did not wolf down the soft warm sandwiches with gusto. Edmund was the only one to take notice of the detective's dilemma.

"It's the curry you're tasting, my friend, a spice blend from India that made its way to England nearly a century ago. Our church started there too so we're rather used to it."

"It never made it's way to Ireland, thank God, but it might have been better than all that grass my ancestors had to eat during the famine."

Edmund sighed.

"Our forebears fought for reasons dark and hidden and the conflict persists to this day. We must turn our backs on those divisions and forge new bonds in this large, diverse nation! Margaret, do we have any peanut butter?"

Tyson swallowed manfully and washed everything down with a swig of coffee.

"Thank you, sir, but I'll get used to it."

Several minutes passed before it dawned on Margaret the men wanted her to lead off the discussion.

"The Episcopal conference of bishops holds a convention every three years in some major city to review and discuss possible changes to liturgy, structure, and mission. The most recent took place in Cincinnati last October. Why don't we consult with hotel management about hosting the next one? We'll need your dignified presence to lead the way, Edmund dear. The rest of us could pass for a group of church dignitaries."

"I doubt the back east boys would travel all the way out to the wild west coast, but I see no reason why not. It's not exactly prevarication and the information might prove useful."

"Seamus, please wear a suit if you have one and uh, maybe, stand behind Edmund?"

"And keep me mouth shut," McManus added in exaggerated brogue.

"T'would be best," Margaret responded, in a vague rendition of Hibernian dialect.

"I, of course, shall take my place by Edmund's side. Cushman, would you be on the other? Maybe utter a few words to make us sound more official?"

"I guess so, and, as you may have noticed, I have no trace of an accent."

"Charlie, would you be willing to come in on your own, maybe as a workman? The four of us can handle the front desk but we'll need your fast feet to investigate open doors and dark corners on every floor."

Tyson nodded.

"Got me some overalls and a toolbox already. Should do."

Cushman scowled, whether at the plan itself or at Margaret for voicing it, she no longer cared.

"We cannot risk further delay. We must meet tomorrow at ten o'clock outside the hotel on the corner of First and Spring. Cushman, Seamus, Edmund, and I will enter through the lobby, then proceed to

Zig Zag Woman

the front desk and ask for the manager."

Both detectives grinned in agreement and even Edmund declared she'd come up with a "capital idea!"

※

The next day was Friday but the Morehouses set out for the Hotel Nadeau dressed in their Sunday best. Cushman wore the same dark vested garb he put on for every occasion.

They met up with McManus outside a glistening wall of glass doors and arced windows. Near the roof, a triangular cornice bearing the inscription "Nadeau 1883" confirmed their location. Tyson whizzed by, toolbox in hand, headed for the workmen's entrance.

After Chicago, Margaret thought she'd had her fill of hotels, but this one was oddly intriguing. The La Salle lobby housed fountains, palms, and many fine eateries within its massive lobby. The Nadeau had all these plus a variety of drugstores, flower shops, hat shops, bakeries, barbershops, and more to meet their guests' needs.

The front desk was located at the back, enticing guests to shop as they negotiated the long marble corridor.

"Ingenious," Margaret whispered to Edmund as they strolled past the store window displays. "Visitors can find anything they forget to pack!"

"Ingenious, indeed" interjected Cushman, "but it makes your search all the more complicated. So many doors to look behind. So many people who might not let you open them."

McManus bobbed his head in agreement.

"Right you are, sir, but my money's still on the hotel proper. A lady held for ransom might need care. Better chance for that in a room with bed and washstand."

Edmund took charge and gestured the others to wait in line behind him. A clerk finally became available after foreign dignitaries and a newlywed couple had been signed in and transported by the city's first electric elevator to the sky-scraping fourth floor. The man, who looked much younger than his mutton chop beard might indicate, listened attentively.

Edmund briefly explained the goals and history of the

convention and emphasized the number of well-to-do hotel guests such a meeting might attract.

"Oh sir!" exclaimed the young man. "With so much time to plan, there is no doubt we can accommodate you! Let me see if our manager is available."

Ten minutes later, Edmund was surprised to find himself shaking the hand of a female manager. Mrs. Winston Rogers strongly resembled Alice in Wonderland's imperious Queen of Hearts. Her squinty eyes regarded them from a fat, square-chinned face jutting over beefy shoulders. A bulging high collar barely contained the fleshy cylinder that passed for her neck. When her scowl lines bent into a smile, Margaret wished the rest of her would disappear like the Cheshire cat.

Mrs. Rogers launched into a narrative promotion worthy of a full-page advertisement in the L. A. Times.

"The Hotel Nadeau is the most desirable place for rest and refreshment in the city. Our 150 sleeping rooms meet modern standards, from coiled springs beneath the mattresses to porcelain tub and basins. A state-of-the-art hot air furnace, along with high ceilings and ventilation, maintain customer comfort throughout the year. Our cafe features expertly cooked market delicacies. For gentlemen who indulge, there is a well-fitted bar stocked with fine wines, liquors, and cigars. Every cultural attraction this city has to offer is nearby and we are within walking distance of the post office."

Edmund folded his arms.

"Not everyone who attends the convention will be able to afford your fine rooms but I dare say we can fill the place, especially if the rate does not exceed three dollars a night."

Mrs. Rogers scratched her chin.

"If, as you say, people from every state will be in attendance, we might do better than that, but they'll be on their own for meals."

Cushman raised a hand.

"The representatives might be here for a number of days. Do you have any rooms large enough for us all to meet in?"

"At the same time? I doubt ..."

Zig Zag Woman

"No need, ma'am," Edmund interrupted. "St. Paul's itself will provide the meeting spaces. What say you we look at the rooms and amenities before making a final decision?

"Many rooms would be best," intoned McManus.

"My colleague is a careful man. That's why he is our treasurer."

Margaret could not resist giving her husband an almost imperceptible nudge.

"Before I forget, let me introduce my wife, the Reverend Mrs. Edmund Morehouse. Could someone show her around the kitchen while we men look around upstairs?"

Mrs. Rogers crooked a finger at the eager-to-please clerk.

"Clarkson here can tour you gentlemen while Mrs. Morehouse and I take a look around at the heart of our establishment, the most up-to-date kitchen west of the Rocky Mountains!"

She waddled down the hall with impressive agility, considering her size, grabbed a large ring of keys off a hook by the back door, and gestured for Margaret to follow.

The room they entered was most inviting. Stacks of porcelain dishes, mostly white, gleamed on floor-to-ceiling shelves. The sinks were deep and wide enough to rinse off everything from fancy seafood to basic potatoes and onions. Margaret admired the enameled cast iron cook stoves and butcher block tables, made practical and movable by the simple addition of wheels. Staples and cookware filled every available space.

I've been relegated, she muttered to herself before inspiration struck.

"What a beautifully appointed kitchen! Everything you need to serve customers and more, but in this warm clime, some things are best served cold. Do you have an ice room by chance?"

"Not by chance, but design," chuckled Mrs. Rogers. "My design, as a matter of fact. Follow me."

She led Margaret outside to a freestanding cinder block structure less than a hundred yards away and opened the heavily padlocked door.

"This is the ice room," she announced. "Small but adequate for our purposes. Ice blocks shrink mightily on the train ride from back

East but enough remain to keep our food fresh and meal costs down. Let me tour you around."

Raising her skirt by at least two inches Mrs. Rogers avoided stagnant pools of water pitting the muddy floor and guided her guest past three large zinc-lined iceboxes filled with perishable food. Misshapen ice blocks, large as steamer trunks, dripped slowly through open metal racks.

Margaret forced herself to breathe through her mouth to endure the fetid air. The light was so dim she could barely make out the long wooden drawers built into the back wall.

"Do you use that cabinet for food storage?"

"It's empty right now but comes in handy when we're at full capacity. As I'm sure it will be three years from now when we host your convention."

With a smirk and a wink, she lumbered on through the dark interior. Margaret followed several paces behind. Something sinister about the place stoked her darkest fears. Could Yvette be nearby, alive or dead?

She pulled off her gloves. One of the drawers protruded, leaving just enough room to slip a hand inside. Her fingers landed on something hard and ovoid wedged into one corner. Probably nothing more than a peach pit, but she pulled the item with so much force it flew out of her hand and splashed into a puddle below.

"What was that?" Nurse Rogers snapped.

"Perhaps I've lost a button."

Margaret felt her way over the muddy floor until she retrieved the object and pressed it into the palm of her left hand.

Margaret sighed. "No matter. I suppose it rolled out of sight. There's a basket full of replacements at home."

She pulled on her gloves. The women exchanged insincere pleasantries and parted ways.

Back on First Street, Margaret found the entire team of men leaning against the buggy. Cushman was gently stroking Jupiter's nose. She wondered why their tour had ended so soon.

"They only let us look at two rooms and a suite," explained McManus. "The clerk began to look suspicious. Didn't want to push it."

"I went upstairs, downstairs, and everywhere BUT our lady's chamber," Tyson panted. "No fancy elevators for me! The only rooms with open doors were full of linens and mops."

"If you would have asked me, though nobody did," complained Cushman, "the likelihood of finding the missing woman in plain view was remote from the start. We're wasting precious time when she might be in mortal danger."

Edmund bristled in Margaret's defense.

"So where do you suggest we look? In my less than professional opinion, ruling this place out as criminal headquarters was nothing less than proper procedure."

"You're both right," Seamus observed. "I'd hoped to make useful discoveries as we went from room to room. What do you think, Mr. Cushman?"

Margaret did her best to maintain a straight face.

"Your example has been most instructive," Cushman dissembled.

Before they left, Margaret asked the detectives for an update on the Pantages case. They still hadn't shared the autopsy report.

"It might be too gruesome for your soft heart." said McManus. "Do you really want to hear this?"

"We're partners, therefore I must," Margaret responded.

He pulled a folded document from his vest pocket.

"Very well. The closing paragraph sums up the coroner's conclusions."

Rigor mortis well advanced. The long bones were fractured and all tendons and ligaments torn. Spinal column is profoundly traumatized at cervical A3-4, thoracic A6-7, and lumbar A3-4. The spleen is ruptured and there is pooling of blood without evidence of organic disease in liver, kidneys, and abdomen.

"Poor girl probably met her fate at the hands of a perverted monster. Sad to come to such a terrible end. No one can save her now, more's the pity."

Margaret didn't know which hurt the most: hearing the tragic end to what must have been a short, hard life or realizing what a wild magical goose chase she'd been on all the way to Chicago.

"We should have found a way to do more," muttered McManus.

"It was our first team assignment and there have been many distractions. You were drawn away by the bombing, and Leland's brush with the law distracted us all. The captain had every right to lose confidence in me."

"On the contrary, he thinks you're the only one of us who has made any progress."

"By eliminating a suspect?"

"That and ruling out one probable identity for the Pantages corpse."

"Does he know about my posing as a showgirl or the trip to Chicago?"

"No, and we'd best keep it that way. Our captain is not fond of deception but we did stretch the truth a bit. Told him the singer you interviewed at Pantages got back in touch after receiving a letter from Marie Levecque. He appreciates your interviewing skills and boasts about how clever he was assigning the three of us to work together."

Edmund looked genuinely perplexed.

"If we don't come up with a suspect soon, do you think he'll force you to abandon the case?"

"Sounds like you've signed on to the team, Reverend! Poor girl never warranted a headline. No one's clamoring for us to solve that one. Money buys interest, I'm afraid, old money like Colonel Otis's."

"And the fact so many lives were lost in the explosion," added Cushman.

McManus nodded his head in agreement.

"The captain's threatened to fire anyone who talks to the press, but sooner or later someone's going to spill the beans about Yvette Morehouse and the strange blackmail scheme. Newspaper busybodies pay well for a scandalous story and some of our boys in blue are not above sharing allegations as fact when offered a buck or two. Young Leland may come to wish he were still under house arrest."

CHAPTER THIRTY-THREE

In dreams that night Margaret danced her way through a swath of stars, clad only in a black satin cape. When the clasp broke, she dropped down into pristine cotton sheets and the safety of her husband's arms.

"Pleasure palls when duty calls. Why is it ever thus?" she murmured and unwrapped herself from his embrace.

Edmund moaned in protest and rolled over to catch forty more winks. Knowing his busy schedule might require Cushman's services, Margaret rode downtown on her own.

The sites she passed were full of people, more than usual for such an early hour. Crowds were growing faster than a swarm of ants on cookie crumbs. Some individuals attempted to form a line while others brazenly wove in and out of it.

Margaret thought they might be waiting for a charity dole until she realized they were mounting the steps of Elvira's bank, First National Savings and Trust, an institution not known for acts of good will.

She reached the police station in four more stops. No officers or petitioners were milling about. Everything was still as a department store on Sunday until triumphant whoops and several gunshots proclaimed Tyson's presence and accuracy on the target range out back. McManus sat at the front desk and grimly handed her the morning edition of the *L. A. Times*.

"My predictions came to pass sooner than anticipated."

Boldly boxed details of Leland's bank position, delay in reporting Yvette missing, and the botched return of the ransom leading to house arrest took up most of the front page.

"Yellow journalism!" Margaret sputtered. "There's no mention of dropped charges until the last paragraph."

"He'll have to watch his every step until we find what happened to his wife. Most folks don't read beyond the first few lines and those who rush to judgment favor vigilante justice. We got word there's a bank run brewing outside First National. If memory serves, he's vice president."

"There's a bank run brewing, all right. I passed by those desperate folks on my way here but didn't understand what was going on. Leland's but one of several vice presidents. Still, it belongs to his family and will all be his one day."

"Only if he and the institution survive."

Margaret paled. Rumors had been undermining banks since the aptly named gilded age. Scions of industry and shopkeepers were equally susceptible to the slightest threat of impending disaster. Malicious gossip often resulted in injury to those withdrawing savings and others trying to stop them. His unwillingness to acknowledge connivance going on behind his back had cost her own father his reputation, and ultimately, his life.

McManus tried to offer reassurance.

"Captain Clarke's dealt with these problems before. He headed out with all the regulars to keep the peace. Our friend Charlie must have had one too many tipples before going to bed, 'cause he looked like something the cats dragged in when he showed up thirty-five minutes late for work this morning."

Another shot rang out. McManus held his hands over his ears.

"Nothing like firing off a few rounds to cure a hangover or make me go deaf. He's not much good for anything else today. I'm not happy with him and he knows it. Instead of writing Charlie up, the captain made both of us stay behind to take down complaints."

"Has anyone come by?"

"No one but you. I want to proceed with ongoing investigations but find myself frustrated at every turn. There's not much one can do behind a desk."

"Charlie may not be ready for duty today but I, my friend, have something which deserves your undivided attention."

Margaret reached into her bag and pulled out the item she'd found at the Hotel Nadeau. She had waited for the privacy of her home before peeling off her gloves to reveal a stunning jewel. By lamplight it gave off a ghostly hue; in broad daylight, the facets glimmered cerulean blue.

Zig Zag Woman

"Where in the world did you come by a gem like that?" McManus asked incredulously.

"At the hotel, when I was touring the kitchen with the manager."

"How did you get such a huge stone past the eyes of that woman?"

"We were touring their ice room. I asked her to show me how they preserve food. We passed a wall of drawers and one of them was open. I felt around inside when she wasn't looking and came up with this. Nearly lost it in the half-light. Fortunately, Mrs. Rogers wasn't paying close attention."

"Do you think someone lost it or left it there on purpose?"

"I have no idea but one of those gut feelings you've told me about made me pick it up. I think it's identical to the sapphire in the Yvette's engagement ring.

McManus examined the gem from every angle.

"The proof is waiting for us just behind that door."

He led the way to the evidence room. Lining the walls were thick plank shelves laden with containers. Some were open and empty, others locked tight. He opened the box labeled "L. Morehouse, January 1911." He took out the ring and using tweezers, dropped the gem from Margaret's outstretched into the setting. The stone fit perfectly.

"No worker at that hotel ever owned a stone like this. Our lady in question may have indeed been held there for some time."

She could almost hear the soft heart beating in his stout chest. His eyes moistened with telltale tears.

"Was the drawer big enough to hold a body?"

Margaret gasped. The puzzle parts were coming together in a most repulsive way.

"It was long and wide but only deep enough to hold a slender woman."

McManus pulled out pencil and notebook from his vest to trace the circumference of the band. He added a quick sketch of the stone with a surprisingly deft hand.

"Charlie's got to take a look at this."

A broken skeleton propped up the row of musty volumes in front of the room's only window. Shoving bones and books aside,

McManus dislodged its skull.

Margaret snatched it from the air, fingers through eye sockets.

"Ty Cobb couldn't have made a better catch."

McManus yanked the window shade down forcefully. It snapped clear up to the top, twisting round and round on its spring-loaded cylinder.

"Tyson, get in here!" he commanded after loosening the latch and pounding the window open.

His partner entered at lightning speed. Margaret directed his attention to the sapphire shining brightly in the noonday sun.

McManus pointed at it too.

"Why don't you do something useful and take a look at this ring this lady found in the hotel kitchen last night?"

Margaret took his words as her cue and continued.

"The stone matches one that belonged to Yvette Morehouse. After she disappeared at the Dominguez Field air show, Leland took several months to make a report, mostly out of concern for his own reputation. The note she left behind indicates she was running away from a loveless marriage. Who knows, maybe there was a secret lover."

McManus looked skeptical.

"You never mentioned a note before."

"It was given to me in strictest confidence."

"A nicety you'd best abandon," he warned. "What's known to one must be known to all or there's no sense working together."

Margaret winced.

"I was inexperienced back then. Compared to you two, I still am."

"Ease up on her, McManus; she's done good so far."

His unexpected support lifted her spirits.

"Let's go back to my house. The letter's there along with Yvette's clothes."

"Very well, but one of us must mind the station," maintained Tyson.

He pulled a half-dollar coin out of his pocket, tossed it while calling heads, caught it, and slapped it onto the back of his left hand. The side he shoved in McManus's face sported the classic feathered

Indian profile.

"Heads, I stay."

"Only way I'll go along is if you man this desk. And I do mean in the manner of a *man*, not wayward boy. Target practice is done for the day. If one of our mates asks you to step out for a beer, say no. If the captain comes in, you can tell him about the jewel and the ring but for God's sake put your coins away. How your wife puts up with you is beyond my ken."

After labeling both parts of the ring as evidence, McManus donned his hat and ushered Margaret back outside. The trolley they boarded rumbled briskly away and maintained that pace until it approached First National Bank. By that time, spectators and journalists had joined the milling crowd. In front of the bank stood a large banner proclaiming in bold black letters:

FIRST NATIONAL IS THE STRONGEST BANK ON THE PACIFIC COAST. YOUR MONEY IS SAFE. ANYONE MAKING A WITHDRAWAL WILL RECEIVE DOLLAR FOR DOLLAR. THOSE WISHING TO SHOW LOYALTY TO FAMILY AND COUNTRY WILL LEAVE AT ONCE.

Two bank employees were passing out sandwiches and coffee to the crowd. When a third picked up a megaphone, out came a familiar voice.

"My name is Leland Morehouse. I stand before you a free and honest man, not the villain depicted in the morning paper. I have been exonerated by the police and reinstated this very morning at First National, one of the finest financial institutions in the nation. Do not let others scare you into making rash decisions. We shall remain open until midnight and reopen at seven tomorrow morning to serve you."

Enthusiastic applause drowned out a few disgruntled jeers. The crowd began to disperse.

"Smart move on your nephew's part. Two days ago, I would have said he didn't have the gumption to face that mob. Brave deed," McManus said softly.

"Brave *man*," Margaret said, a sentiment she was anxious to repeat to Edmund.

CHAPTER THIRTY-FOUR

She thought the day would not get more convoluted until Cushman, swifter than a charioteer, drove the buggy right past them.

By the time they caught up, Cushman had stabled Jupiter and told Edmund all about Leland's courageous stand.

For Margaret, the look of relief on Edmund's face more than made up for not being first to share the news.

"Please excuse my reckless driving earlier. You must have noticed the large sign I posted in front of First National."

Cushman's apology softened his boastful tone.

"That was your doing? How did you manage to have it installed in such a short time?"

"It took a carpenter, painter, financial backing from Thomas Warren, and my own two hands. We shoved the boards sideways across the carriage, making it look like a horse-drawn airplane with wings. I overheard a passerby say, 'What will they think of next?'"

"Did the workmen ride with you?"

"They met me there with paint and nails and went straight to work. The carpenter built the sign at the top of the stairs, the painter lettered it — rather neatly, don't you think? — and the three of us propped it up in place. Did you see it?"

"Seamus and I could read your sign all the way from the street. It calmed the crowd, as did Leland's speech."

He beamed with pride.

"I had a short talk with your nephew, as well. More to him than meets the eye."

Margaret felt like hugging him but restrained herself. She wouldn't have hugged him in private, either. As often as her affection for such a difficult man vacillated, at that moment it ran deep. The only times they'd physically touched happened when he was helping her on or off the buggy or during those painful moments back in Chicago. The support he'd given her in recent weeks had gone a long way to restoring her trust.

Inspired by Leland's strides on the road to redemption, Edmund went upstairs to work on a sermon. Cushman brought the hatbox of Yvette's personal effects downstairs. Margaret laid out the haute couture clothes across her dining room table. Seed pearls held fast to the embroidered bodice and the blue satin sash was still bright, but the flat ensemble looked crumpled and forlorn.

Who else would wear so much finery to an airfield? Margaret wondered, hoping if Yvette was still breathing, she'd shed her haughty attitudes along with the clothes.

McManus maintained a cool, professional attitude as he examined the apparel, but blushed deeply when he picked up her corset and bloomers.

"Looks like everything a lady should wear. How in tarnation did she change her clothes underneath that grandstand without anyone seeing her?"

"A woman of her upbringing would never chance being caught nearly naked. She is slender and the corset could hold another layer in place."

Margaret worried Cushman would recall how light costumes worn under outer clothing had fired a magician's passion. Instead of disapproval, he gave her a knowing look.

"She must have worn pants under all that getup. Even Leland with his fancy binoculars wouldn't look twice at another man running around the field."

McManus held the dress up to his shoulders. The ruffled hem barely touched the floor.

"She was tall for a woman."

"Right you are. No one would think it odd to have an extra hand around to turn propellers or hold back the crowd if that person wore trousers, loose shirt, and maybe a cap big enough to cover his, or in this case her, hair."

"The ring arrived on your doorstep along with a one of her curls. Would she have had enough time to cut it off that day?"

As Margaret recalled, Yvette's upswept hair had been secured by a hat. Trimming a wayward lock was not out of the question but could have happened weeks beforehand.

She shook her head and plucked a note from the bottom of the box.

"I don't see a word here about where she was going or how she planned to get there."

"What's the writing on the other side?"

"Maybe a sketch," Margaret suggested.

She turned the sheet over and flattened it against the table. At first glance, the markings looked like scribbles. As she concentrated, patterns began to appear in the faint penciled spots.

"Could this be a diagram?"

She pointed to an X marked across rows of broken lines. The thickest mark extended across two-thirds of the page and ended in an arrow pointing to a spot within the crease.

Cushman peered at it intently.

"Someone tried to draw her a map."

Margaret pointed to the cluster of broken lines.

"Those might indicate the grandstand. The fenced-off portion was rectangular. That smaller dark square on the upper right-hand corner could be the judge's stand. Look at the corners — see the large dots? They correspond to the pylon towers. The arrow looks to be pointing to a particular location on the field."

"Pretty clear to me," McManus observed. "Once on the field, finding what she was looking for must have been easy."

"But it doesn't make sense," Margaret persisted. "Let's assume she was running away with some French aviator taking part in the meet. No matter how skilled the pilot or how far they flew, she had to end up stranded in the middle of nowhere."

"How can you be so sure?" queried Cushman.

"Edmund and I followed the newspaper stories to the very end of the meet. Many planes reached great distances that week, but not all."

"You're forgetting how the Frenchmen and their airplanes arrived in the first place," McManus added. "Their planes couldn't cross the Atlantic. Louis Paulhan sailed over with airplane parts, wife, family, and that pampered poodle we all read about in the papers. They took the train like a bunch of carnies from New York to

California and hired a dozen or more helpers to assemble their contraptions a few days before the show."

"They may have taken off from the field," speculated Cushman, "and landed safely enough. I'm putting my money on them landing miles away, hiking to a station, and boarding a train headed for New York or some other East Coast port."

"Before sailing away to France. Problem is, according to Leland, the family never heard from her again," Margaret reminded him.

"Her family *says* they never heard from her. She could be in hiding. All we can go on right now is a sapphire ring."

Catching Cushman's confused expression, Margaret caught him up on her ice room discovery.

"Whew!" he let out, "this case, and you, continue to confound me. We've wandered into a labyrinth. Maybe we should go our separate ways for a while if we ever hope to solve it."

Once again, his demeanor transformed from faithful servant to officer in charge. Pinkerton's finest had taken the lead and they might end up the more successful for it.

"Madam," Cushman continued, "if anyone can contact this branch of your family, it would be you. You should talk to Leland once more and, disagreeable as it surely will be, his mother. McManus, Tyson, and you were assigned to the Pantages case in the first place. Why don't you nose around the theater and see what you can find? As for me, I'll track down the identity of all the pilots at the Meet and see if any of them left early."

McManus nodded. Always a practical man, he seemed to have no issues with following Cushman's lead.

"Sounds like a good plan; I'll do my best," Margarette said, trying to hide her distaste. "As for the ring, perhaps Yvette didn't want a souvenir from a bad marriage and gave it away."

"Maybe she removed it while she was shedding her lady clothes," suggested McManus.

"Or a scoundrel stole the ring and gave it to someone else," added Cushman.

They looked at each other, perplexed. Margaret kept reevaluating clues and contradictions before making one more observation.

"The stone is worth a small fortune. No one fond of finery as Yvette Morehouse would willingly leave it behind. It can only mean the gem was lost, as Seamus proposed; stolen in the way Cushman described; or something went terribly wrong."

CHAPTER THIRTY-FIVE

The next time Margaret visited Leland Morehouse, he greeted her with respect and cordiality. After sharing a pot of tea and polite discourse, he handed her a message addressed to Yvette's younger brother, Julien LaRoche.

"My wife's family is the most outrageous bunch of status-seeking profiteers I've ever known. Yvette's brother is the only exception."

Margaret's dubious expression made him chuckle.

"No one outdoes Mother, but for sheer numbers of grasping connivers I've never seen their equal. When we went to France for the fateful introduction to Yvette, Julien and I got along well at first. We shared many interests though I could never understand the bond he shared with his shallow sister."

"You never had a sister, nor, to my knowledge, an example on which to model a good relationship."

"I ignored a fine example right here in Los Angeles. You and Uncle Edmund are the only family members I trust, although at times I find his self-righteousness irritating."

"He's compelled to take the high moral ground; he's a minister, after all."

"His morals came under public scrutiny when he married such a young, pretty woman. Even I questioned his judgment. I have never shown you the respect you deserve although you've always been kind to me."

Margaret was stunned. Edmund's protectiveness and her own naiveté made her oblivious to gossip. Twelve years hadn't seemed like all that much. They were so deeply in love she didn't want or worry about anyone else's approval.

"Whatever your opinion of us, you've kept a civil tongue, Leland, at least in public. He may not always show it, but Edmund loves you. That love and all the good qualities you try so hard to hide oblige me to take your side too. Tell me, dear nephew, why should *I* be the one contacting Mr. LaRoche and not you?"

"He does not respect or trust me, perhaps with some cause. At first, I was intrigued by Yvette's stunning miniature and exquisite daguerreotype. The opportunity to meet such a divine creature while going on a Continental holiday prompted me to arrive in France a week before Mother. When Yvette left word she was indisposed, Julien came to my hotel.

"What an adventure that was, two bachelors seeing the sights of Paris and the countryside! He professed to be a painter, though I never saw his work. His reputation was growing in artistic circles and he introduced me to many interesting people. If I could paint, sculpt, or write poetry, his was the life I would have chosen."

"Your Uncle Edmund and I believe you were never given the opportunity to develop talents beyond balancing ledgers. When did you meet Yvette?"

"At a ghastly formal dinner. Mother presided, as she always does, even when it's at someone else's home, or in this case, I should say castle."

"Castle?"

"At least a hundred rooms full of LaRoche sisters, brothers, cousins, uncles, aunts, and their Louis Quatorze furniture. Julien refused to set foot inside. Yvette looked like a Dresden doll but her behavior made her just as brittle. She made no attempt at civility until days later when our parents announced our betrothal."

"Did Julien advise you against the arrangement?"

"Yes, until he realized I was too weak to go against Mother's will and our relationship soured. He acted as if Yvette was making a great sacrifice and I was the fortune hunter. With or without the bank acquisition, I stand to inherit more than enough fortune for any ten men. If Mother ever disowned me, I'd lose everything."

"Couldn't you find a position at another bank?"

"Not any institution dealing with Elvira Morehouse."

The note Margaret unfolded disclosed Yvette's disappearance, the threat on her life, and need for immediate help.

"What do I do with this?"

"Take it to a telegraph office. There's one less than eight blocks from here."

It was a simple enough request. Before another hour passed, Margaret found herself in a bustling office waiting for the words to be codified and tapped out on a fancy contraption. It seemed impossible those precise keystrokes would transform into an inquiry and cabled across the Atlantic, but the operator assured her the message would be in Monsieur LaRoche's hands by nightfall, Paris time.

Three days later Margaret found herself standing on Elvira Morehouse's doorstep, calling card in hand. She would have far rather faced her mother's judgmental spirit in the hereafter.

It had taken hours to locate the paper-mâché case of engraved cards Edmund had a printer make for her when they were newlyweds. The practice was old fashioned, yet she was not about to breach etiquette on such a delicate mission. While Elvira's motivations might be ruthlessly Machiavellian, her outward social interactions were rooted firmly in Victorian manners. Margaret bent down one corner above the words *Mrs. Reverend Edmund Morehouse* to indicate she was calling in person.

Elvira's brownstone mansion made the home Margaret grew up in look like a doll house. A dozen peaks and spires topped by gaping gargoyles and underscored with architectural furbelows pointed towards the sky.

She lifted a brass lion knocker and let it fall. A gangly butler opened the door and bade her sit on a tufted settee. He took the calling card upstairs on a silver salver. Margaret stared at the cobalt blue walls, which would have been attractive in another setting. Situated above mahogany wainscoting, they made the vestibule look funereal.

She half expected the butler to turn her away, but moments later Elvira herself descended the staircase.

What happened to all that fabled beauty? Margaret wondered. The hardened features, permanent scowl lines, and ghostly pallor of the woman looking down on her were unnerving. Elvira's figure remained slim and posture stately but it took a high lace collar and cameo choker to camouflage her drooping jowls. Her mound of pewter hair secured by ivory combs still glistened rich and thick.

The turquoise eyes of girlhood had taken on an avaricious glitter behind pince-nez glasses.

"Margaret, my dear," Elvira declared. "How good of you to call! I have been remiss in expressing gratitude."

She extended her large hands towards Margaret's shoulders and tapped them briefly before pulling swiftly away, neatly avoiding an embrace.

"Leland has told you about my work on his behalf?" Margaret asked.

"Not directly, but a mother always knows; ah, pardon me, I am forgetful at times, you probably never will ..."

With that acid remark and a self-satisfied smirk, she preceded Margaret into the parlor. If the visit had been merely social, Margaret would have left immediately, knowing Edmund would support her action. Acting on the presumption Elvira might be in some way responsible for Yvette's disappearance, she followed.

The sunlit parlor was a more pleasant setting. Margaret thought the wall and rug patterns too ornate for her taste and the artfully posed marble statues better suited for a mausoleum than a home.

At the sound of Elvira's silver bell, a housemaid appeared pushing a lacquered cart topped with a tea service, a tray of cookies, and crystallized fruit. Elvira sat on one end of the gold watered silk covered sofa. Margaret laid her shawl down on a gilt drum table and sat on the other. She accepted sweetmeats Elvira proffered and picked up a cloisonné-framed picture of Leland and Yvette on their wedding day.

"What a beautiful couple! How happy they looked back then."

"Looks can be deceptive. By now you must know Yvette has left him. She even fooled me, and poor Leland had no idea how to handle her. I wish he had consulted me before their problems began."

"How did you learn about the part I played in his release?"

Elvira looked at me smugly. "I have my resources. I was bereft when they arrested my poor son, and they wouldn't let me post his bail although I did — how shall I put this delicately? — *donate* sufficiently to the Widow and Orphans' Fund to keep him out of jail."

She chuckled when Margaret choked slightly.

"Women of the world have much in common, although I am better at making a profit than you or your do-gooder Edmund."

Margaret smiled sweetly, "Doesn't the Bible say it is easier for a camel to go through the eye of a needle than for a rich man to enter into the kingdom of God?"

"The Scriptures say nothing about women, my dear, though one day we'll rule the world. In many cases, we do already but have to hide it. I have it on good authority it was you who came up with the necessary evidence to clear Leland's name."

"It was a minor achievement and shows how useful we women can be in police work. I believe our gender has a sharper eye for detail."

"Your skills match those of many men in my employ. You've been held back by your husband, your conscience, and a lack of sophistication I find puzzling in a woman your age. Idealism be damned. It takes money to care for the masses and keep them in their place."

Her words, her sneer, her arrogance hammered steel into Margaret's spine.

"You are the wealthiest woman in Los Angeles, but I've yet to see your name on any donor list."

"Touché. My fortune builds banks. The poor can prosper through my efforts, provided they work hard and save. If you had a business bent and could learn to think in larger terms, I would face a formidable rival. Or ally if you so choose. Right now, all you seem capable of is falling into one scandalous situation after another."

Elvira's expression hardened as she leaned forward. She wagged a bony finger in Margaret's face.

"Don't think your escapades have gone unnoticed. Women must exercise more caution than you've done in recent weeks, my dear: consorting with those rough policemen; traveling to Chicago with your butler, or however you choose to use that odd fellow; appearing half naked in a magic show."

Sickened by the disclosures, Margaret rose to her feet. Before leaving, she turned to face Elvira.

"Edmund had full knowledge of my actions, and they may have

saved your son."

"Every cloud may have a silver lining, my dear, so be on your best behavior. There is a storm brewing over Edmund's pulpit. All I need do is hurl a single lightning bolt and he'll be finished. He might stand accused of borrowing from church funds to finance your escapades."

"Any monies we used to fund my investigations were a gift from my father."

"Oh, I believe you, but accounts can be altered in various ways. Both the St. Paul's and your husband bank with me."

"So, you think you can force me to abandon my work?" Margaret sputtered, shaking with fury.

"I could do that easily enough. Up until now, you've been useful, and I am confident you will continue to keep my interests in mind from now on. All you need to do is drop that misguided Joan-of-Arc manner of yours, guard your reputation, and remember who really runs this city. If you manage all that, you'll still be standing even if I topple your infuriating husband."

Margaret's mind spun the wall patterns into a massive web with Elvira the monstrous spider and she her hapless prey. God only knew how many victims the woman had dismembered over a lifetime! The most pitiful was her own son and his scarred psyche. Without question, she could harm anyone and take as much time as necessary to achieve her ends.

"My guest is not feeling well. Escort her to my automobile and take her home. Make sure she wants for nothing."

Elvira tossed a drawstring bag in her guest's direction. Feeling coins through the cloth, Margaret threw it back.

Despite her years and arthritic hands, Elvira's caught the sack neatly. She bounced it in the palm of her hand, taunting Margaret with the clink of at least twenty gold eagles.

"That was intended for the babies in that home you used to run, my dear. I know what a wonderful favor you did for Mrs. Mobley. Pity the child looks so much like his nanny."

With Elvira's malicious words and virulent smile searing her brain. Margaret backed out of the room, toppling statuary along the way. The lanky butler held open the passenger door of Elvira's

Stanley Steamer and extended an arm to assist. Exhaustion, part physical and completely emotional, compelled her to climb in, knowing no comfort would be found in the dark upholstered seats.

"Thank you," Margaret said perfunctorily, wondering where she'd seen his flat-nosed, chisel-chinned features before.

CHAPTER THIRTY-SIX

Although certain the butler would inform Elvira, Margaret asked him to drop her off at Pantages Theatre. In her mind he'd become the mythical ferryman taking her on a reverse course out of hell.

He steered the car past street cars, buggies, and other autos until they came to a halt in front of the box office entrance.

Margaret jumped from her seat and ran straight into the theater. Whether henchman or lackey, the coachman was Elvira's employee and therefore, dangerous.

Dimmed lights and a hushed audience signaled the afternoon matinee was about to begin. Most of the watchers, and even Margaret, thought the three men chasing each other up and down the aisles were part of an opening act until Pantages' voice bounced back from the proscenium.

"No idea where that infernal rug came from and don't expect I ever will!" roared the maestro.

Suddenly aware of audience reaction, he balled up a sheaf of papers, flung them over his shoulder, and hurried off. The wad sailed over the orchestra pit and landed less than three feet away from where Margaret was standing. With nothing to stand in her way, she quickly retrieved and read it.

"What you have in your hands, Mrs. Margaret, is a search warrant," came McManus's mellow voice.

"Might as well be a bunch of scribbles for all the attention Mr. High and Mighty Showman's going to pay to it," growled Tyson at his side. "What brought you here, might I ask?"

"I had a strange feeling I needed to be at this theater in this moment...that, and I needed to cleanse my psyche of anything remotely connected to Elvira Morehouse."

"It must have been a difficult interview," McManus observed.

"If it only had been an interview! She hurled so many threats and insinuations my way I haven't had time to sort them out. Speaking of time, how long have you been here?"

McManus checked his pocket watch.

"An hour, although it feels like weeks. Must give the devil his due. How he's going to keep this show together on a day when an acrobat fractures his ankle and a comedian staggers in too drunk to remember his jokes is beyond me."

"Surely even Alexander Pantages won't be able to ignore you or the search warrant for long."

Tyson put on a mischievous grin.

"He's treating us like fleas on a dog. We decided not to press the issue for now. We're just going to hop off his hairy back and nose around these sets and props one more time. Sooner or later, he'll have to talk to us. For now, I think he'll leave us to our own devices. Care to join us?"

Dancing dogs cavorting to The William Tell Overture distracted both audience and crew. The trio went out the front door and made their way around the building to the back lot.

The main door stood open. Tyson crooked his finger and bade Margaret follow him through a maze of sets to a wall of gauzy curtains left over from the ballroom dance act. Every time they pushed a panel aside, another dropped down to enmesh them. McManus slit the flimsy cocoon with a pocketknife before they did any more damage.

"Clean cut, no one will notice," he muttered.

"At least not from the audience," Margaret replied with regret. Her recent brush with show business made her cringe at the thought of damaging anything artfully created.

She shifted her attention to rows of prop tables carefully aligned along the back wall. Signage clearly indicated which items belonged to which act.

"I wonder if any of those objects might have been used for more nefarious purposes."

McManus shrugged his shoulders.

"It's been a long time since we found the body, but we might as well take another look. I doubt these props ever get wiped completely clean. Dried blood would look more like rust from the audience."

They inspected the tables for items with lethal potential. Aside from the sword swallower's rapiers, the only weapons were made of balsa wood and painted silver for effect. McManus toyed with the juggler's pins and concluded they were too lightweight to inflict bodily harm, even in the hands of a strong man.

A couple of stagehands questioned their right to be there until Tyson waved the warrant in their faces.

Margaret took charge of the costume racks. Most of the gaudy outfits were in good condition; others were a bit worse for wear. Seen from afar, all would be passable. They inspected each garment for unusual tears or vestiges of blood but found nothing noteworthy.

Tyson confiscated a foot-long screwdriver and ladder from one of the stagehands and climbed halfway to the rafters. He began to scrutinize the stacks of containers lining the inner walls.

"Whip out your notebook, McManus," he yelled down. "I'm about to read off labels and addresses."

After jumping from one shipping crate to another like a bipedal mountain goat, Tyson stepped onto a freestanding wardrobe. Propped on top of it was a six-foot-long crate with Santa Fe station tags. He pried the slats open, let out a horrified gasp, and lost hold of the screwdriver.

A cry of pain rang out as the tool fell into an open barrel below. The cask fell over onto its side and rolled out an open delivery door. McManus and Margaret were too stunned and Tyson too high above the ground to respond quickly.

The wayward barrel rolled towards Spring Street, where it smashed into a lamppost. By the time they caught up to it, all that remained was a pile of broken staves, sprung hoops, and the sight of Walters' backside swiftly running away.

"Persistent fellow, isn't he?" Margaret ventured. "Shouldn't you give chase, Charlie?"

"We have far more important matters to attend to. All the stains on the lining of the crate look and smell like blood."

Tyson returned and climbed back up to the crate while McManus took charge of the situation below. Wielding badge and Irish persuasiveness, he recruited four crew members to set up ladders around the wardrobe. They flung ropes across and around the crate and lowered it to the ground.

Tyson jumped down and lifted the lid. Satisfied his evidence was intact, he warned everyone not to disturb anything while he walked off to the police station.

Workers, performers, and even Alexander Pantages himself clustered around the open container until odors more pungent than a slaughterhouse assaulted their senses.

The Greek gagged. At his direction, dancing girls tore down the curtains Tyson and Margaret had shredded, then ran back and forth with their newly formed gauze banners fluttering behind. The source of the smell needed no translation for the Chinese acrobats, who waved fans and opened windows to clear the air.

The animal act onstage continued to delight and distract the audience. Pantages led his crew and any performers who happened to be backstage outside and sniffed the air with his prodigious nose. Tyson's grim discovery had given the detectives the upper hand.

Crisis averted, the maestro allowed them to question him, although his answers remained defensive.

"Don't you maintain a shipment log?" queried McManus.

"I'm running a theater, not a factory. We empty out crates too quickly to catalogue what was inside."

"If it was empty, why hold onto it when your backstage is so full of scenery, props, and costumes one can hardly navigate around them?" growled Tyson.

"We never throw away a piece of good wood. That crate might have turned into steps, swords, ladders, or whatever we needed. It was only a matter of time before we found it."

"Believe me, I have no idea how and when that crate got into the building in the first place. The box looks like all the others. There was no reason to look inside."

Tyson snorted louder than most horses whinny.

"And if you'd found one, a fine upstanding citizen like you would to the police station the minute you saw the blood stains. Don't give me that! I'm on my way out to find someone to pick up that crate out of here before you lose track of it again."

As Tyson sprinted out the back door, Pantages turned to

McManus and Margaret. He stroked his beard and spoke with a thoughtful air.

"Maybe someone cut himself nailing the slats together."

"Let me remind you, sir, the stains were on the lining, not the exterior. Whatever bled out was nailed up inside."

The maestro's face blanched.

"Marco the Magician... Marie Levecque...You don't suppose?"

"We've ruled out that possibility," answered McManus. "I have it on good authority they will soon be back in our fair city as headliners."

The news was as much a shock to Margaret as it was to Pantages. Why, oh why, had she forgotten about Marco's obligation to the Grimaldi brothers?

"The woman who rolled out of a carpet in your back alley has not been identified. On the other hand, the rug itself is a match for the ones we've seen in your office."

"No two of those are alike, sir," Pantages protested.

"In pattern, yes, in pile and quality, no. You, sir, are one of the few people in the theater world who flaunt personal luxuries backstage."

"Are you trying to say I'm a suspect?"

"We're not trying at all; we're *telling* you. In addition to your fancy carpets and reputation with women, your associate Walters has gone to great lengths to divert our attention. Did he tell you he was going to hide in a barrel underneath the spot where Detective Tyson found the bloody box, or did you put him there?"

"He is nothing but trouble, that one! Last week, I found my office door open. The oil painting hanging over my safe was pushed to one side. The safe, of course, was empty. By the time I rushed back out, he had just made it to the end of the hall. I ran him down and fired him, how do you say, on the spot? Then I seized the satchel he'd been dragging and kicked him down the stairs. He must have left the theater, although it would have been easy to hide anywhere in this big place."

Margaret eyed him coldly.

"Where is the bag now?"

Pantages's tone became defensive when he realized even

Margaret had come to suspect him.

"In my safe. I carried it with me everywhere until the locksmith arrived. He must have stuffed all the money in his pockets. Contracts and bills-of-sale were still in it. Please, please, come see everything I'm telling you is true."

Leaving Tyson behind to guard the crate, McManus and Margaret followed the Maestro to his office. He emptied the bag onto a table for their convenience. They spent an hour combing through vouchers and assorted deeds before heading back downstairs.

Tyson was nowhere to be found. McManus recruited a burly stagehand to guard the box.

"Don't take your eyes off of this or let anyone touch it! Keeping this thing intact and delivering it to the station is our top priority."

The rumble of a horse-drawn paddy wagon and motorized hearse interrupted him.

Police and personnel ran into the alley. Tyson was directing the vehicles with one hand and waving a pair of handcuffs with the other. Eyes blazing, McManus pulled his partner aside.

"If those manacles are meant for Pantages, you're way out of line, boyo! No one, not even you, can directly connect the body and the crate. Not yet."

Margaret stepped in between them before the conflict could escalate.

"Even if our suspicions are correct, Pantages employs several men desperate enough to commit barbarous acts, or pretend they did, for money. Maybe one of them was trying to impress the boss!"

Tyson's freckled face reddened deeply and he sputtered words neither of his partners could understand.

"Calm down, my friend. Our showman has friends in high places. You make one stupid move, our case against him could vanish completely."

Reluctant as a child giving up sweets, Tyson told the paddy wagon driver to turn the horses around but remain ready to return when they made an arrest.

The ivory hearse with gilt embellishments looked like an upside-down wedding cake and shook from side to side. The driver pulled up to the backstage door and asked for a body.

Tyson told him the corpse had already been laid to rest in Potter's Field. They his vehicle to transport the crate to the station without damaging crucial evidence. Even McManus had to concede the logic behind the solution.

The driver turned out to be Tyson's cousin, who either valued family ties to an unusual degree or didn't mind someone taking advantage of him. He lifted the box into the ornately decorated vehicle with the same care he'd use if it were a made-to-order coffin.

"And all of this has become necessary," Tyson announced with a meaningful look towards Pantages, "because someone around here is guilty of murder."

CHAPTER THIRTY-SEVEN

Margaret returned home, weary in body and spirit. Another day passed before McManus and Tyson appeared again on her doorstep. Dusty with flour from all the baking she'd done to take her mind off Elvira, Margaret took them to the kitchen.

Between spoonsful of cookie dough, they described the Captain's reaction. He had been in a rare foul mood when the hearse arrived. A light drizzle did not help matters. Even with the lid nailed back on, the container reeked. The Captain would not let anyone haul an empty, blood-soaked box inside.

"Why didn't any of us catch a whiff of it earlier?" Margaret asked.

"It was high up off the ground with air circulating around it. And it was nailed up pretty tight until Tyson pried it open."

"So where is the crate now?" Margaret persisted.

"The Captain declared it must have been used to ship meat but let us take it to the coroner's office anyway," answered Tyson. "As the little kit belonging to our friend here was not up to the job, he gave us a blood testing requisition. Without it, the City Morgue attendant would have turned us away."

A muffled cough announced Edmund's presence. Cheered by unexpected company after a tedious council meeting, he poured them all a round of sherry.

Tyson downed his glass in a single gulp but McManus hesitated.

"Where's that Cushman fellow of yours? He's been on the job for all of us in one way or the other. He deserves some of this fine wine too."

Edmund and Margaret looked at each other in puzzlement. For the first time in nine years, neither could recall seeing their butler since the previous evening.

Just before they knocked on his bedroom door, Cushman rushed in, shaking from what Margaret hoped was excitement rather than a lapse in sobriety. Tossing aside coat, hat, and muffler in uncharacteristic haste, he launched into what was for him a torrent of words.

"Jacques-Yves Bertrand's our man," he pronounced, "He left the meet on the first day in his Frenchified aero plane."

He arched his bushy eyebrows for dramatic effect.

"I'd bet my last dollar Yvette Morehouse was with him."

What might have taken the rest of them weeks to discover, Cushman accomplished in a matter of hours. He'd started the day at Gilroy's saloon, a dangerous setting for a man with his weakness, but the best place for *L. A. Times* reporters to seek respite from deadlines and irate editors. After treating several of them to a round or two, Cushman sparked a debate about which local events of 1910 the writers thought most newsworthy. Many suggested the bombing while others cited the Halley's Comet furor. Most agreed the Dominguez Air Meet had made the greatest impact and given the nation a glimpse of the global future.

Lewis Rutledge, a seasoned reporter with an eye for detail and gift for storytelling once his tongue was properly lubricated, shared an anecdote that hadn't made the papers. On the first day of the meet, he claimed, Paulhan's cousin Jacques-Yves Bertrand, took off in a biplane and landed nearly sixty miles to the east in San Bernardino. Although his flight had a strong enough showing to win a prize, the Frenchman didn't stick around to claim it. He hopped aboard a train and headed towards the Atlantic coast, even though there were nine days of competition left and plenty of money for the taking.

While most Los Angeles residents were eating breakfast, Cushman, fueled only by peanuts and lemonade, rushed to the telegraph office. Throughout the morning, he exchanged telegrams with H. R. Jamison, a station agent in San Bernardino. Jamison verified seeing a passenger wearing aviator togs board a Southern California Railway train headed east at 6:10 PM on January 10th. He was traveling alone.

"Alone, eh?" mused McManus. "What did he do with Yvette Morehouse?"

"Maybe they landed in some field and she left of her own

accord," Margaret added hopefully. "Perhaps another man, maybe her real fiancé, met up with her in San Bernardino."

"And they all lived happily ever after!" Cushman scoffed.

Tyson and McManus did not react but caught him up on their part of the investigation. Margaret disclosed Elvira's knowledge of her activities and the threats about Edmund. He, in turn, snarled an indelicate but accurate description of his sister-in-law.

"We'll outwit her yet. There's more than enough money left over from your Chicago trip, dear, to send you and Cushman to San Bernardino. Taking into consideration what you've just revealed, I want to leave money in that account. This means there will be no hotels or restaurants."

"I'll pack a hamper," Margaret offered, overjoyed at the chance to make progress.

He paced the room, possibly reviewing the bank balance in his head.

"And I shall be coming along too."

McManus gulped.

"Why would you want to do that, sir?"

"First off, my presence won't interfere with your investigation and might throw off Elvira's minions, who, by your account, must be everywhere. Secondly, we'll save money. The pastor of St. John's in San Bernardino is a good friend and former mentor. He's in poor health and wants to retire soon to his native Virginia. No one should find anything unusual about my paying him a call. I might even preach a guest sermon."

"If you're joining us, we can't leave until you find someone to fill in for you on Sundays," Margaret said, trying to hide her disappointment.

"Right you are, my dear, and that could take a bit. Perhaps the delay will reassure our parishioners we still maintain a normal family life."

"You've heard rumors?" Margaret asked.

"Let's begin with these facts: you have consorted with vaudevillians; you travel to Chicago with a man in our employ; you've been flashing a police badge all over town. These are laudable pursuits to those who know and love you as I do. Of course, there are rumors. A few verge on scandal."

"No man I've ever worked with has more insight or determination than your wife, sir!" asserted Tyson.

Edmund nodded, letting only the faintest flicker of a self-satisfied smile show he knew he'd regained a measure of control. Victorian values had left their mark on Margaret's beloved, however enlightened he might have become. Cushman's amused expression was equally unsettling.

Tyson changed the subject. Margaret could almost hear his mental wheels turning. The man might have been more physically than intellectually adroit, but he never missed a point of reasoning.

"We have a missing woman and a pile of clothes. We have a Frenchman who left the meet early when he should have stuck around to claim a prize. Your nephew gets a ransom note. A body shows up outside Pantages. A bloody box big enough to hold a body shows up *inside* Pantages. All well and good, but how do we link 'em?"

"Well stated, detective," declared Edmund, "although I fail to see the connection. The air meet took place more than a year ago. If the Pantages girl had any flesh left on her bones, that death had to occur later."

"Not necessarily, sir, but there's one thing more. The tags we found on that box said Santa Fe, which is in New Mexico. Maybe you should take that train a bit further east."

McManus took his turn.

"I doubt the airplane ever got that far. San Bernardino might be exactly where we need to go. Last year, I took the Southern California Railway back east to my grandmother's funeral. We left in the evening. I might have slept most of the way if the train hadn't stopped at San Bernardino to pick up passengers. I remember being confused by a Santa Fe sign I saw hanging in the station. Couldn't figure how we'd traveled that far in such a short time. A fellow passenger told me we hadn't yet crossed the California border and the train was operated by the Atchison, Topeka & Santa Fe line, hence the name."

"Then to San Bernardino the three of you must go," concluded

Tyson. "We'll keep an eye on the Greek while you're away."

Margaret hated to see their team head off in different directions. Cushman, of course, would be indispensable. Climbing stairs and wielding a pen were the only forms of exercise in which Edmund regularly indulged. He might not be able to deal with dangerous situations, not that any were likely to arise during such a brief excursion.

"As long as the captain has sanctioned our working together, would he let you go with us?"

McManus shook his head.

"Captain's under tremendous pressure to bring the *Times* bombers to justice. There should be plenty of officers available since the Boyle Heights Rapist and Parlor House Horror haven't struck in weeks. Reassigning us wouldn't set well with the bigwigs, therefore the Captain would never approve our absence or pay our way."

"Find the motive for that bombing and you'll find the perpetrators," pronounced Cushman.

"It's a long list," responded Tyson, "motives, I mean. We're nowhere near to finding the guilty parties."

"Wouldn't be so sure about that, my friend," said McManus, pouring himself a bit more cheer. "Colonel Otis and his cohorts are unapologetically anti-union. Local labor leaders find it curious all the editors and owners happened to be out of the building when the explosions occurred. Others say there's no point in having authority or pulling down big salaries if you must work all night. Of course, the ones who say that loudest were all home safe in their beds."

"Although the unions have legitimate axes to grind, nothing can excuse what happened," Cushman asserted. "The explosion might have been bigger than planned and only intended to scare the bosses. Twenty-one people lost their lives and mark my words, no matter who's responsible, it'll be union men who pay."

CHAPTER THIRTY-EIGHT

Cushman volunteered to take the detectives home, a great convenience since Margaret had filled Easter baskets for the children. Their sweet, chocolate-smeared faces were all she could think about while greeting the congregation alongside her husband and singing her way through three services.

Their anniversary fell on the day after Easter that year. Edmund delighted her with a silver Waterman pen crafted for a woman's hand, and a bottle of walnut ink.

Cushman surprised them both with hand-tooled, leather-bound notebooks, Edmund's capacious enough to hold a minister's writings and Margaret's a scaled-down version small enough to carry in a pocket. He had cunningly added spring devices to both so papers could be neatly taken out and new sheets added. Neither Morehouse had ever seen the like. Edmund suggested getting a patent.

"You'll be rich as Croesus, my friend. Can't think of any professional who wouldn't want one. How excellent it will be to keep only the best of my writing! I can add more paper and throw away the mistakes. Only hope you remember all your friends at All Saints when the money starts rolling in."

Margaret caught Cushman's uncomfortable look and felt his pain. Applying for a patent might mean having to disclose one's past. No way could he risk it. Pity.

Newspaper headlines put a damper on her Easter cheer. Another bomb had gone off, this time at the Llewellyn Iron Works Plant. No one died in that explosion.

To prepare the group for San Bernardino, McManus arranged a meeting next day with the coroner, Dr. Erasmus Singleton, as somber a fellow as ever wielded a scalpel. Bristly beard bobbing, he recited his findings in a lugubrious tone. After a lengthy litany of anatomical terms and conditions, he gave them the information they wanted.

"In summation," the doctor intoned, "last September, Detectives Tyson and McManus brought me the body of a woman who was most probably in her early to late twenties, about five foot nine inches tall. Her blood type was O, quite common — you've heard about blood types, haven't you?"

They all nodded, although Margaret was sure the men had far more detailed knowledge of this recent discovery.

Dr. Singleton eyed her uncertainly. "Are you accustomed to discussing such sordid details?"

"I've never seen a dead body but taking part in a murder investigation has more than prepared me to separate evidence from emotion."

"Then by your leave I shall be blunt. Her body might have once been inside the crate and her blood, also Type O, soaked up by the lining.

"The lining was stained with *human* blood!" Margaret exclaimed. "The proximity of body and box has to be beyond mere coincidence."

"Your original notes about the deceased's battered internal organs intrigued me, Doctor," said McManus. "If we assume the crate once contained *our* body, do you think she was harmed before being killed or perhaps compressed post-mortem when the culprits nailed it up?"

Dr. Singleton gazed up at the ceiling.

"Both explanations are possible, although in my career I have only examined one other body in such a wretched state. That poor fellow committed suicide by first scaling a tower, then flinging himself to the ground. In such cases, the body exsanguinates, much as a sponge hurled against a stone wall. I would advance the notion this poor woman met her untimely death falling from a tower or rooftop."

A kaleidoscope of images, some real as Dominguez Field, others dark and imagined, played before Margaret's mind's eye.

"Or an airplane," she added quietly.

CHAPTER THIRTY-NINE

Six weeks later, Cushman and the Morehouses arrived at the Santa Fe Depot platform in San Bernardino. Railroads had transformed that once-sleepy town into a bustling city, even at night.

Station Agent Theodore Jamison met them on the platform. Cushman had made the arrangements beforehand by way of telegram requesting help with an official police matter and signed himself as lead investigator. He made no mention of Margaret, the only team member with official ties to the force.

She was not offended. New ideas about female equality needed time to take root, and time was not on their side. Agent Jamison had been sufficiently impressed by Cushman's initiative to arrange a horse and carriage for their use.

They rode for half an hour before pulling up in front of St. John's, a sturdy stone edifice with copper-plated steeple had oxidized green as the surrounding forest. The air was brisk but Reverend Archibald Meeks greeted them warmly and clasped Edmund with a fervor Margaret would have thought impossible for a man with such an emaciated frame. When the men retired to the rectory, Cushman and Margaret felt no need to stay around to exchange family pleasantries.

Her star had risen considerably in Cushman's estimation since she'd uttered the word "airplane" at the coroner's office. At last, he considered her, if not his equal, a bit more deserving of collegial standing than a mere New Woman.

Before their departure, they'd studied maps of the San Bernardino area. Their evidence led them to believe the Pantages girl and Yvette were one and the same, but there was a time discrepancy. To the best of their knowledge, the body had never been inside a coffin and should have decomposed during the months between the air meet and McManus and Tyson's discovery. The initial report mentioned vestiges of flesh and cloth clinging to the bones so they kept those conclusions to themselves.

Cushman and Margaret proceeded on the premise Yvette's fall caused her erstwhile suitor to panic, land, and run away. They plotted a course outside the town perimeter, looking for any area free from brush and buildings that might attract an aviator's eye.

Unless they found evidence preserved in the dry climate, suspicion would continue to plague Leland. Clearing his name meant preserving Edmund, his pulpit, and Margaret's peace of mind.

They boarded the station carriage, anxious to follow the route they'd planned. Cushman kept the mare at a slow pace while Margaret twisted left and right, scanning everything between the road and horizon with binoculars. At first the homes stood cheek-by-jowl, then farther apart, until mostly crops and trees dominated the landscape.

"Look at those farmhouses!" Margaret called out when an odd pair of buildings appeared before her lenses. "Mirror images, far as I can see: same white painted clapboard, same rose windows. One's porch is on the right; the other's is on the left. There's not fifteen yards between them."

Cushman pulled the horse to a halt and took the binoculars from her hand.

"Chicken coops and a big barn over there; maybe a dairy farm. The one on the right is next to fields. Bet alfalfa's growing there; and my, oh my, is that a Model T Ford I see before me?"

Margaret had been examining the houses so closely she'd neglected to see the black four-seat open touring car with its brass radiator and headlights gleaming in the shade of a towering eucalyptus tree.

Cushman grinned broadly as if he'd just struck the mother lode.

"Tell me, Madam Detective, which farm would you choose to launch your investigation?"

Silence revealed her confusion. Without so much as a condescending remark, Cushman set her reasoning skills in motion.

"Either they brought in an awfully good crop this year or discovered an alternative source of income."

"Then I believe, Mr. Cushman, it's time to say we are visitors who went for a ride and lost our way. Let's ask those folks with the brand-new auto for directions."

The sign on the gatepost read "Furman's Farm." A chubby-cheeked woman who turned out to be Ruth Furman opened her door for Mr. and Mrs. Cushman, a respectable-looking couple from Los Angeles asking for directions to St. John's. Coincidentally, Ruth and her family were parishioners. Pleased by the prospect of unexpected company, she gave them detailed directions and invited them in for lunch.

They left the picnic Margaret had packed behind in the buggy and went inside. Ruth laid out a spread the like of which Margaret had rarely seen: potato soup garnished with bacon strips and laden with cream, glazed ham taken from the haunch of what must have been an immense hog, and beans bubbling in molasses and brown sugar. Her well-padded frame filled the room, along with warmth and good humor. She heaped on second helpings and afterwards led them proudly into her parlor.

The furnishings, probably hand built by Farmer Furman, were dark and sturdy, all right angles with not a single curve. Ruth had done what she could to soften the room with lightweight cotton curtains and an assortment of hand-hooked rugs. Nothing except the shiny black auto parked outside suggested harvests large enough to buy luxuries.

They sat cautiously on the sofa. The springs did not protrude through the fabric but were perilously close to the surface. A crocheted afghan folded neatly over the back hid years of wear.

Their conversation began with the usual polite exchange. Ruth and George Furman's thirty-two-year marriage had produced two sons. Albert was the oldest. Steven was "a sweet boy though not quite right," and still lived under their roof.

George built and Ruth furnished the house next door as a wedding present for their eldest son, setting the stage for the younger Furmans, also parents of two sons, to duplicate their lives. Margaret told her she and Cushman were newlyweds, no family but "hopefully, some day."

Fidgeting like a silly schoolgirl, Ruth asked the question she'd wanted to pose since they first mentioned Los Angeles.

"What's your city like? I've heard tell there are ice cream

wagons, vaudeville shows, skating rinks, and even pictures that move! It sounds heathenish to a God-fearing woman, but I'd like to go just once and see for myself."

"It's not at all depraved. There are museums, public gardens, grand houses of worship, and beautiful homes, though ours is modest by comparison. Take it from me, ice cream on a hot Los Angeles day is a reasonable version of heaven. I've bought one on a waffle cone from a truck and had a banana split in an ice cream parlor."

"Banana split with what?" she asked.

"Ice cream, of course."

Ruth nearly swooned.

Cushman, who had mostly remained silent, joined in.

"My dear, don't forget to tell our hostess about the Dominguez Air Meet. First in the nation, remember. One day soon those pilots will be flying all the way out here."

Ruth bounced up and down like a schoolgirl who knew the right answer.

"One already has!" she blurted. "Late last fall, we had our own private air show when a Frenchman did a loop-de-loop and landed in our field! Didn't speak three words of English and wouldn't stay for supper, but he paid my husband handsomely for the damage to our crops."

It took all Margaret's newfound acting skills to contain her excitement.

"How interesting! Please tell us all about it."

Ruth was relishing their attention and wanted to everything in her power to prolong it.

"First, we'll have dessert."

"Thanks, I could not eat another bite."

Ruth eyed her much as a mother would an insolent child. "I'll bet that tall husband of yours wouldn't turn down a slice of chocolate cake with a glass of cold milk to wash it down, would you, sir?"

Cushman grinned. "It would be against my religion to say no."

Ruth gestured for Margaret to accompany her to the kitchen. "My dear, you may not have much of an appetite right now because you are, shall I say, a bit unwell?"

"Unwell? I'm in perfect health."

"I'm not talking about an illness. You're obviously expecting."

Expecting what? Margaret wondered before the full meaning of Ruth's words dawned on her.

"I couldn't. I'm not," she protested, touching her slender form.

"Tall woman like you won't show for a while. I can tell by the look in your eyes, the glow of your skin. I'm never wrong. How late is your flow?"

No one had ever asked Margaret such an intimate question before.

"Oh, only a few weeks. That's perfectly normal for me."

To silence her nosiness, Margaret unlatched the largest door of the oak icebox and downed a glass of the cold, white liquid, the freshest she'd ever tasted.

Ruth handed her three nested glasses and, self-assured as a maître d'hotel in a fine establishment, bustled ahead with a tray full of cake and a pitcher of milk.

"He doesn't know?"

Margaret shook her head vehemently.

"Not a word of this to my husband, please. We've only been married a short while. I don't think it's possible!"

"All it takes is once, if you catch my drift."

"I'll see a doctor when we get back home and then, if you're right, break the news."

"If?" Ruth laughed. "Mark my words, not so many months from now, you'll be cradling a babe in your arms. Good thing you're starting a family right away. Man like that is getting up in years, must be anxious for a son."

Ruth sliced the cake decisively.

"Time you put meat on your bones. There's milk in the ice box. Have another glass now and more with your cake."

Cushman devoured the great gooey chocolate slice Ruth handed him with gusto. Margaret's cake and milk went down so easily she knew Ruth had to be wrong. Her female relatives in a family way were invariably sick to their stomachs in the early months. Margaret had just consumed a feast large enough to satisfy a lumberjack and all she felt was pleasantly full.

Licking the last crumbs from his fingers, Cushman returned to the earlier conversation.

"The airplane you mentioned must have made a loud clatter."

"Yes, I was in the middle of kneading bread at the time. I did not pop my head outside until I heard a thump, like a rock dropping out of the sky. Albert yelled at me to stay indoors until the airplane landed."

"So, you heard loud noise before the airplane landed. Did you have the chance to see it up close?"

"I could hardly take my eyes off that strange contraption. It just missed smashing into our icehouse. Looked to be made mostly made of sticks, paper, and a few wires. George told me they call it a biplane 'cause it has one wing above and one below. I touched the metal parts and couldn't believe how hot they were. George made me go inside while he bargained with the man who was flying it."

"Did you see the pilot before he left? Was anyone else with him?"

"Now that you mention it, there may have been someone else waiting outside. The only person I saw up close was that flying fellow. George brought the man in, sat him down on that very chair so's I could bind a wound on the back of his hand. Told me it was a burn which makes sense since he'd been sitting near that hot metal."

"Do remember what he was he wearing?"

"I was very much taken with his tall leather boots and fine silk scarf. The rest of his clothes were pretty torn up. They must have cost a pretty penny: cap with a visor, double-breasted leather coat with fur lapels. He filled them out well and when he washed the dirt off his face, I thought he looked mighty fine for a foreigner."

Before they could continue questioning, Farmer George and his hulking, blank-faced son Albert tramped inside.

"Who we got here, Mother?" growled George.

Cushman jumped to his feet and proffered a hand.

"Harold Cushman from Los Angeles and my wife, Margaret, at your service, sir."

"These lovely people came knocking on our door asking the way to St. John's. I couldn't let good Christians go off without offering our hospitality, could I?"

Ruth's situation was painfully clear. Mistress of her home when alone, domestic servant in front of her husband.

"They were telling me about the wonders of Los Angeles. I couldn't top them with anything in San Bernardino until Mr. Cushman here bragged about the big air meet they had last winter. I told them we had a show of our own right out there in the alfalfa field."

The farmer's face turned livid and Margaret feared he might burst a vessel or harm Ruth if they weren't around.

"Get them outta here and get me my food if they haven't eaten us out of house and home already. And if they have, woman, so help me ..."

He plucked the empty plate from Margaret's hand and waved it threateningly in front of Ruth.

Cushman responded nobly.

"We shall take our leave immediately, good sir, with thanks and payment. Our cousin is visiting Reverend Archibald; we'll be sure to tell your pastor about the Furman family's generosity when we join them."

He pressed a five-dollar gold piece into the farmer's hand and bowed slightly. The gesture made George Furman relent. His son lumbered off, sensing no need for further confrontation.

Cushman led the way out and Margaret followed. Turning around to wave goodbye, she overheard Ruth whisper audibly to George about the guest being in a family way and the husband not knowing. She was asking him to help Margaret down the hill, not at all necessary but not unwelcome, considering Cushman's haste and the Margaret's delicate boots.

Until they reached the carriage, Farmer Furman was as good as the gold Cushman had given him. After helping Margaret up to the plank seat, his eyes fell upon the well-marked map she had used to cover the picnic hamper.

They were headed for trouble the instant he picked it up.

"You knew where you was goin' all the time! And look at your basket under here, with enough food so's you didn't need none of ours. Who sent you? You must be spies!"

Cushman cracked his whip; their carriage sped down the dirt road, leaving little dust cyclones and an irate farmer in its wake.

Above the clopping hooves and my pounding heart I heard George Furman yell, "Albert, Albert, fire up the Lizzie and bring me my shotgun!"

CHAPTER FORTY

They could have easily outraced the Model T if volleys of buckshot overhead hadn't frightened the horse. Even Cushman's powerful hands could not control her, and she fell, poor thing, into a ditch. Bellies to the ground, they crawled a few yards away under cover of low brush and hunkered down. They took shallow breaths, fearing any movement would rustle the grasses.

George and Albert brought the metal monster to a halt beside the empty, upturned carriage and went to the opposite side of the road to search through the overgrown field. Each time they cursed or whacked the alfalfa, Margaret and Cushman inched a little farther away.

"It's the only place those nosy parkers could hide," Margaret heard George growl.

Peering up through a fringe of grasses, she watched them return to their upended carriage. Albert kicked the injured mare; she whinnied feebly in pain. George placed the barrel of his shotgun to her head and put her out of her misery. Margaret shrieked, knowing they too could be dispatched that easily.

Like hunting hounds, they turned their eyes in the direction of her cry. Cushman pulled Margaret to her feet. They ran for their lives. Margaret hoped her mother was watching from the hereafter, deeply regretful of any attempts to curb her daughter's love of exercise.

The hulking farmers were strong but too bulky to keep pace with two lean people frightened out of their minds. The rounds of firing overhead ended, giving them hope father and son had run out of ammunition.

Before exhaustion claimed them, Cushman and Margaret came upon a harvested field. Margaret brushed her clothes, hands, and face against a bale of hay, exchanging a layer of dirt for a few shallow scratches.

"Four-thirty, maybe five o'clock," Cushman determined from the sun poised over a distant mountain peak. "We drove here heading east; we'll get back to town by going west."

He barely missed stepping in animal droppings. "Equine," he concluded.

"Is there any way we can hire a horse?" Margaret asked, realizing the only way to avoid similar messes would be to keep her eyes on the ground.

She already knew the answer. Her purse was gone; any money Cushman had brought was either buried beneath the carriage wreckage or lining the Furmans' pockets. Cushman looked like a wounded soldier and Margaret felt that she, no doubt, looked worse.

Cushman studied the horizon and motioned for her to follow.

Enclosed inside a hexagonal corral were three grazing steeds.

"I'm afraid we'll have to borrow one," he sighed.

The gate was latched but unlocked. With a handful of grass and a soft voice he never used around people, Cushman cajoled a strong chestnut to feed from his hand. Minutes later, he mounted the horse, extended an arm to Margaret, and pulled her up behind him. Eyes shut, she held tightly to his waist as they rode towards the pending sunset.

They must have looked quite a sight trotting down Main Street in such a deplorable condition. Looks on the faces of passersby registered everything from amazement to disgust. Waiting on the church steps, as he'd been for hours, was Edmund.

Cushman dismounted leaving Margaret, paralyzed by pain, atop the horse until he could ease her down. Edmund rushed to her side and began to brush straw off her clothes and wipe her face with a moistened handkerchief. He combed his fingers through her hair, windblown wilder than a Medusa's snakes. Slowly the trio stumbled their way inside.

Reverend Meeks listened intently to every detail of their adventure. Edmund had already told him about Leland's predicament and Margaret's position with the Los Angeles Police Department. When she wryly confessed to being a horse thief, he only laughed and said the felony was a justifiable act of self-preservation.

The pastor appeared to be all too familiar with the Furman family; he thought Ruth well-intentioned and offered no opinion about husband's character. His disapproving expression spoke volumes.

With safety and home only a train ride away, Reverend Meeks offered to drive them to the station.

A sound of pounding horse hooves grew menacingly near the moment they'd settled into his buggy. Hayforks pointed upward and torches burning, a party of eight vigilantes materialized from the darkness. A boulder-sized man, eyes smoldering like embers, blocked their path while his cohorts surrounded them. He drew a rifle from his saddle scabbard and aimed it directly at Cushman.

"Hand over those thieves, Reverend, or you'll have blood on your hands."

Reverend Meeks addressed him in a voice worthy of an Old Testament prophet.

"Any blood spilled tonight will be on your hands, Alf Reardon. Haven't seen you for quite a while. I recall you being much more respectful when I christened your son. These good people are engaged in the Lord's work and I've granted them sanctuary. As we speak, your horse is being curried and given a full share of oats."

No orator ever projected his voice more forcefully than that outraged member of the clergy. Almost on cue, the assistant pastor, collar askew and shirt sleeves rolled above his elbow, led the chestnut out of the barn. The horse glistened in the half light as it nuzzled the young man's hand.

"Take him, safe and sound as your souls will still be if you put down your weapons immediately," Reverend Meeks commanded.

The chastened band departed. Margaret wouldn't have pegged them for regular churchgoers. Still, they were letting them go.

Despite her husband's tender ministrations, Margaret fretted all the way to the train station. Her disheveled state and the late hour would be almost as difficult to explain to Stationmaster Jamison as the loss of his horse and carriage.

Once again, Cushman came to the rescue. With eloquence and a near attorney-like flair for summarizing facts, he informed the stationmaster his efforts would soon lead to the capture of a fiendish criminal. The man merely shrugged and clapped Cushman on the back. All was forgiven, including any need to pay for damages.

"Call it my way of making things right," said Jamison. "I wouldn't have lent you the rig in the first place if I didn't have a few to spare. I've trusted you from the first time we corresponded. Many suspicious characters pass through here and I am honored and obligated to assist in police matters."

Cushman's face registered mild surprise.

"Many a thief has eluded the law aboard this railway," Jamison continued. "They pay their fare; I look the other way. Even with a warrant, if there isn't a poster to go with it, all I can go on is my suspicions and there's never enough time or manpower to act on them.

"Above all, I don't trust the outlandish men and women who head your way along the vaudeville circuit. Praise be, none of that public wantonness is allowed in this fair city."

"Dancing is against the law in San Bernardino?" Margaret asked.

"We've got an ordinance against it, except for square dancing at church socials. Keeps out the riffraff. One of your Los Angeles vaudeville showmen kept sending an odd-looking fellow out here to meet gents and ladies and escort them back to his theater. Guess he was afraid they'd go elsewhere if anyone offered more money. The man he hired guarded those performers, especially the ladies, like a sheepdog, and a vicious one to boot. I was relieved to learn they weren't going to spend much time in this city but couldn't help wondering what made them choose such a dangerous path. Most of them looked terrified."

Margaret felt a shiver go up her spine.

"When did you last see this man?" Cushman asked casually.

"Hmmm, it was a while ago. He started coming out here every other week, strutting about the platform like some little fop with his starched collar, velvet cuffs, and coattails. Always wore a brocade vest and carried a pocket watch on a chain. I used to worry about the way he'd sidle up to the ladies and..."

Mr. Jamison suddenly remembered Margaret's presence and blushed.

"I beg your forgiveness, madam, I got carried away. Not used to female company when I'm at work."

"Don't worry, sir. We're all tired."

He smiled weakly.

"That we are! I just recalled the first time I laid eyes on that fellow. It was January of last year when I sold the French fly boy that ticket. The small man seemed to pop out of nowhere and kept pestering him for money but all he got was a blackened eye. Only thing for certain is, Bertrand boarded the Atchison, Topeka & Santa Fe headed east. An hour later, the other man boarded a train for Los Angeles. Didn't see him again for many weeks."

CHAPTER FORTY-ONE

As usual, Thomas Warren was waiting for them at the station. The ride back home was blissfully swift. Margaret was surprised and a little frightened to see a Model T, identical to the one that had pursued them in San Bernardino, parked in front of her house.

Still stiff from earlier exertions, she stumbled up to the porch while Cushman and Edmund approached the vehicle. Two people emerged. One was Leland, moving awkwardly; the other was a large, liveried stranger holding a knife to his back.

A tall blonde gentleman fanning a small pistol at all of them came round from the passenger's side, ready to strike down anyone who got in the way.

"Ne lâchez pas ce lâche!" he commanded his knife-wielding lackey.

From her smatterings of French, Margaret translated: *"Don't let go of this coward!"*

The reason he spoke French finally dawned on her.

"Are you Monsieur Julien LaRoche?"

"I call myself that, Madame, and you must be *la femme ingénieuse* who intends to clear this one's name."

As Edmund and Cushman looked on stunned by the bizarre situation, Margaret approached M. LaRoche.

"Welcome to America. Your outrage is understandable. Threatening our nephew is not. Although Yvette has been missing for several months, there is no reason to suppose she has come to harm."

"I'm listening, Madam."

Margaret's sleep-deprived brain struggled to engage him.

"We need your help to find her. Suspecting Leland of foul play is only natural but please keep in mind both he and your sister were little more than puppets manipulated by evil hands."

The stranger's eyes glistened. "His mother and our father! You are right in that, Madam. Yvette gave up every chance of happiness for the sake of her mother, brothers, and sisters."

"What a close bond you had, er, I should say *have*."

"We can only hope. Our father treated Yvette like common stock and did everything he could to manipulate her."

"Please tell me more about Yvette. We never had the chance to become very well acquainted."

"She took it upon herself to save our family's fortune but this man, this country, ah, it was all too much. She was, how do you say, playacting the part of the *enfante terrible* when this young prince and his *vieille sorcière* of a mother were around."

He signaled the chauffeur to surrender his knife to Margaret and release Leland.

Although they had reached an accord, Margaret did not take her eyes of the French visitors.

"If it is any comfort, this young man told me you were the one member of Yvette's family he respected. It was he who suggested I send you the telegram. No matter what we discover throughout the investigation, I pledge to keep you fully informed."

Julien bowed to Margaret and climbed back into the vehicle.

Leland looked dazed as the car drove off. "He and the driver kidnapped me just as I was leaving the bank!"

"Keep this," Margaret said, handing the knife to her nephew, "and stay with us tonight. I'll have nightmares enough without worrying about anyone else terrorizing you at knifepoint. You get enough of that treatment from your mother."

∿

It was days before Margaret was able to sleep for more than an hour at a time. The trip had produced more questions than facts. The harrowing adventures replayed in her head like a badly edited nickelodeon show. If a solution to the mystery lurked within those images, she was too tired and upset to see it.

The combined physical and emotional challenges confined her to bed for almost two weeks, except for an occasional effort to sup lightly or attend to bodily functions. Little by little, her strength returned.

One Sunday morning, Margaret caught the strong odor of the honing oil she used on her kitchen knives coming from Cushman's room. With both he and Edmund at St. Paul's until at least mid-afternoon, she had no qualms about trespassing.

Margaret hadn't set foot in the room that had once been their study for years. Edmund and Margaret had agreed keeping Cushman on the first floor would give them all a welcome measure of privacy. She left freshly laundered linens outside his door weekly and counted on Cushman's natural fastidiousness to keep the space tidy.

His room was spare as a monk's cell. The bedclothes were pulled drumhead tight. One suit and three perfectly pressed shirts hung in his closet above a pair of well-worn, polished shoes. Across the oak dresser he'd lined up a bar of soap, straight-edge razor, comb, and box of shirt stays. A porcelain washbasin and pitcher, glaze crackled from decades of use, provided the only decorative elements.

She half expected to find a small stack of the risqué French postcards she'd heard about, but if Cushman had any, he had hidden them well. His bookshelves held only an atlas, a Bible, and a few gun catalogs.

Where pictures had once graced the walls, he'd tacked up newspaper clippings about Boyle Heights, the bombings, and other cases under investigation. The graphic articles and pictures lining the walls were disturbing. She gritted her teeth, deciding this was his room after all, and she could always paint over the holes if he ever moved out.

He should return to investigative work, she thought. *I've never known anyone half as thorough.* She promised herself once her cases were solved, she'd search for a way for a way he could be reinstated. They owed him that much and more.

On a low table she found a small metal jar topped with a conical spout. She poured a few drops of the pale red liquid onto her fingers, sniffing and feeling the viscosity to confirm its use as a honing fluid.

One end of a long, wide leather strop had been nailed into the table's edge. Next to it, a dozen knives stood blade down in an empty bucket. Among them she recognized the Italian-designed stiletto and a blade wide as her palm and long as her forearm that had to be the famous Bowie.

Margaret turned to leave when a dull glint of steel and sheen of dark wood against the far wall caught her eye. On wooden pegs hung a dozen firearms arranged in two rows according to size: three Derringers, three Smith and Wessons on top; two Civil War-era Remingtons, three versions of the Peacemaker, and a Winchester .44 below. Thanks to McManus and Tyson's tutelage, she had a smattering of knowledge about these weapons but no direct experience. She wondered whether Cushman still carried his Pinkerton service revolver.

Margaret had never seen so many weapons in one place outside the police station. There was no time to speculate about his reasons or means for getting them. Impulsively, she pocketed a tiny Derringer, hoping he wouldn't miss it, certain he wouldn't approve. She recalled how Marco secreted objects up his sleeve and found she could easily do the same.

CHAPTER FORTY-TWO

Edmund and Cushman waited on Margaret hand and foot until she declared herself well enough to return to duty at the police station. She hoped that's where they would think she was headed when the door slammed shut before either had arisen, but Margaret had other plans. Kerchief hiding her hair, padding round her middle, and a large nondescript dress borrowed from the church's poor closet, she headed for the Pantages Theater in the guise of an older woman.

Head bowed and feet shuffling, she blended into the backstage mêlée without difficulty. No one questioned the right of a cleaning woman to appropriate a broom propped by the back door. She swept her way around workmen and rehearsing acts to the women's dressing room.

It took a measure of courage to reenter the place where she had first appeared rouged and bedecked in revealing satin.

Whatever happened to that emerald-green gown? she wondered, glancing in the mirror with disapproval at the foolhardy woman who'd worn it.

Almost all the ladies were onstage but from the other side of a dressing screen came trills so pure and high they could only come from the American Nightingale. Posters, handbills, and glowing reviews framed three sides of Miss Wetherby's space along the wall of mirrors. A spray of exotic flowers and half-eaten box of chocolates, tributes from her many admirers, lay on the shelf below. Emerging in all her porcelain prettiness, Amy Wetherby was pleased to find Margaret combing platinum strands from her hairbrush.

"How thoughtful of you!" she gushed. "Please, have a chocolate. What's your name, dear?"

Margaret had been rehearsing the next sequence of events in her mind for the past week. The moment Amy Wetherby handed her the candy, Margaret grabbed her wrist and thrust the barrel of

Cushman's Derringer against the actress's back.

"Margaret Morehouse. We've met before." She hissed in her ear. "If you scream, I'll pull the trigger and no one will hear the shot above all this noise."

Amy turned to flee. Margaret turned with her, maintaining her hold. Their new angle reflected in the mirror confirmed the gun's reality. Margaret released Miss Wetherby and let her sink into the chair, sobbing.

"After you brought me the poster, I left the theater not knowing whether to suspect Mr. Pantages or Marco the Magnificent. Your words made me waste precious time investigating the magician. You may be happy to learn your friend Marie Levecque is very much alive."

"I already know that. She visited me the same day she returned to Los Angeles. We have plans to go shopping together tomorrow."

"She's back here already?" Margaret gasped.

"Marco and she had to return to Los Angeles and perform for the Grimaldi brothers. Marco tried to worm out of his contract and take off for Europe but couldn't do it no matter how hard he tried. She said he'd found a replacement for a while, a tall redheaded woman who probably looked a lot like you."

Margaret's expression gave her away. Realizing she had the upper hand, relief filled Miss Wetherby's face, followed by puzzlement.

"So, it was you after all! I had my suspicions, but no idea police work would give a woman so many travel opportunities. Don't tell me you succumbed to his charms, too."

Something between a sob and a moan escaped Margaret's lips. Amy Wetherby took control of the situation and gently pushed the gun away.

"Take it from me, he's not worth your while. Marie may hold his heart for the moment, but if she adds a single wrinkle or pound, he'll find someone new."

The room began to spin around. Margaret fell to the floor. When she returned to consciousness, the songstress was holding a jar of smelling salts under her nose.

"Never know when these will come in handy. One last thing I

heed to know: if she's alive and he's not guilty, at least of murder, why are you still harassing me?"

"My fellow detectives found the body in question less than a hundred yards from here. Now that we know Marie is alive, we must find out who she was."

"How does that concern me?"

"I believe Alexander Pantages used Walters and you to make me think Marco was a murderer. During that little skirmish I witnessed in the alley, Walters said you didn't properly deliver the lines he'd rehearsed with you. Tell me exactly what he wanted you to say, and I promise to leave you in peace."

She laughed softly.

"How do you manage to be so right and so wrong at the same time? I was worried when Alexander Pantages came to the door. I've heard he's had girls roughed up by hired thugs. Without my looks, I could never get another job no matter how sweetly I sing. Everyone thought Walters was Pantages' right-hand man, but it was the dwarf who promised me fifty dollars if I could make you think Pantages was a murderer. That money would have bought my ticket out of here."

Her words could not have been more devastating if she'd wrested the gun from Margaret's hand in the process and pointed it in her face.

"Do you think Mr. Pantages is capable of murder?"

"Not intentionally. He has an awful temper. Could have been accidental, maybe, with all his fooling around."

Feminine voices were fast approaching; the chorus would soon outnumber Margaret twenty to one.

She mumbled an apology and asked Amy Wetherby to keep the discussion confidential. No one followed Margaret when she exited the building faster than any elderly cleaning woman could possibly run.

The Derringer tucked back in her sleeve took on the heat of Margaret's body and began to chafe. She wrapped it in her kerchief and let her hair fall loose as she walked towards the police station.

Margaret's brain was beset with questions: what was Walters trying to achieve by bribing the girl? Where would he have gotten the fifty dollars if not from the Maestro? Was he working for one of Pantages' business rivals? There were plenty of impresarios who might want Pantages out of the way, and she remembered McManus's tale about the woman scorned in the Yukon.

Before reaching First Street, she spotted McManus and Tyson outside a local public house. Their welcoming expressions turned to alarm as she shouted *Hallo*! and crossed a busy intersection, startling a horse and nearly colliding with a careless driver.

"You look like a ghost," said McManus, helping her up from gutter to curb. "Sit down before you vanish altogether."

Tyson also offered a hand and brought her a glass of lemonade.

They'd been celebrating the capture of an elusive cat burglar with thick corned beef sandwiches and beer. She asked why they hadn't visited during her illness. They assured her they'd tried several times, but Edmund and Cushman turned them away.

Keeping in mind McManus's earlier warning not to withhold information, she described every event from the San Bernardino trip to her recent rash actions in the back of the vaudeville theater. Nothing she said seemed to surprise them, not even her resorting to firearms.

Both men were intrigued by the Furman's Farm episode, as well as Agent Jamison's description of Pantages' malevolent minion.

"Walters," they said almost in unison when she was done.

"I might agree if I could figure out his motive. If it's purely monetary, who's footing the bill?"

"We can find that out on our own," offered Tyson, "and you'll be the first to know. Now please go home and complete your recovery."

"You can't expect me to stay in bed when there's all this work to be done."

"I don't understand what's driving you," added McManus. "You've taxed yourself and the good Reverend mightily in your efforts to solve this murder. Without your persistence, I must admit, the victim would remain another body buried in Potter's Field. Well, we're halfway to finding her identity, and whether she was a fine French lady or a woman of the streets, we'll follow this case to its conclusion."

Tyson interrupted in an uncharacteristically concerned tone of voice.

"Let McManus and me take the lead for a while until you get your strength back and we can work together again."

Their words made sense. She drained the lemonade, its sweet tartness the first taste as appealing as the milk had been in Ruth Furman's kitchen.

The men saw her aboard a streetcar and hurried off. Her body swayed to the rhythm of the wheels, perhaps from weakness or an attempt to fall into its tempo and forget the recent past. If her folly had rekindled their interest in the case, perhaps she was not such a terrible person after all.

Back home, she boiled several kettles of water and filled the claw foot tub. Hot water up to her sternum buoyed her nearly as much as her colleagues had. On the morrow, she would ask Cushman to take her to the Morehouse Home. There she could check in on the wonderful people she'd neglected for so long and consult Dr. Sherman on a private matter. The words that hefty oracle pronounced back in her San Bernardino kitchen had most likely come to pass.

CHAPTER FORTY-THREE

Tuesday was laundry day at Morehouse Home. A banner line of sheets and shifts waved them welcome under an uncommonly warm sun. Cushman declined to come in but made himself useful by locating a hand tool in the shed and pruning the bushes.

Four out of six unmarried girls, all under eighteen, had just given birth. Margaret held the smallest baby, a boy, in the crook of her arm. Listless at first, he instinctively nuzzled her finger when it brushed his cheek.

Once the baby latched onto his mother's breast, Nurse Fulbright conducted Margaret to the kitchen, where Dr. Sherman was rolling down his sleeves. She told him her monthly flow had stopped. He escorted her to his examining room, prodded gently, then told her to come to his office as soon as she was dressed.

When she joined him, he was positively beaming.

"You've restored my faith in miracles! I know how much you've wanted a child and I've long feared the Reverend and your busy schedules would stand in the way. Yet here you are, almost one-third of the way along. Does your husband know?"

"Of c-course not," Margaret stammered. "I wasn't sure myself. We'd given up after ten years."

The doctor chuckled. "More couples would be successful at conceiving if they worried less about it. You're carrying a fortunate child, with two intelligent, loving parents."

Margaret took her leave, barely listening to the doctor's advice about getting more food and rest. All she wanted to do was go home, lock herself inside, and pray for divine guidance to solve this case.

It was not to be. One of the patients went into labor complicated by breech delivery. Dr. Sherman succeeded in turning the baby but required the nurses' assistance. Margaret sent Cushman into town for supplies and stayed until nightfall, changing and feeding infants, holding mothers' hands.

When they returned home, McManus and Tyson were waiting outside. Margaret had come to love them dearly but that night they were the last people on earth she wanted to see.

"We've arrested Walters on conspiracy to commit murder!"

"How in the world did you manage that?" Margaret asked wearily.

"Wouldn't have thought it likely myself. Very often one question produces several answers," explained McManus. "Please let us in; there's much to explain."

"Couldn't you tell me out here?"

The men shook their heads.

"Never know who might be hiding in the bushes," said Tyson.

Margaret groaned. For all she knew, Elvira's minions might be lurking in the greenery. She gestured them to come inside.

"What questions did you invent that turned out to be so all-fired revealing?" Margaret began once they were settled.

"Quite simple," McManus explained. "I asked myself, who hated Pantages enough to make him look like a villain? Could anyone else could have bid on the property Pantages turned into a theater?

"I went down to the Hall of Records, expecting to find rival developers like the Grimaldi brothers or one of the nickelodeon houses. It turned out to be our friends at First National Bank. They wanted to convert that building into offices, and I'm sad to report Leland's name was on the bid sheet."

"He probably signs a dozen such forms every week as part of his duties," Margaret protested.

"Maybe, but according to the record, a courier named Wilfred Walters brought in the bid."

"And the Wilfred Walters you have in custody is the full name of Mr. Pantages' toady?"

"One and the same," said Tyson triumphantly. "We took a chance and went back to the theater. Found him lurking around the alley looking like he might try to break in through a window. No problem getting Pantages to sign a complaint. We hauled Walters to jail on breaking and entering charges to make him squawk. No luck with that. He's close mouthed as a clam."

"Maybe he's afraid."

"Let's hope the bloke he's sharing a cell with terrifies him into singing like a canary."

McManus did not entirely share Tyson's jubilation.

"Funny thing how everyone gets up in arms about us putting a gentleman like your nephew behind bars. Not even the captain minded us bending the truth to nab this scoundrel. Almost makes me feel sorry for him."

"Don't waste your sympathy on that one," Margaret said, recalling every nasty encounter she'd had with him. "Los Angeles streets are safer without him."

"Perhaps young Morehouse merely signed off on the transaction," suggested Cushman. "Many rich men work with that institution."

"One wicked woman controls them all," Margaret reminded them, "and we happen to be related by marriage, not blood. Leland is Edmund's beloved brother's child, and until you have proof one way or the other, your suspicions will only hurt them both. Please leave before my husband comes home. He has more than enough burdens to bear right now."

Her voice crackled. When they first worked together, McManus and Tyson tended to overlook Margaret's occasional displays of temper. Her growing abilities helped them achieve a good working relationship. Watching her tremble for reasons unknown, they rose to their feet and turned to leave, hoping an evening of rest would calm her.

As she opened the door, a hulking form stepped out of the darkness to block their exit. Only a horn and tail could have made the man uglier.

"We... has...Michael Tyson," the immensity rumbled. "Wee baby boy. You let our Wilfred go or we keeps him, raise him like our own. Eye for eye, son for son."

Tyson lunged at the mountain of flesh but the giant stepped aside and lumbered off into the night. The dazed detective scrambled to his feet and gave chase.

"That's the creature Charlie tackled at the bank," McManus moaned. "How did we ever manage to lose track of anyone so large?"

He too, ran into the blackness, hampered by his own size and considerable outrage.

"There are others where he came from," Margaret said to herself somberly, realizing at last how much the giant's features resembled the flat faces and leering eyes she associated with Wilfred Walters and Elvira's stony butler.

CHAPTER FORTY-FOUR

Of three things Margaret was certain: somewhere last night's behemoth had a safe harbor; Tyson and McManus would never snare him on their own; and, despite her vulnerable state, she might be the only means through which justice could be served.

Balancing roles of dedicated policewoman and devoted wife had been difficult, but it would take at least one more day to clear Leland's name. Her first task would be to inform Edmund about the pregnancy and assert her need to solve the case. The baby wasn't real to her yet, but the danger to the man she loved all too clear.

Talking to Edmund in person would have undoubtedly closed the door on any further investigation. Writing a letter seemed the coward's way out, but the only way to proceed.

Edwin was the cornerstone of her life. Before they met, she had been a headstrong girl with only creature comforts and an unconventional upbringing to define her. He'd nurtured Margaret's social conscience and encouraged her to act upon it.

The little life growing inside had survived so much already, she rationalized, as she took up pen and paper. Making several starts and stops, the letters she ripped up were full of guilt. If she did not rise to the challenge of Elvira's evil, their entire little family would be destroyed.

The words she finally wrote read like a clinical check off list without a trace of emotional nuance, except for the underscored "Love, Margaret" at the closing.

It was nearly midnight. Edmund came home late and trundled straight off to bed. Margaret folded the note into a vellum envelope and left it on his writing table.

Jupiter was chomping at the bit when Cushman brought the buggy around the next morning.

"Where to, Madam? Your husband tells me you're closer to solving the mystery."

"The Tysons' to start with."

She hesitated. For the second time in their acquaintance, Cushman had been missing while danger was on the doorstep.

"While you were out last night," she began slowly and with just a trace of venom, "a man came to our doorstep. Our friends have arrested Walters. The monster said he had baby Michael and the only way to get him back would be to let Walters go. Seamus and Charlie ran off after him but I was too exhausted to follow."

"That little fiend! I blame myself for not being here. I, uh, I sometimes visit a lady friend."

So, he is human after all! she thought and immediately softened her tone.

"If we can round up Charlie and Seamus, let's proceed to the station. After that, I'm afraid we'll have to pay another visit to Elvira Morehouse."

"Careful, the Greeks said the Chimera could bring on natural disasters even when curled up in her cave. What do you think she's hiding?"

"A motive linking her to Walters," was all Margaret shared.

Little Mary Catherine let them in when they knocked on the Tysons' door. Charlie Jr. crouched in a corner, keeping a fixed gaze on the regiment of toy soldiers lined up around him. Mary Ellen's puffed eyes and mottled skin distorted her features.

Margaret tried to console her, but no amount of reasoning could relieve a mother's anguish.

"The windows were closed, and the door locked when we went to bed. Only evil spirits walk through walls. You know how loud our Michael can be, yet the poor babe made no cry when they grabbed him. 'Tis cursed we are for Charlie always catchin' killers and thieves, the devil's own. One of them he sent to the gallows has come back to haunt us."

Margaret put her arms around her and glanced at the hearth, thinking it and the chimney above were a more plausible portal once the embers had died and the family was fast asleep. Mary Ellen kept twisting Michael's blue flannel blanket through her fingers.

"They pinned a note to it," she sobbed, handing me a scrap reading *Gone forever.*

Evil spirits don't wield pens, but there was no way of reasoning with Mary Ellen that morning. Cushman and Margaret fixed a small breakfast for the children and departed.

〜〜

The minute Cushman and Margaret entered the station, they heard Tyson and McManus and the Captain embroiled in heated argument.

"Can't you see we're onto something?" the Captain reasoned. "We shouldn't give in to these ruffians, not even for the sake of your child. Once we give these criminals the upper hand, they'll take over the entire city."

"My son will not be sacrificed to solve a crime!" bellowed Tyson as he circled the room, fists cocked.

"It won't come to that, dummy. Don't forget I'm a family man myself. We have who they want, and I call that a stalemate. Your child is reasonably safe, at least for now."

Margaret stepped into the midst of the fray, surprising the men into silence.

"No one can be safe in the hands of villains who resort to blackmail and kidnapping. Tell me, Captain, do you recall who brought in the money to bail out the man Mr. Tyson arrested last March on the steps of First National?"

"Not by name but I won't soon forget his face. Said he was a lawyer representing Mrs. Elvira Morehouse, even produced a letter with her signature. Looked and sounded more like an undertaker. Seemed strange at the time, but we had to release him. After all, he was only trying to make a deposit."

"One could easily take Elvira Morehouse's butler for an undertaker."

"Whoever he was, we set the prisoner free. I thought the lady might have a soft heart after all. Now it seems she was only covering up for her spoiled son."

"Except for the soft heart, I would have agreed with you, More information has come to light. My husband, Mr. Cushman, and I traveled to San Bernardino almost a month ago. By chance, we learned someone matching the description of the man you now have in custody visited that town on occasion. Also, not long after the Dominguez Air Meet, a witness remembers seeing him argue with a Frenchman, most likely Jacques-Yves Bertrand, a pilot who left the air show early, probably with Mrs. Leland Morehouse."

If she'd been in his seat and heard such a story after the fact, Margaret would have been angry. The Captain appeared pleasantly surprised, however. Perhaps she'd just handed him the key to solving an important case, one that would reflect well on his record.

At mention of the Morehouse name, station chatter ground to a halt. Captain Clark led Margaret and her cohorts into his office and closed the door.

"Don't want this to hit the papers until we're sure of our information. One of our officers might be looking for some ready cash and itching to spill the beans. Tell me what you think the connection is and, if you want to continue in this line of work, back it up with facts."

"Amy Wetherby, one of the vaudeville performers, said Walters offered her a bribe to implicate Alexander Pantages in the alleyway murder. My sister-in-law wanted to buy the land where Alexander built his theater. She does not take defeat lightly. Walters was on Pantages' payroll, and I believe he also was, and probably still is, on hers."

The Captain glowered in disbelief.

"How could a pillar of our community be capable of such deceit?"

"If he were here, my husband would confirm my speculations. He's witnessed her behavior for over thirty years. Reverend Morehouse always looks for a saving grace and rarely calls anyone evil. This practice does not apply to Elvira Morehouse."

The air around her was clearing. Tyson and McManus were less angry. Captain Clark looked thoughtful.

"What do you propose?" he asked.

"The detectives, my associate Mr. Cushman, and I must go immediately to the Morehouse mansion. Detectives McManus and Tyson should go covertly, perhaps in disguise. Please release Walters to our custody. Mr. Cushman can corral him once we enter."

The captain rolled his eyes towards the ceiling seeking divine guidance. Several moments passed until he spoke again.

"I agree your relationship with Mrs. Elvira Morehouse gives you a distinct advantage, but you're not the strong, confident woman I hired a few months back. Pardon my saying so, the chaos involving your family seems to have taken a tremendous toll. Are you sure you're up to it?"

She smiled weakly, ready to sacrifice anything for Edmund.

"More certain than anything that's happened to me in recent weeks."

The captain reluctantly agreed to her plan. McManus and Tyson grabbed tools and overalls left behind by workmen replastering the station's back wall, recently cracked by an earthquake.

What a fortunate coincidence! Margaret thought. Elvira's mausoleum, as Edmund liked to call it, was in constant need of repair.

The Captain took it upon himself to thrust Walters into the back of their carriage. Cushman gagged and bound the poor creature like a malevolent turkey. Margaret pulled her bonnet down over her ears, trying to block out his pitiful moans.

CHAPTER FORTY-FIVE

It took every ounce of Margaret's courage to knock on Elvira's door.

The grim butler opened it. Cushman crossed the threshold carrying a trussed-up Walters, back and bottom hanging low.

With a snort and swish of satin, Elvira descended the staircase. Throughout their acquaintance, Elvira had regarded Margaret through lizard-lidded eyes sunk in a mask of sneering condescension. This day, her livid features revealed the greed staining her soul. She held a riding crop and would have struck Margaret had Cushman not stood between them.

"You are undone!" she screamed. "You and your spineless husband and anyone else who stands in my way!"

"I'll be leaving the police force, Elvira. If this meeting does not go well, I have written an article for the Times exposing what I know about you and all your criminal acts. Believe me, there's more than enough to lock you away forever.

"Edmund will remain virtuous before my critics, making it impossible for you to sully his name. He will keep his pulpit and continue to champion the people you exploit, since I have the means to undo *you*."

"Not if you're dead," snarled the butler, putting his hand into a cerulean blue pottery umbrella stand. A menagerie of carved animal heads topped the umbrella handles; from amongst them he withdrew a three-foot-long rapier and thrust its tip towards Margaret's neck. Cushman deflected the blow by tossing Walters in the way. The sword sliced through Walters' ropes, sending him flailing to the floor.

In a move so quick Margaret could scarce believe it happened, Cushman pulled out two Derringers and pointed them at their adversaries.

"No one's dying today," he growled, "at least not us."

Margaret turned her attention to Walters and untied his gag. Instead of talking, he tried to bite her. Margaret discouraged him by boxing his ears.

"Walters, why were you pestering Jacques-Yves Bertrand last year in San Bernardino?"

"How did you ...?"

"Know? The Stationmaster told me but seeing you lying here like a badly wrapped present makes me think there's more to the story. The farmer's wife said she'd bound a wound on the pilot's hand while someone else waited outside. Were you that man? Did you stow away with Monsieur Bertrand? Did you push Yvette Morehouse to her death?"

Walters looked up helplessly at Elvira. Cushman cocked one of his guns.

"That was the original plan. Young Mrs. Morehouse had given her serving girl time off and an extra dollar to mail letters to France from the post office at Seventh and Grand. The girl is my sister. She noticed it was not addressed to the LaRoche family and brought it to Mrs. Elvira instead."

"Was the letter addressed to Jacques-Yves Bertrand?"

"Yes," answered Walters. "Elsie helped Mrs. Elvira steam open the envelope. Mrs. Yvette was once betrothed to Bertrand and still in love with him. She had a plan for them to meet at the Field and fly away together."

"Silence that Judas-tongue!" snarled Elvira.

The muzzle of Cushman's gun brushing the back of his neck made Walters babble on.

"Now that she had his address, Mrs. Elvira made Bertrand a generous offer to sponsor him at the meet and sweetened the deal with a small fortune in cash. When Bertrand's crew reassembled his biplane, he had to make them build a storage box underneath the passenger seat. He was to look the other way when I snuck aboard and scrunched up inside it, just like *she,*" he jerked his head towards Elvira, "told me to."

"How did young Mrs. Morehouse get on board that day without anyone noticing?"

"She dressed like a man."

"We were right all along," Cushman whispered. His gaze never left Elvira; neither did Margaret's.

"You must have felt every inch the conqueror when you popped out of your hidey-hole and pushed Yvette Morehouse to her death. How could you be sure she wouldn't survive the fall?"

"She didn't fall. Trouble was I couldn't push the lid open. We circled round and landed in the field, almost knocked over a shed. I had my pistol ready to shoot her, if necessary, but it turns out she had one too."

"That must have quite the standoff. Who paid the farmer for his silence?"

Walters wasted no time taking credit.

"The Frenchie would only pay for crop damage. I had to shell out more than he did to keep those hicks' mouths shut. Yvette waved her pistol at all of us and ran off into the night."

Margaret looked at Elvira's face and retched.

"Why in God's name did you arrange such a heinous crime?"

"Yvette was craftier than I suspected. Don't know and don't care what happened to her or if she ever made it out of the country. After all, she was abandoning my son."

"Who hated her."

"Dissolution of that marriage would have devalued my European investments."

"The truth at last," chuckled Cushman. "but not all of it. He gestured with the guns. "Mrs. Morehouse and I located those farmers a short while ago. They were covering up a lot more than crop damage. We must continue this conversation in the comfort of your parlor."

Keeping his guns still trained at their backs, Cushman stayed half a pace behind Elvira and the butler. Margaret followed, rolling the still-bound Walters with the toe of her boot until they nearly caught up with the others.

She shouted a warning, remembering too late the embroidered satin bell pull. Elvira reached it first and tugged repeatedly. Within seconds, a dozen creatures of varying shapes and sizes rushed into the parlor through French doors and adjacent rooms. Most were flat faced like the butler and Walters. The men were armed with rifles;

one woman, a disarmingly pretty misfit, cradled baby Michael in her arms.

Elvira glared triumphantly.

"Let me introduce the Walters family."

༄

Although Cushman was armed and Margaret held Wilfred Walters immobile under her boot, odds for survival were not in their favor.

"These people have proven invaluable in all my dealings," continued Elvira.

"Such as shooting people on their doorsteps or loosening carriage bolts?" Cushman asked.

"I merely wanted to stop your involvement, Margaret. You are, after all, family, and far more intelligent than your cohorts. I never dreamed you'd be headstrong enough to ignore those warnings."

"Who did you hire to derail the investigation?"

The giant who had loomed above her the night before stepped forward.

"Missus don't need to hire no one. We all knows how to handle a gun, and I knows how to fix or break down most contraptions."

"Are you also clever enough to make Alexander Pantages look like a murderer?" Margaret persisted.

Elvira cracked a malicious smile.

"That's where I take over. Leftover bodies have their uses. And we had one. Wanted to ship it back to California when Walters remembered the Furmans' freestanding root cellar. We paid them handsomely upfront but those greedy farmers kept demanding more money. After we came to an understanding about how I deal with blackmailers, Wilfred went back there to pick up the body of Olivia Warren."

"Olivia Warren?" Margaret and Cushman gasped, almost in unison.

CHAPTER FORTY-SIX

"Once Olivia and her brood were back home in Tennessee, we made short work of her."

The smug satisfaction in Elvira's voice intensified her repulsive words.

"But Thomas thinks he's going to get his children back and expand his business!" Margaret sputtered. "I know he sends Olivia's parents money regularly but they blame him for her despondency and forbid him to see her."

"You can hardly blame them. They found her hanging from a rafter. Not sure how my man made that happen, possibly poison before he slipped a noose around her neck. They think she's buried in the churchyard, but I had other plans.

"When Pantages dared usurp my land, I asked Wilfred to arrange shipment of the corpse by rail, first to San Bernardino and later to Los Angeles. It ended up very much worse for wear due to all the jostling and ice melting in transit.

"We stashed it in the ice room outside the Hotel Nadeau, an institution patronized by many of my business associates. When the theater was about to open, I gave them some publicity. I wonder what we should do with your bodies? Student doctor cadavers along with an endowment, maybe?"

"I thought she didn't give make donations," Cushman grumbled under his breath.

"Only when it suits her," Margaret murmured back.

Elvira scowled and resumed her ghastly lecture.

"From there it was a short ride to Pantages Theater. That greasy Greek's building should have been mine. He left the doors wide open, making it easy for my fellows to leave the crate backstage and Olivia's body outside where even your bumbling friends couldn't fail to find her."

"Given the stench, I'm amazed the theater folk didn't find her

Zig Zag Woman

before the detectives. You must have tracked the body, and by association, me, every step of the way!"

"You'd best believe it, my dear. I followed your progress closely from the day you were named to the force. Sometimes you performed well, a little too well, the coroner has informed me. All too often you bungled situations as badly as those two dummies who took you on as an apprentice. If you had ever hoped to succeed, you should have modeled yourself on someone competent. Mrs. Rogers at the Hotel Nadeau comes to mind."

"I should have known she's one of your informants, too."

"She told me all about your little visit. There's a professional woman you should have emulated. Canny, completely loyal to me, knows how to get ahead. You, my dear, are far too naive."

"If you think I'm so inept, why did your let your spy tour me through her kitchen icehouse?"

"She was only attending to business and had no idea we'd ever stashed human remains there. There was no need for her to know."

"Who in their right mind would overlook the sapphire from your daughter-in-law's ring? I found it in the storage room and recognized it as Yvette's."

"Sapphire?" For the first time since Elvira began her tirade, she sounded confused.

"Someone left a box containing a lock of blonde hair and the band and setting from Yvette's engagement ring on your son's doorstep. The note accompanying it reads the same way the huge man who came to my door talks. That huge man to be precise."

Margaret pointed to an immense figure standing against the opposite wall.

"Conrad?" Elvira screeched. "Did you leave that ring where my son would find it?"

"Yes'm," the giant answered sheepishly. "Young Mrs. Morehouse gave it to our Millie over there three days before the meet. Said she didn't want no reminders of your son. I was just tryin' to help my Wilfred. Millie passed it on to me, good lass that she is. We was over at the hotel, so I pried out that big blue rock and hid it in the ice room 'longside the body you had us stash there. Kept fergettin' to send someone back to fetch it."

229

"You fool. I've fed, clothed, and coddled you and your clan of misfits for years."

Conrad glowered with unrighteous indignation.

"And we's done your dirty work so your hands stay clean."

A sneer crossed Elvira's face. "You couldn't survive in this world without me. They'd lock you up in carnival cages. People would come from miles around to throw rotten fruit at the freaks."

Tears welled in Conrad's eyes. Elvira's bullying attempts seemed to be working.

"The only way you can stay in my favor is to pull the trigger and get rid of the evidence. Dump all the bodies at sea if need be."

As the giant shouldered his rifle, she turned to look at Cushman. "Try to save your mistress, and the Tyson baby dies. Do nothing and my friends will raise him as their own."

More than one baby's life's at risk here, Margaret thought desperately, and parried with a few facts of her own.

"If I were a gambling woman, I'd wager members of the Walters family used that ring to extort money from your son, then for a completely unfathomable reason, returned the funds to his account."

She pointed to the woman holding Michael and the man aiming the gun.

"The detectives told me a pretty girl took the money from Leland and a large man took it back to the bank."

"That was my boy Wilfred's idea," Conrad admitted. "He grew up with Mr. Leland, who always treated him real snotty-like. Allus told my son we had to put up with it, but my Wilfred ain't got no tolerance. He's smarter than Mr. Leland, for all that fancy education. Wilfred gets in and out of banks and rich men's houses without anyone bein' the wiser and can copy almost anyone's writing."

Elvira's face twisted with rage. "You implicated my son!"

"I never took no money for all my trouble, Ma'am. If I shoots the both of 'em, can you forget about what me and Wilfred did?"

A corner bookcase swung open. Out stepped Leland, heir-apparent, so grimly determined Margaret almost failed to recognize him. The elegant man beside him had to be Julian LaRoche. Both brandished guns.

Julian LaRoche doffed his hat and as a mane of blonde hair fell on his shoulders, transformed into Yvette Morehouse.

"I knew you must be involved, Mother, once Walters' sister showed up to collect the ransom, but I never realized to what extent. Aunt Margaret has supported me more in recent weeks than you've ever done. I should let you take my life instead. After all, you never let it get started."

Leland's angry eyes met his mother's.

Stunned by his presence and the disclosure of events over which she exercised no control, Elvira looked confused. She hesitated, and, in that moment, saved them.

CHAPTER FORTY-SEVEN

"Fire!" came a shout from outside the window. "Run for your lives!"

From the reflection in the glass-paned doors, the Walters family saw their servants' quarters engulf in flame. They scrambled away like jackrabbits. A swift slender man wearing workmen's overalls whizzed right past Margaret clutching baby Michael.

A rock shattered the main stained-glass window and someone hurled a burning branch into the parlor. It struck the floor and spewed sparks in all directions. When Elvira's skirt caught the brunt of the blaze, she rolled out the back door in a vain effort to extinguish the flames.

Margaret could think of only one strong arm capable of such precision. Seconds later, McManus confirmed his presence. He covered Margaret's head with his coat and carried her to safety. Tyson stood outside, comforting his son.

Cushman was the last one out. "Without a doubt, your sister-in-law will go to blazes. I fear today's not the day. We saw her limp away with those poor devils. She'll probably be scarred for life, but who's going to notice?"

Margaret shushed him. The fire's flaming arms had beckoned the fire department. Soon they'd be surrounded by horse-drawn or automated trucks. All that mattered was her friends were safe and the conflagration did not spread.

Yards away, Leland and Yvette regarded the charred ruins with grim satisfaction. They glanced at her, bowed slightly, and walked off hand-in-hand.

It was clear they would all be headed in different directions that day, perhaps forever due to Margaret's condition. She wanted to hold on to their tattered camaraderie a little bit longer.

"Dear Cushman, if you drove slowly, could we possibly all fit in the carriage together? I want to make sure everyone gets home safely tonight."

Cushman eyed massive McManus and grunted. "The ride will be slower with him aboard. If you take the reins and I sit astride Jupiter, we just might make it."

CHAPTER FORTY-EIGHT

Joy burst from the Tysons' house in the form of two lively children and one relieved wife. Mary Ellen rubbed the tear darkened skin under her eyes. The gratitude suffusing her face revived her beauty.

Saying good-bye to Seamus was the most difficult. He was Margaret's first male advocate on the force; without his continued backing, she might not have been able to continue. She hoped one day he'd turn on that Irish charm long enough for a good woman to claim him.

Their long evening was ending. At half past midnight, Cushman pulled up in front of an ornate house. Laughter and music streamed from it in a way not entirely pleasant. He seemed familiar with the place and tethered Jupiter to the railing.

"There's something here you should see," he said, helping Margaret to the ground. "I think it may surprise you."

He picked up the lantern they always carried and led her down a graveled path to a small barn. It looked like a suitable place to raise a colt or create useful gadgets like her notebook. Looking back at the main house, Margaret noticed a rowdy couple dancing on the back porch and a lit red glass lamp in the window.

"Is that a bordello?" Margaret gasped.

"The place where you belong."

Cushman shoved her into the barn and swiftly trussed her up tighter than he had Walters. She cried out but no one came.

"Most of those drunken sluts and their johnnies think screaming is part of their play. I was ridding our city of them one by one until distracted by your police work. At first you seemed intelligent and brave, an exception to your gender. Then, like so many others, you fell into sin and betrayed me."

From beneath his vest, he pulled out a grey flannel roll and spread it out on the ground revealing a dozen pockets. Each contained a sharp silver implement.

"As you may recall, I once studied to be a doctor. Surgery would have been my specialty. I'm about to rid the world of you and that abominable creature you're carrying."

He turned toward her, a long blade in one hand.

"This is Edmund's baby!" Margaret gasped.

"Your husband confided the nature of your relationship to me long ago. You should have burned the letter you wrote last night instead of leaving the torn-up sheets lying around. And you're three months along? The exact amount of time that's passed since we left Chicago."

He pinioned Margaret and was about to slice off her clothes when a gunshot rang out from the doorway. His chest dropped down against her face and warm blood oozed across her cheek.

"You're all done, you self-appointed inquisitor, and may all the tortured souls you've killed chase you straight to hell!"

From the rafters above descended a familiar female form, graceful as a trapeze artist. With uncommon strength, she kicked Cushman's lifeless body aside.

"Alice???" shrieked Margaret, certain she must be hallucinating.

"LAPD's first policewoman with arrest powers, and temporary vigilante, at your service, ma'am."

"But how...when...why?"

"Hush, don't overexert yourself. I try to control my competitive nature but must own up to some professional jealousy. Your role appeared to be much more adventurous than mine, so I began following you whenever my regular schedule of duties allowed. When we had our tea, I recall saying I didn't know who had captured your heart. After a while, I began to suspect the butler!"

"How could you ever come to such an outrageous conclusion?"

"He was always by your side! Like Abe Lincoln, he was attractive in a homely way. It took time for me to discover the darkness within him, although I never suspected how deep it ran.

"I'll have you know he was a former Pinkerton agent. What made you follow us?"

"I was genuinely concerned. Something just did not sit right with me about that fellow. I asked a young friend to keep an eye on your house. Every time Harold Cushman left your house late at night, satchel in hand, another woman was found mutilated."

"We would never have gotten as far in the investigation without him. I owe him my life!"

"You mean the life he just tried to terminate? He must have been skillful at solving mysteries or Mr. Pinkerton would never have employed him. I didn't begin to suspect his penchant for butchering fallen women until too many had bled their lives out in the gutters and the patterns coincided.

She paused, eyeing Margaret suspiciously.

"Whatever could a pious preacher's wife do to test his faith in her so grievously?"

"That's my business."

Margaret struggled to her feet, brushing soot and straw off her slashed garments.

"My heart bleeds for those poor women! We must get ourselves and Cushman's body out of here, but I must know more before we continue. If he was the Parlor House Horror, the scales of justice will never be balanced."

Alice rolled her eyes impatiently.

"He dispatched his first victims by various means, baffling authorities. They thought it impossible for one man to have committed all the killings and abandoned their investigation, since the victims were from the dregs of society. Only a few self-righteous editorials acknowledged their existence."

"He left the Pinkerton Agency under a cloud years ago. Why didn't they ever manage to locate him?"

"Because he found you. He lied to you and himself as well. Cushman wanted to play the hero. He silenced his demons by serving you and yours."

Alice kicked Cushman's corpse.

"Now that I've revealed enough about him to write a Penny Dreadful story, we are facing a dilemma. Should we haul him to your buggy or leave him here to rot? What's your pleasure?"

"The buggy if you don't mind. But before we go, I need to know if your talents include driving trolleys."

"Only empty ones late at night. I was aiming for an evil man out to commit murder. Never dreamed you were along, safe and sound for the moment. Sorry to spoil the evening."

Margaret groaned.

"For all Cushman's sins, he helped me out more than a few times. I could never have solved Yvette Morehouse's disappearance without him. Strange as it seems, he saved my life at least once. He carried two souls within him, each warring with the other. He deserves a decent burial."

Alice shrugged and shouldered most of Cushman's weight.

"I know it's late and you've had a strenuous day, but we must make this look like a spontaneous attack, and for that, your antihero needs to be in the buggy's driver seat."

Summoning her last ounce of strength, Margaret helped load the body onto the buggy. Alice leapt into the front seat and tugged his arms while Margaret shoved from below. Sitting in the moonlight, Cushman and Policewoman Number One made a grotesque pair until she elbowed his chest and toppled him into the cart.

"Tragic loss," she said dryly. "The headlines will probably read, 'Faithful Servant Gunned Down by Assailants Unknown after Rescuing Courageous Mistress.' Take the reins. I'll ride alongside you."

"Not until you tell me what happened to your gun!"

"What gun?" came the haughty reply. "You of all people must be aware Los Angeles Policewomen are not permitted to carry firearms. We must keep the peace in some unsavory spots, but unlike our male counterparts, we're out there on our own."

Margaret knew better than to press the matter. Stranger characters had entered her life than those she'd found in fiction. Part guardian, part avenger, Alice outdid them all.

"How long have you been following us?"

"Not long, maybe four months," came the tacit admission. "Mostly tried to keep tabs on him. Caught your magic act once."

She eyed Margaret coolly before making a final revelation.

"Your detective friends merely started the Morehouse fire. It was I who kept it going."

"We could have all been killed."

Alice shrugged. "Then I wouldn't have had to waste a bullet on Harold Cushman."

CHAPTER FORTY-NINE

No more words passed between them until they reached the rectory. At the sound of Margaret's key turning the tumbler, Edmund rushed to open the door.

He held her at arm's length, inspecting top to toe for injuries. Seeing none, he stood motionless, not knowing what to say or do next. Alice stepped between them and gently led him to the buggy where Cushman lay, mouth grimaced in surprise, torso dark with blood.

Edmund recoiled in horror. Alice told him how she'd been on her way home from a mission of mercy and heard shots ring out past midnight.

"Imagine my surprise to find your wife and butler stranded on the highway in such a deplorable situation!"

A boulder falling out of the sky could not have dazed Edmund more. Nevertheless, he helped Alice move the body to the backyard, where it would remain until they summoned the undertaker.

There seemed no end to Alice's talents. She unhitched and stabled Jupiter, accompanied the Morehouses back inside, brewed and poured a pot of tea, then departed.

Edmund and Margaret fell into a wordless embrace and clung to each other for the rest of the night. Any need for explanation was cast aside. All either one needed was certainty of the other's presence in their life.

Panic overtook Margaret the next morning however when she reached out to find his side of their bed was empty. Could he ever truly forgive her reckless disregard for the life of this most wanted child?

The sound of hammer on wood interrupted her thoughts. Rushing downstairs, she was amazed to find Edmund, trousers hastily pulled up over long johns, using the kitchen table as a work bench to repair the cradle he and his brother had used in infancy.

"Sturdy enough to last for generations," he called out, looking up at me hopefully. "Let's set it up in our bedroom."

Margaret nodded. It was a heavy little piece of furniture but once they'd filled it with cushions, love, and best of all, baby, it would become their most prized possession.

The coroner's arrival in a black coach and four struck the only sour note that morning. Edmund recounted the details of Alice's report with so little emotion Margaret wondered if he too had come to suspect Cushman's true nature.

Deluding a man with Edmund's insight would be difficult, though they'd both been hoodwinked for years.

"Did you ever harbor doubts about Cushman?" she began.

"Not until yesterday. He'd become a fixture, always there, always indispensable. After reading your letter, it was impossible to continue writing. I was angry, although I knew the sacrifices you were making were for me.

"I remembered loaning Cushman my copy of *Paradise Lost*, the very state I would sink to if anything happened to you. Thinking to use lines from that masterpiece, I took the liberty of going into his room. On his desk was the bottle of white paste he had used to reassemble the torn-up version of the note you'd written me. He'd weighted it with the volume of Milton's poetry and penciled lewd drawings and words around it on his desk blotter.

"The contemptible words he'd written were all directed at you. I feared for your well-being and went to Leland for help. The Frenchman was still with him. Without hesitation, both men agreed to follow your trail, which I assume led straight to Elvira's."

"Without a doubt, their appearance changed the course of events. And that French*woman* was none other than our missing Yvette. I have yet to hear her story."

Edmund's face froze in astonishment.

"It also took Seamus, Charlie, Alice, and even Cushman to save the day."

"I should have been there, too."

"It would have only added to the chaos. Someone had to have the presence of mind to seek more help, and that someone turned out to be you."

Edmund squeezed Margaret's hand.

"It was you who saved my life many times over by gracing it. I blame myself for not perceiving his duality."

"Cushman was a modern-day Jekyll and Hyde. He deceived us all, but in the end, himself, and most grievously. As Robert Louis Stevenson wrote, "Man is not truly one but truly two.""

A persistent reporter interrupted their discussion. He came to the door with questions about Cushman and the fire. Margaret refused him an interview, but he kept repeating impertinent questions until Edmund escorted him off the property.

Margaret had been on a confidential police investigation, he told the reporter, and would henceforth be devoting herself to family matters.

CHAPTER FIFTY

It would be grand to end this tale with "and they all lived happily ever after." They had joyful moments, to be sure. Son Justin was born on Edmund's late August birthday, a sign from God, the Reverend said privately.

Elvira did not rebuild her mansion. She was never seen in public again. While she remained influential in banking circles, her stranglehold on Los Angeles's development weakened and eventually came to an end.

After Cushman's demise, the Parlor House Horror never struck again. Several months following McManus and Tyson's night on the town, however, the Rape Fiend of Boyle Heights resurfaced in Omaha, Nebraska. He was apprehended by an officer in women's clothing and shot dead trying to escape.

Leland severed all ties with his mother and began financing airplane design and construction while learning to fly his own.

As for Yvette, the realization of how thoroughly she had fooled him before, during, and after their marriage only heightened his respect. Three years after their original wedding, they fell in love and remained side by side.

Edmund continued to champion the downtrodden and kept his pulpit to his dying day.

The Tysons brought their brood over so often that Justin regarded their children as rowdy older siblings. McManus learned to be as charming around eligible young ladies as he had been to Margaret. He met Maggie O'Dowd at the 1912 county fair and in five years they produced more children than the Tysons.

Marco never fully left Margaret's consciousness, primarily as a cautionary tale. Eventually he performed for the crowned heads of Europe with a new assistant by his side – blonder, bustier, and younger than Marie.

As McManus predicted, blame for the *L. A. Times* explosion fell on trade unionists, though Edmund and Margaret remained skeptical. Three men were arrested: Ortie McManigal and the McNamara brothers, James and John. To secure a light sentence, McManigal confessed but implicated the brothers.

Union fundraising secured them representation by the eminent Clarence Darrow, whose ill health and prior conviction for jury tampering undermined their case. Held in solitary confinement and unaware of public support, the brothers confessed before the year was out. James McNamara was convicted on twenty-one counts of manslaughter and sentenced to life in prison. John received fifteen years for setting the Llewellyn Iron Works bomb.

Alexander Pantages' ability and lust for power made him one of the most influential show business moguls of the time, rivaling P. T. Barnum. His stage productions lit up theater districts throughout the United States and Canada. He introduced motion pictures into his establishments and would have become a leading producer had he avoided scandal. His unfortunate penchant for the ladies played into the hands of competitors, who drove him to financial ruin on trumped-up charges.

Despite the mishaps, Margaret longed for the excitement of police work. When she was a married childless matron, Captain Clarke wanted her on the force; once she was a mother, he had no further use for her services. For a while, she managed to settle into a pattern of placid predictability devoted to Edwin and Justin, the loves of her life.

She satisfied her need for adventure by reading and, whenever they could leave baby Justin at the Morehouse home, going to motion pictures with Edmund. By 1913, most nickelodeons were out of business; movies had become longer, more expensive, and thoroughly respectable. Edmund became enamored of the Keystone Kops and offered to buy her a high-domed hat as a gentle reminder of her former career.

Then fortune intervened, and a tidy one at that. Its source was Leland. Within days of the fire, he had combed the ashes of his mother's estate to find means for funding his freedom. Elvira escaped with her life, minions, and bank accounts intact. The flames had not destroyed her gems but she made no effort to reclaim them.

Zig Zag Woman

Auction proceeds from what he scavenged gave Leland the necessary capital to launch his aeronautical enterprise.

Within a year, his investments doubled. One day he brought Margaret a check, not drawn from a bank owned by his mother, in the unheard-of amount of two thousand dollars.

He shushed her the moment she began to protest.

"This money is for you alone. It is small recompense for the new life you've given me. I wouldn't dream of telling you how to spend it, but there is a storefront office available next to mine near the Bradbury Building on South Broadway. There's a large room and a small grassy area in back where Justin could play when you're busy. I even have a suggestion for the sign: Distaff Detective Agency."

Margaret shared his vision but changed the name. With Edmund's moral and physical support, Morehouse Investigators opened for business on Valentine's Day, 1914.

And so, Margaret went from Zig Zag girl to Zig Zag woman, no longer cut in two but headed on a clearer path. At first, the office was little more than a furnished space where she kept one eye on the front door, hoping for trade, and the other on her child.

Alice Wells dropped by on occasion. Any concerns she'd had about Margaret were long gone and each found in the other a forthright, intelligent friend.

Paying clients were few and far between. Locating a pooch and runaway bride were fun adventures but not fulfilling. Margaret was thinking about turning the place into a cake shop when her old detective chums came by asking for help. Comedian Charlie Chaplin, about to go into rehearsal for a Keystone comedy called "Making a Living," was missing, leaving only a bowler hat and bloody kerchief behind. Foolishly, she took the case.

THE END

ABOUT THE AUTHOR

Early experience as a staff greeting card writer introduced Roberta Tracy to witty people who shared the writer's dream. Marriage, motherhood, and career intervened, but she maintained that creative desire. A degree in nonprofit management led her to work situations where newsletters, grant proposals, and business correspondence took precedence. Still, she wrote poetry, some of which won prizes and publication, and children's books set in worldwide locations. Recently, she co-authored Come Dream With Me, a part travelogue, part hippie nostalgia work of creative nonfiction, detailing the adventures of colleague Inese Civkulis. No matter what writing projects unfold in the future, she'll never find enough words to thank family and friends for their inspiration and encouragement.

Follow Roberta Tracy at
www.thehistoricalfictioncompany.com/roberta-tracy

or at the author's website at

HISTORIUM BOOKS

www.historiumpress.com